Jessica was a successful IT Director, but now she is on the run. Accused of fraud and orchestrating her company's downfall, she travels as far as the island of Lindisfarne in Northumberland before breaking down.

There, an American, Anna Meyer, takes her in and offers kindness without questions. As they become closer, Jessica soon discovers Anna has her own much bigger problems and a past that comes knocking.

# THE ISLAND ANGEL

*Alex Slorra*

A NineStar Press Publication

Published by NineStar Press
P.O. Box 91792,
Albuquerque, New Mexico, 87199 USA.
www.ninestarpress.com

# The Island Angel




Printed in the USA
First Edition
December, 2018

Print ISBN: 978-1-949909-65-4

Also available in eBook, ISBN: 978-1-949909-63-0


Warning: This book contains sexually explicit content, which may only be suitable for mature readers, references to domestic abuse, a brief reference to a homophobic assault, and the death of a secondary character.

To Mabel, who always sat beside me and put her feline
paw on my leg when I was upset.

# Chapter One

ANNA'S EYES WERE shut tight. She held a coffee cup in both hands below her chin.

It had been a mistake, a huge rotten awful mistake, and now, as some additional sadistic punishment, Anna would have to pay. No, make that two mistakes. First, marrying him, and second, buying an overpriced dump she couldn't afford to sell.

She remembered a third, signing the divorce papers without really understanding what they had owed on the farm. No, the last wasn't a mistake. It was the only way out.

Forcing herself to lift her gaze above the rim of her cup, she focused on her mother across the table. Tourist season had not yet started, and they were the only people in the Crown Hotel.

"Honey, sell and come back to the States," her mother pleaded.

"You know I'm not doing that!" Anna slammed down her cup, before noticing the shock on her mother's weary face. "I'm sorry."

Her mum had flown all the way from Michigan after hearing how distressed she'd been on her daily calls home. "Anna, how are you paying the mortgage at the moment?"

Anna leaned back in her seat. "In the divorce, John signed the house over to me with enough money for six months. So, right now, I only have four months left."

"I don't understand why you would agree when you don't have any income. He's a lawyer, you should've asked for a lot more."

"Mom, I'd expected to get the business going, you know, I told you... And I wanted to see the back of him. But now, I couldn't even sell up if I wanted to. When I had it valued, the farm was worth thousands less than what we paid for it. And then I found out what we owed. If I sell, after all the costs, there'd be nothing, and I'll still owe what is on my cards."

Anna rested her chin on her chest, and her blonde hair fell forward, concealing her eyes. She hated that her marriage had ended. Hated that all her plans to turn the old farm into a business were now broken. Her sanctuary had become a burden.

"Oh, darling, talk to John. Can't he—?"

"Mom, I'm not talking to him."

A moment passed before her mother continued. "Why not come back home and wait for prices to go up? They always do, you know."

"I can't. I feel safer here. Abbie is safer here."

Her mother leaned forward. "Just come back. It would be all right. He won't bother us, I'm sure."

"He was released last month, you said. And he's still in Michigan?"

"As far as I know... But enough about that. You know, you could just default on your house payments, and it'll be repossessed. The banks won't chase you."

Anna had considered the idea of going back home, but she couldn't face it. She knew the fear would return. Especially now he'd been released. She had to keep Abbie safe. But also, the thought of being a barista at twenty-nine, while listening to whispers about her British husband leaving her for a younger woman, made her stomach turn.

She'd rather drown in the cold North Sea outside her kitchen window.

She put on a brave smile. "Well, I've got four months. Things will improve. Maybe I can make enough from pony trekking this summer." She didn't want to worry her mother more than she had, so she didn't mention she only had one pony and the stable's roof needed to be repaired. It was another thing she couldn't afford.

"There you go." Her mum squeezed her hand. "Darling, do you have a friend here to help you?"

"Yes, a few." It was a blatant lie, but she couldn't have her mother concerned that she was alone. The truth was the people here weren't very friendly. They seemed to stick together in groups as if they might catch the Black Death from someone new. Being the American who had bought a croft on their holy island, she hadn't been welcomed into the tight-knit community.

Anna reached into her pocket to retrieve her watch and check the time. The strap had broken earlier in the day, and it wasn't as if she needed it. She had her phone, and there was always a clock somewhere. It was just, since she was sixteen, she'd always worn it. The thought reminded her of her older sister, Emma, and caused tears to well up in her eyes.

She blinked to clear them and forced herself to damp down her emotions before her mother noticed. "I'm sorry Abbie wasn't here to say goodbye."

"I understand. The timing wasn't good," her mum offered. "It was nice to see her on the weekend. It must cost a lot to have her go to boarding school?"

Anna shook her head. "It's free. The council pays, it's the local government. There's no secondary school on the island and, because of the tides, it's nearly impossible to cross and get back during a normal school day. So, kids older than ten have to go to the boarding school on the mainland. Right now, there's only three students from the island who do it, though."

"She's happy there?"

"She never says she doesn't want to go back and she's picking up an English accent."

"I noticed." Her mum chuckled. "She's becoming an English rose. Emma would be proud."

Anna didn't want to disagree. At fourteen, Abbie was more like a thistle than a rose, at least with her anyway. One minute they were fine and having fun, the next they would be at loggerheads. *Perhaps, in the holidays, things will be better between us.*

Anna remembered why she had looked at her watch and touched her mother's arm. "It's time for your bus."

"I wish I could have stayed longer." It was her mum's turn to lie. Anna knew her mother thought England was too cold, as well as expensive and inconvenient.

Anna's mother got up and took hold of the handle of her cabin bag. "I know you don't want my help with money, but it's there if you need it. And do come home. I worry about you and Abbie."

"I know. But you don't need to. We're fine, really."

Outside, they hugged goodbye. It was still pretty cold for mid-May, and the wind cut through the fibres of Anna's burgundy all-weather coat. She buried her hands in her pockets and watched as her mother boarded the small bus that would cross the mile-long causeway back to the mainland before the tide covered it.

Anna's hair was blowing into her eyes. She brushed the wavy strands aside, before bursting into tears and darting back in the direction of her home.

Hurrying through the small village with her head down, she soon left the few buildings of the hamlet behind.

The island was small, only a few miles in both directions. In the winter, no more than a hundred people braved the North Sea storms. Spring was not much better, with high tides and cold easterly winds from Norway. It was a suffering romantic's paradise. For Anna, only the suffering part seemed true now. She passed the ruins of the old monastery, said to be the birthplace of Christianity in Britain. Beyond it, waves crashed against the rocky coastline.

She tried to put her predicament into words, but all she could think of was a swimming lesson from her grandfather at his cabin in Michigan. As was the tradition, Grandpa Brent had the job of teaching the younger family members how to swim. Anna had begged her way out of swimming until, at eight years old, her mother insisted she must learn. It was apparently a necessary life skill. So, there she was standing in her newly purchased white-and-pink one-piece at the end of the dock with Grandpa Brent behind her. He was explaining how to move her arms and legs. Looking back, she should have questioned why the man was fully dressed. Next thing she knew, he'd picked her up by her waist and had thrown her off the end of the dock into the lake.

Anna would have drowned if it wasn't for the end of a bamboo fishing rod the old idiot offered her when she managed to surface. She'd desperately grabbed the thin yellow pole and used it to get back to the dock. Sobbing and hunched over, having literally been fished out of the water, she looked at the person she had trusted and screamed at him before running back into the cabin where her mother and older sister were making lunch. She still hadn't learned how to swim and, now, she felt like she was underwater again.

On the exposed barren land, she followed a single-track road that hugged the jagged coast until Lindisfarne Castle could be seen on the south-eastern corner of the island. It was perched on a pinnacle, half-hidden by sea mist. Anna found some solace in the old fortress, knowing it had been there for four hundred years, withstanding all that had been thrown at it. But more so, it comforted her knowing people had lived, worked, and survived in its walls. If they could, so could she. She turned down a narrow muddy lane and scampered towards the eighteenth-century farmhouse that was her home.

SITTING ON HER sofa, Jessica felt a warm breath on her neck.

"What are you doing?" Victoria asked, leaning over Jessica's shoulder, while she opened her laptop and logged in.

"I won't be five minutes. Just need to check today's release status," Jessica answered, now regretting having invited Victoria in for an after-movie drink. The woman had asked her out after meeting her through a colleague at a pub close to the office. And, now, it was clear she intended to stay the night.

Long fingers slid down Jessica's neck, then along her shoulder. "Don't be long. I'll be waiting," Victoria said in a sultry voice. The redhead kissed Jessica's cheek before heading into the master bedroom of her Docklands flat with a filled-to-the-brim glass of white wine.

Reaching up, Jessica rubbed off the red lipstick she knew had been plastered on her cheek. She sighed. *I should've told her I'm not interested... Fuck. Bloody too late now, you idiot.*

All the indicators for the release were green, and she authorised its upload. She closed the lid of her laptop. Jessica really didn't want to sleep with Victoria. But, right now, she couldn't face telling her to go and having to deal with the drama. *Just do it. A romp might make you feel better about things.* She knew it was a coward's lie. She should have sent her home hours ago. Sighing, she headed into the bedroom.

Victoria headed out early the next morning, and Jessica was pleased to see the back of her. At work, the day was pretty uneventful. When she left the office, she went straight home, spending the evening looking at holiday destinations online.

In the early hours, her mobile rang. She focused on the blurry digits of its display. It was 02:00 a.m. She hooked her short chestnut hair around her ear and glanced at the woman sleeping beside her. It had been the first time she'd slept with someone in a number of years, and she'd forced herself to go through the motions. By the time she picked up her mobile, it had stopped ringing.

She slipped out of bed and carried her phone with her into the lounge, where she dialled the number of the missed call.

"What's up, Chris?" Jessica asked when she was connected.

"Hi. Can you hang on? I need to take another call." He sounded under duress.

"Sure."

It wasn't unusual for her to get calls at this time of night—they went with the territory. A territory she was finding hard to endure. She'd spent the last month with the thought something was missing. A fact she discovered by stopping and listening. When only silence answered, she knew she had gotten everything wrong.

Victoria, as she liked to be called, rather than Vicky, had been Jessica's attempt to fill the void. But the encounter had just added to it. *I'll tell her it's not working in the morning.*

She glanced at her guitar propped in its stand. It was another part of her past she'd left behind.

At thirty-three, she'd spent all her years since university focusing on her career, and now it felt like she was at the centre of a sphere filled with dark, acrid treacle. She had to escape. Having exercised most of her share options a few days before, cashing in on her hard work at Hokthorn, she was ready to quit her job. She wished her previous employer, Genism Systems, one of Hokthorn's competitors, had been more successful, as she still held a large amount of their stock. As it was, she didn't think she would have enough to start her own business, but at least she could take a year off and travel the world and perhaps write a book.

Chris joined the call again. "We have a big problem."

"Give me the specifics." While listening, she sat on the sofa. "How many customers are affected?" It sounded bad, very bad. She dropped herself onto the sofa and cursed with her hand over the mic of her phone. "Give me a moment to log in." She flipped open her laptop. All she knew at this point was a routine update had gone horribly wrong.

Emails were coming into her inbox at a rate of knots, and Jessica skimmed the subjects of each email: *twenty thousand servers at TicoCorp down, New Hong Kong Bank offline, NYC Webster Hospital systems unresponsive.* The list continued with new entries appearing with every passing second.

*How? We just audited the test rigs. Why has this happened?*

Her insides twisted, and she fought the sensation to be sick. She jerked up off the sofa and walked over to the southwest corner of her flat. Ceiling-to-floor windows offered a panoramic view over the Thames and beyond to the City of London. Tail lights from a taxi streaked across Tower Bridge, a barge glided as a dark mass discernible only by its navigation lights, and a police siren wailed before its source sped past.

"Fuck," she whispered and dialled her QA Senior manager. "Chris, what's going on?"

"We released a bad update. Our QA system designed to check this scenario reported an internal error—a problem with the rig itself. And, well, the aggregated reporting process didn't recognise the failure, so it defaulted to marking the test as passed. This was an old issue we fixed years ago. It shouldn't have happened... We're investigating."

"Wait, back up. What's wrong with the update?"

"It corrupts system files, breaking the operating system and, well, making it impossible for us to release a new update to fix the issue."

"Great... Do we know how many customers received the update?" She expected the damage should be limited as they always released to a handful of customers first as a precaution.

There was silence on the line before Chris answered. "We blocked the update, but it was too late. The staging didn't drip feed it out. Well..." He cleared his throat. "Again, we don't know why. But—"

"Chris, please answer this, how many customers got the update?"

"I guess the estimate is 60 percent of our customer base before we blocked it. So, well, you know...possibly eighty million systems."

Jessica's throat went dry, and she couldn't speak for a moment. She tried to still her shaking hands. As VP of product release, this was her responsibility. Her head was on the block. She pushed the thought aside. She needed to find out what had gone wrong. *These failures don't make sense!* She was gripping her phone so hard her knuckles turned white. *First, we need to mitigate the damage and protect our customers' businesses. God, lives could be at stake.*

"You there still?" Chris asked.

"Yes. Has a support call been set up?"

"Yeah, the Disaster Level Four process kicked in five minutes ago. But Carter is calling for it to be a five. I'm dialled in on my desk phone. It's pretty...unpleasant. And the CEO is on as well, but he's not saying much. Can you join us?"

Jessica tried to concentrate on what Chris was telling her, but she was struggling to take in his words. Disaster Level Five meant a full meltdown of all customer systems. Her chest tightened, and the freefall of her stomach threatened to drag her down with it. After a moment, she found the strength she needed. It was another problem to solve; a huge one that would likely end her career, but she needed to do the right thing before facing that inevitability.

"Yes, I'll join now."

# Chapter Two

A LOT CAN happen in two weeks, especially when nights are spent awake. In a sterile meeting room, Jessica sat opposite Mrs Kapoor, a stern woman and the HR Director for EMEA. To Jessica's right was her boss, Brian, senior VP of Product Quality.

"I'm sorry we have to do this, but the severity of the impact on the business means we must take appropriate action," Mrs Kapoor stated quickly.

A drop in share price of 54 percent, potential class actions in the billions, and the loss of key accounts to their main competitors were all going to be seen as her fault.

Jessica sighed. *At least no one died.* Although, she had heard there'd been severe delays in hospitals that used their software.

"We'll need you to hand in all company property," Mrs Kapoor said. "Where's your company phone—"

"I've already collected them," her boss cut in.

Mrs Kapoor closed her mouth like a chick that hadn't been given a worm. She stared for a moment at Brian. Her posture and expression poised for an ice-cold reprimand. "And the company car?"

Jessica chucked her keys onto the table. *I was going to resign anyway. This doesn't matter.* But as much as she tried to rationalise what was happening, it felt wrong.

"Thank you. I'm afraid there won't be any notice period as you're being dismissed from Hokthorn for gross negligence. But you may be called to answer questions as part of an enquiry. Are your address and home phone number up to date?"

Jessica nodded.

"Good. Now, I just need you to agree to this declaration."

A document was shoved under her nose. Jessica skimmed the words. It was asking her to agree to the termination of her employment and stated all the share options she held were now null and void.

Once she had signed the paper, Jessica stood abruptly. She didn't want to attend her own funeral any longer. "Are we done?" Her words were edged with an undertone of fear that she hoped no one else would notice. She wasn't sure if it was because of what had happened over the last fortnight, but, for some reason, she was struggling with a deepening foreboding.

"Please sit," Mrs Kapoor said with twisted charm and another icicle smile. "We are done, but you're not. Please stay seated."

Jessica sighed and sat back down. Everyone else left the room. After a minute, a man and a woman entered.

"Jessica Cox, I'm Adrian Chapman from the Serious Fraud Office." The man didn't offer his hand, nor did he introduce the female colleague who was with him.

She'd thought she had just survived the worst couple of weeks of her life, but apparently something else was about to slam her in the chest. "What's this about?" she asked, but it was obvious—it could only involve fraud of the serious kind.

After the SFO officers sat, Mr Chapman continued while the robot beside him said nothing. "Miss Cox, it's about insider trading and market manipulation."

"I've not been involved with any—" *Shit*. A thought occurred to her.

Mr Chapman leaned forward and tilted his head. "Go ahead, please finish."

"Well, I sold most of my share options just before we had the problem with the update. You see, I was thinking about resigning and taking a career break. But I don't see how—"

"We are aware of those transactions. But that's not the whole problem."

"What is then?" She twisted her hands in each other where she sat. She was petrified to the point she found it hard to breathe.

"The difficulty is..." He paused as if on a talent show waiting to announce the winning act. "The shares you hold from your previous employer."

Mr Chapman was now watching her intensely. If his eyes were hands, every part of her body would have been violated.

"My... What?"

"Yes. You worked for Genism Systems, right?"

"Five years ago. I don't see—"

"We've been informed you hold a considerable number of shares in Genism. Shares now worth three times their original value as the result of the disaster at this company that you may have deliberately caused."

Jessica blinked and gathered her thoughts. She needed to fight back. "Look, first, I've not done anything with those shares. Second, as VP, I take responsibility for the problems we've had with our update, but I've by no means purposefully caused it."

Mr Chapman sat back in his chair. "That's yet to be determined."

The unreadable android-like woman beside him continued to stare.

The room was silent for an uncomfortable period, forcing Jessica to fill the void. "So, if I haven't done anything wrong, why are you here?"

"That will depend on the investigation your company is doing. An investigation we are assisting with." He half smiled, before continuing, "I should have said ex-employer as I understand you were dismissed today."

Jessica kept her mouth shut. She was desperate to leave, and it was hard not to make a run for the door.

"But, to get to the point, I'm here to inform you that all your financial assets are frozen until the circumstances around what has happened is determined."

"What do you mean? My bank account is frozen—"

"That is correct, a court order was granted. So please don't leave the country. We'll need to ask you more questions as our investigation proceeds." He slid his chair back and stood. "I suggest you find yourself a lawyer, Miss Cox, if you haven't already." He turned and exited the room with his mute shadow following close behind.

Jessica dropped her head into her hands, pushing her fingers into her hair, before letting out a sharp exhale. "I've done nothing wrong..."

The door opened again, and Brian's face appeared. "I'm to escort you out."

THE WALK BACK to her flat hadn't helped to ease the tension in her chest and, once inside, Jessica paced back and forth, while talking on her hands-free phone. "So there's no way I can take out any money?" Three of her cards had already been swallowed by a cash machine.

"Sorry, no," the woman on the line said.

"Do you know when it will be unfrozen?" Jessica's words were edged with frustration.

"No, ma'am," the woman told her for the third time. "We don't have that information. Is there anything else I can help you with today?"

Jessica closed her eyes tight and rubbed her temple. "No."

She hung up and threw the phone across the room. It hit the wall and split into fragments.

"What the hell am I supposed to do? Shit... Calm down," she told herself.

She went back to pacing. She could think better when letting her body burn off some of the energy blurring her thoughts. "Just get some money to tide you over. But from who?" She tapped her forehead with all four fingers. "Darren. Hell, there's no one else."

She went to the broken handset and tried in vain to piece it back together. "That was stupid. God! And I don't even have any contact numbers."

Back at her laptop, she mined her emails, social media, and the internet for numbers she thought she might need, writing them down on a small pad. At least she could still email or Skype, *but who?*

She didn't have many friends, at least not the sort she could discuss her current predicament with, since they were all work colleagues, except perhaps Chris. Any friends from her childhood and university, she'd simply left behind. All she had was a brother. Her father had passed away five years ago, and she'd last seen her mother in an open coffin at a crematorium a year ago. Her mother had worn a smile fixed in place by embalming fluid. It had been so hard to consider the staged construction as the woman who raised her, and she couldn't bring herself to pay her final respects at the casket.

*Why am I thinking about my mum's funeral? I don't want to, not now. Just borrow some money from Darren, assuming he has any. Things will work themselves out once the investigation is done.*


IT WAS DUSK, and the sky was threatening to rain when the train screeched to a stop at Brimsdown station. Jessica had just enough cash in her purse to get a train ticket to North London, and now she hoped her brother was home. Otherwise, she'd have an impossible journey back. She walked slowly through the station, checking the shadows. Her heels clacked on the platform as she passed the closed ticket office. Some of her tension eased once she was outside.

Jessica hurried along the pavement until she came to its junction with Green Street. It was a street she never wanted to see again. She hated the hypocrisy of the place, which started with its name. Nothing was green here, except for the household rubbish bins. Post-war semi-detached houses filled both sides of the road with the exception of a gap for a few run-down shops and a pub. All along the street, front gardens of the houses had been covered with concrete slabs to make parking spaces.

The Jade Garden Chinese restaurant was on her right as she turned the corner. It also wasn't anything like its name. A "To Let" sign was visible in its large window. Someone had graffitied an "i" between the two words.

Her steps faltered as a shoeboxed memory tried to wriggle its way to the front. After what had happened in the restaurant, the smell of Chinese food still made her want to throw up.

She lowered her head briefly, before raising it again and crossing the road.

This had always been an area where people lived by abusing the benefits system and bending the law. Here, the sun didn't lift off the morning's paper, and, as a teenager, Jessica was forced by circumstance to rub shoulders with thugs, drug addicts, and alcoholics who thought they were God's gift to women, boasting about their sexual prowess at every opportunity. She was always polite to them, not because she wanted to be, but because she was afraid. One evening, her fear had become reality in the cruellest way. She didn't want to think about that day and pressed on.

In front of her was the home where her parents had moved twenty years ago. Now, she was back. Back because her brother had never left, staying put even after their mother died of lung cancer. Jessica had wanted to sell the semi-detached house and forget about every particle of the place, but Darren wouldn't budge, oblivious to her need to forget. He had all he wanted in life: Sky TV, a pub across the street, a betting shop a few doors down, and an Indian takeaway around the corner.

When the doorbell didn't make a sound, Jessica stabbed at the letterbox, causing the metal flap to snap back with a clapping noise. She repeated the action three times, before yelling through the gap. "Darren, it's Jessica!"

There was no answer.

Light was visible from the front room window, and she squeezed around a dirty old Saab convertible with its roof covered in a blue tarpaulin. It looked like it hadn't been driven in months and areas of the black bodywork were green with algae. She walked around it, banging her shin on the tow bar of the car.

"Fuck!" She rubbed the bruised area, before heading to the window. After rapping on the glass, she could still see no movement through the nicotine-stained lace drapes.

The neighbour's door opened. "He'll be in the pub," an old woman said, waving her hand jerkily towards the Black Horse tavern across the road.

After a nod, Jessica turned and crossed the street. All the cells in her body told her she should stay away but, with no other choice, she forced herself to enter the rundown public house.

All eyes were on her as she walked inside, looking her up and down, before returning to their pints of beer. Her brother beckoned her over and patted the stool next to him at the bar. "Long time no see. So, what brings you here?"

"I need to talk to you about something." She was glad she had changed from her business suit into jeans and a thick navy sweater; this was not the place to look professional. She kept her handbag on her lap and was about to reach for her purse when she remembered she had no way to pay.

"You could have just phoned. Oh, yes, I remember, you don't do that," Darren said.

"Look, I'm sorry. I actually don't have a phone right now." She looked at his face; he had aged a lot over the past few years. "Can you get me a Diet Coke? I can't pay."

"Okay, sure, coming up." His tone was jovial, and Jessica suspected he had already put a few pints away. Darren waved the bartender over. "Mel, a Diet Coke for my sister."

The bartender looked like the type of person a prison warden wouldn't confront, and she served the drink without any camaraderie.

Jessica said nothing until after she had a sip of her Coke. "Darren, I'm a bit stuck. A problem at work caused my bank account and cards to be frozen. It will clear up in a week or so, but, until then—" She paused, having to swallow more than her pride, before asking, "I was wondering if you could lend me some money?"

"So, my sister, with her job in the City, needs money from me? What's wrong? Spent it all on prosecco?" He laughed and called to the bartender, "Mel, do you have any prosecco for my sister?" The woman didn't hear him over the din, or perhaps she just ignored him.

"Darren, I just need some money for the next couple of weeks. There was a big problem at work and—"

"Listen," he said, interrupting her. "You think you have problems." He pointed across the bar. "You see that woman, there, sitting with that asshole?"

Jessica sighed and glanced in the direction of his chubby finger. There was only one female customer other than her in the place, so she wasn't hard to spot. "With the man with greying hair?"

"Yes." He leaned close. "She's my girlfriend, and that's Greg, her husband."

Jessica frowned.

"He suspects something's going on between us, and now she has given me the shoulder. What the fuck am I supposed to do? He's a complete snake in the grass, but she won't leave him because he's minted." Darren finished his pint and ordered another while bemoaning his situation.

Jessica found it hard to empathise. She was here to get his help, not listen to his half-cut ramblings about what sounded like a sordid affair.

Then she saw him, sitting at the other end of the bar. She should have known the bastard would still live here. She needed to leave and leave now.

She put her hand on her brother's arm. "Please, let's go."

Darren hadn't heard her. His mouth was twisted into an enraged grimace.

"Please don't have any more." Her tone belayed her desperation. "I need to talk to you about our options. Maybe you can get a small loan against the house for me."

Still, he ignored her. Jessica tracked Darren's gaze to see him watching his "girlfriend" kissing her husband.

"I'm going home," he announced. "And you should go to yours." Darren slipped off his perch, before sauntering to the exit.

Outside, Jessica hurried after him but had to wait for two cars to pass before crossing the street. By the time she caught up, he was already inside and had latched the door.

"Darren!" She banged on the door. "Come on, please. God damn it! I can't even get home!" After a few more attempts to be let in, she checked her watch. It was close to eleven. "I bet the slob is in a drunken sleep on the sofa. Hell," Jessica mumbled to herself, leaning against the old car in the drive.

She tugged the cuffs of her sleeves down over her hands to keep them warm. *I can walk home. But it's twelve miles.*

She left the short drive and took a single step onto the pavement when she saw him. From his staggering gait, it was clear he was drunk. She slowly backtracked and ducked behind the old Saab. Her fingers curled into fists, and her heart raced with fear. There was no way she wanted to face him. She tried the door of the car. It was unlocked and creaked open. She quickly slid in. Through the driver's window, she could just make out the evil fuck who had nearly killed her and Myra.

He fumbled with his keys at a parked car and got in. After what seemed like an eternity, he slowly drove off. The headlights of his car turned on when he was some distance beyond the level crossing.

"God. I should've never have come here." Afraid, she didn't move, still waiting, and unsure of what to do.

Perhaps half an hour went by before Jessica managed to calm down and suppress the spectre from her past.

A thought occurred to her, and she reached up to fold down the car's sun visor. A key fell to the floor, and she groped in the dark to find it.

"Why does this car stink of damp?" she whispered. But the real question was *will it start?*

The engine barely cranked over before the lights on the dashboard went black. She tapped the accelerator. "I must have used up all my shitty luck today. Come on, stinky car." She knew the words wouldn't help, but they couldn't hurt. "Start!" She twisted the key. After the second crank, it sputtered to life.

Without hesitating, she reversed into the street. But as she passed the brick posts, marking the drive's entrance, the tarpaulin caught and was ripped off, leaving it behind.

She sped along the empty, grey street. The only light came from the dim tungsten headlights of the Saab. She was pleased with her first success of the day and maxed the heating settings. She considered turning on the radio but suspected it was tempting fate. Her day had been one disaster after another, but at least now she could get home. *I'll have to find Megan and ask her to help. No choice now— I should've done that first. Why is my thinking so screwed up?*

"Shit. Fuel..." She checked the gauge, almost full. "Wow!" She turned the radio on and tuned into Radio One, happy for anything that seemed normal. Her mood dissipated when she remembered she was broke, had no insurance, and you can't eat a tank of petrol. She was so hungry. *I'll just get back to the flat. I can live off pasta and stay put.*

Only five minutes had passed when the passenger side front tyre blew out.

"Piece of shit car!" Jessica screamed. "Kill me now, already! This is too much! I've not walked under a ladder, run over a black cat, or broken a mirror, so what is it with this day?"

It had started to rain, and she drove the lame car into a closed service station to the sound of the rubber flapping around a rim. *Why is this happening to me?* She got out and found that, in the boot, the spare was in good condition. Lifting and yanking, she was able to pull the wheel out. She knew how to change a tyre. Her father had shown her how to do many things before he died. It was odd she was thinking about him. It was something she rarely did. *First, my mother, then my brother, then Megan, and now my father. And none of them are here to help me!*

The rain was starting to soak through her jumper. She hurried to position the jack, but it was hard to see with only streetlights that seemed to emit shadows instead of illumination.

Jessica managed to loosen three of the lug nuts, but the last wouldn't budge. Using all her strength, she shoved at the tyre arm, but it slipped off, causing her hand to slam into the lip of the wheel rim and scraping the skin off two of her knuckles.

"Fuck!" She slapped her hand over her bleeding wound and got back into the car. She had seen a pack of tissues in the glove box and used them now to cover her injury.

A lump formed in her throat. The universe was out to destroy her, but she'd done nothing wrong.

Unable to cope with any more of tonight, she crawled into the back seat and yanked a musty tartan blanket over herself. She wanted to cry, but, somewhere, as she had transitioned to adulthood, she'd forgotten how. Her head felt waterlogged, and her breathing was shallow and fast. Most of all, she was afraid and didn't want to move.

Tired and hungry, she listened to the rain on the car's canvas roof leaking onto the passenger seat. There was an inch-wide gap where the left clasp for the convertible's top was broken, allowing in a steady trickle. She pulled the blanket over her head and, with her knees close to her chest, she fell asleep.

# Chapter Three

JESSICA WOKE TO tapping on the driver's window. Not sure where she was, it took a minute for her mind to replay the sequence of events that had taken her to the here and now. She folded the driver's seat forward, yanked the door handle, and climbed out of the old Saab.

"You can't stay here," a rotund man in a hi-vis jacket told her.

"I have a flat tyre."

"Let me guess, you don't know how to change it," the man sneered.

Jessica ignored him and fitted the tyre arm onto the same bolt she'd struggled with last night. She stood on the wrench and was finally able to loosen the nut.

"Do you need help?" the man asked, his tone having flipped to friendly.

She continued to ignore him, and he wandered off to the service station.

When the tyre was changed, she checked her watch. It was after eight in the morning. All she wanted was to be at home on the sofa with her duvet wrapped around her.

*Home... Is it really my home?* On the few occasions her girlfriend had stayed over, Megan had commented on the fact that Jessica's flat felt like a hotel room. Megan was her opposite, and the attraction hadn't lasted. When they had split up a couple of years ago, Megan had moved to Edinburgh to do a doctorate in European history.

Jessica shook her head; she had been sitting in the driver's seat, staring off into middle space while thinking about the past. *Just get back and Skype Megan. God, I really need a coffee.* She started the engine and drove twenty minutes to her flat in the Docklands.

Once there, she parked in her reserved space and entered the four-storey glass and brick building, which was wedged between others and surrounded by waterways and a marina.

Inside, Jessica came to a shuddering stop and ducked back into the stairwell. A man, a woman, and two police officers stood outside her door.

With her back against the wall, she could hear the voice of Adrian Chapman from the Serious Fraud Office.

"Officer, break the lock," Adrian ordered.

*Shit, they must have a warrant! If they have that then... They've come to arrest me!*

Her brain raced. Should she turn herself in and hope she would be proven innocent or run and make time so she could talk to Chris and find out what the hell had happened? The more she thought about it, the more she suspected someone had set her up. Events had been too perfectly timed for it to be a simple software bug. She needed a fucking phone to find out what had been done to the systems and who had orchestrated her downfall.

She slid along the wall, withdrawing on quiet footsteps. When the staircase turned a corner, she leapt down the steps, three at a time, and raced out of the building back to her brother's skip-on-wheels.

Minutes later, she had joined the A12 to head north out of London. Her thoughts were a muddy grey mess, and the best she could come up with was to drive to Edinburgh. *Megan will help, if she still lives there.* They had parted with slings and arrows, and Jessica wasn't sure Megan would actually help, but she desperately hoped so.

ANNA STOOD AT the bottom of the stairs. "Abbie, come down, breakfast is ready! I won't call again!" Anna yelled.

Abbie had arrived home from her boarding school late last night. As was their weekend tradition, Anna was making American flapjacks and already had a stack of twelve. It was too many, but Anna still hadn't got used to cooking for just the two of them. She had set out breakfast on the old elm table situated at the centre of the spacious, if dated, kitchen. Worn handcrafted cabinets ran in a U-shape along three walls. A window above the sink overlooked a narrow muddy lane that was their drive. At the opposite end, an archway stepped down into the small lounge, while a short hallway connected Anna's office and upstairs.

"Why don't you make pancakes instead sometimes?" Abbie asked, slipping sideways into her chair at the table and hooking both feet on the stretcher of the chair next to hers.

"You mean crêpes?"

"Yes."

"You don't like these now?" Anna asked, serving three flapjacks onto Abbie's plate.

"I do... It's just, in England, they eat pancakes. They're thinner."

Anna took a seat at the table with a mug of coffee. "Well, we are pretty close to Scotland, perhaps we should eat haggis for breakfast?" She wasn't very hungry, and the thought of boiled sheep's organs served in the lining of a stomach put her off completely. She watched as Abbie woofed up another flapjack covered in golden syrup.

"There's no hot water, and it's freezing," Abbie said, after finishing another mouthful.

"The boiler's broken. I'm waiting on a quote." In truth, she had received the quote yesterday. It had recommended a complete replacement, and the cost was £3,450.95. She couldn't afford anything like that as it would cut into the money she needed for another pony. She wasn't even sure she had ninety-five pence to spare. *I wonder what part of the boiler costs ninety-five pence?*

Anna didn't want Abbie to know about it, because she hadn't yet formulated a plan that didn't involve selling her own kidney.

"Mum, you're staring at nowhere again."

"Oh." Anna shook her head, as if her troubles could be got rid of as easily as a drenched dog shakes out water. "Are you going to help me today?"

Abbie glanced up from her breakfast. "Doing what?"

"Clearing out the old stables."

"Why? Daisy already has one."

"I want to get another pony before half term in two weeks."

"But we need the roof replaced. And I have homework."

"I might be able to put some plastic over the roof."

Abbie wrinkled her brow and grimaced. "Really?"

"Yes, really."

The rose-gold iPhone buzzed where it sat beside Abbie's plate, and it drew her attention.

"No phones with meals. Put it away." But Anna's request was ignored. "I'll take it from you."

"It's my friend!" Abbie flicked her fingers along the phone while forking another portion of flapjack into her mouth.

Anna missed Abbie when she was at school, but there were times like this when everything seemed too much. About to be overwhelmed, she swallowed down her emotions with a sip of coffee. "We'll start on the stables after your homework. First, I'll go into town and get some trash bags and gloves."

Abbie's head darted up. "Get me some chocolate Mini Eggs?"

"*Please?*" Anna insisted. "Is it just me you talk to without manners?"

"Yes," Abbie said under her breath, but then looked up and added, "All right, please, Mum. Some Mini Eggs, if they still have them."

"Okay." Anna stood and went over to the kitchen counter to plug her phone in to charge. "You can do your homework downstairs. I lit the fire in the lounge so at least it'll be warm there."

"Can I go to Katy's to do my homework?" Abbie's pleading was echoed in her big blue eyes.

Anna sighed. "It'll be warm there, I suppose. All right, but be back after lunch. And make sure you've done all your work." She grabbed her purse from the counter, went to the peg rack, and unhooked her coat.

When she opened the front door, a light rain promised a day that would chill her bones. "Don't be any later than one," she said, glancing briefly at Abbie, her sister's mirror, before exiting their home.

THE NEEDLE HAD read empty for the last sixty miles. It was seven in the morning, and Jessica hadn't found an open petrol station. She'd hoped to beg someone for a few litres of fuel.

"Keep going... Just keep going, stupid, stinky car!"

Since London, she had been travelling north, stopping halfway at a motorway service station when the engine temperature gauge was on "about-to-explode." There, she had convinced a woman let to her use her phone to make one call. But Megan hadn't answered. She had fallen asleep waiting for the engine to cool down. It was 04:00 a.m. when she woke and set out again.

She had decided to divert to the eastern coastal road. She wasn't sure it was a good idea, but she didn't want to break down in the middle of a major motorway and be picked up by the police.

Two hours later, she knew the car would sputter to a stop any minute. A sign showing a petrol pump flashed by, and she took a quick right turn. Three miles on, it was obvious it had been a mistake.

To her left and right, in the dawn drizzle, there was nothing but sand and sea. She was halfway along a causeway, with no possibility of turning around.

As she drove, the sea gave way to sandbanks, then firm fields and, finally, a village. She steered into a public car park and switched off the ignition. Dead tired and with her eyes closed, she listened to the wind and rain. She knew she was on the island of Lindisfarne with no fuel, no money, no phone and still seventy miles from Edinburgh, the city where she hoped Megan would be her salvation.

ANNA REGRETTED TAKING the longer route back to the farm. She was walking east out of the village and had just diverted down a small path, which ran along the large visitors' car park, when the gentle raindrops turned to a downpour.

After getting her supplies, she had been to Priory's Cup coffee shop to ask about part-time work. The owner, Linda Conway, must have taken pity on her or known about her situation, since she'd been offered a trial as a barista to start the next morning. It was a big conflict for her, taking on other jobs to pay the bills or focusing on what she had intended—namely, getting the pony trekking business ready for the season.

Normally, she was an optimist, but there was a huge amount of work that needed to be done to the farm. Most of which, she hadn't a clue how to do.

As she marched on, the fears she'd put aside were slowly inching their way back into her present.

"Morning." A familiar face poked out of a hooded anorak. Mr Foster was walking his dog in the rain. The Border collie didn't appear too happy about its forced exertion.

"Morning, how's the piglets?" Anna asked. It was clear the man wanted to chat, even though they were in the middle of a downpour.

"The piglets are doing fine. I'm glad we decided to bring them home. But they're getting big now. Almost ready to be pork chops."

Anna failed to hide her shock at the remark. She didn't know Mr Foster well. In fact, she didn't even know his first name. She knew he was a farmer on the island and harvested hay in the fields next to hers. She thought the sheep on the island were likely his. She knew of him because he was Abbie's friend's grandfather. Abbie and Katy had gone to see the piglets two weeks ago. "I didn't know pigs were kept on the island."

Mr Foster smiled. "My oldest, Daniel, runs the farm on the mainland. He keeps pigs and dairy cattle. Me and my youngest just have sheep here. I'm too old to do much more. And my youngest is too lazy." The man appeared to be in his late sixties and was a picture of health, with rosy cheeks and strong hands. He looked as if he could still fight an ox and win. "Daniel has been doing pretty well. He's been diversifying. It's all the rage. Diversifying."

"Diversifying?" Anna asked, glancing down at the dog, shivering beside its master's legs.

He nodded. "Yup. It's camping now. Why anyone would want to sleep out in a field of cowpats, I have no idea. Edward says he has many bookings already, and the volunteers are building a toilet block." His eyes flicked up to the grey clouds. "But not today perhaps."

"Volunteers?"

"Foreigners mostly. He puts them up in return for work." The collie whimpered and weaved around his legs, tangling its lead. Mr Foster rotated on the spot as if he was an unravelling barber's pole. "Yes, from the Interweb. He has a website." He leaned down and patted the dog. "I better take Fairweather in. Good day, Anna. Well, good grey and raining day." He laughed and walked past her back towards the village.

Anna paused, watching him head out. Wondering how he knew her name. She guessed Abbie must have told him. But, then again, everyone except her seemed to know each other on the small island. She should probably be more social, but they had always been outsiders. And John hadn't helped. He had a knack of rubbing people the wrong way.

The rain had eased up. Anna yanked down her hood. She started along the footpath that paralleled the car park.

A woman was leaning against an old convertible. When she spotted Anna, she headed in her direction.

*She's in trouble?* As the dark-haired woman got closer, Anna wondered if she should've ignored her. The woman's posture was intense, her shoulders jutting forward and her pace urgent. *Mentally unstable?*

"I was wondering if I can borrow your phone to make a call," the woman asked in a refined accent, but her words wavered.

Anna blinked a few times, trying to decide if she was a friend or foe. The woman, despite being attractive, looked like a drowned rat. An expensive wool sweater hung heavily on her slender frame, weighed down and distorted by being damp.

"What is the problem?" Anna asked.

"I'm a bit stuck. I need to call a friend to see if she will come and get me." Her long fingers pushed her wet hair around her ear. "I'm sorry to bother you. I guess you're visiting."

"Why do you think that?"

"You have an American accent."

"Actually, I live here. But I don't have my cell with me. Sorry."

"It's fine." The woman turned away and started back to her car.

*She needs help. The question is... Do I want any more problems to deal with?* Anna turned away and took a few more steps along the footpath. *I know it's a holy island, but I'm no Mother Teresa.* She stopped in her tracks. *What if it was me?*

Her decision made, she stepped onto the tarmac of the car park. Anna caught up with the woman and put her hand on her shoulder. "Wait a second. What's your name?"

The woman spun around. Her eyes were red. She might have been crying. "Jessica." Her voice was laced with desperation.

"I'm Anna. I live over there." Anna pointed to her farmhouse, beyond two hedgerows in the distance. "I have a phone at home you can use. It's a ten-minute walk, or if you drive, I can show you the way. You'll get soaked if we walk."

Jessica wiped her eyes. Obvious relief lifted her lips into a smile. "That's... That's very kind."

Anna took hold of Jessica's forearm and squeezed. "It's okay. Let's go."

At the car, Jessica opened the passenger door for Anna. She let out a long, frustrated breath. "I'm sorry the seat is soaked. You can't—"

"I can sit in the back," Anna suggested, before noticing Jessica's eyes were fixed on the refuse bags she carried in her left hand. "Oh, yes." Anna unfolded the pile and passed one over. Jessica placed it on the seat.

"It's not my—" Jessica had stopped in mid-sentence.

When nothing more was said, Anna climbed in. After a few attempts, the car started, and they were underway.

"To the left here. It's narrow." Anna pointed to a small lane between stone walls.

Water was dripping through a gap in the roof directly onto her thigh, and she brushed the splashes off.

"I'm sorry. The latch is broken," Jessica said.

"Not a problem." Anna glanced at the woman's profile as she drove. She was pale, and there were dark shadows under her eyes. "Where have you come from?"

"London."

"Take the next right." She positioned her stack of refuse bags to protect her jeans from the steady drips. "Where were you headed?"

Jessica didn't answer.

Anna noticed her hand where it gripped the steering wheel. "How'd you hurt your hand? Were you in a fight?"

She realised she had switched into question mode. *Maybe she'll start cutting my fingers off or just mug me and take all my money.* Anna frowned at this last thought. She didn't have any money, and Jessica looked as if a moth would win a one-on-one with her.

"Well, I was changing the tyre, and the spanner slipped."

Anna kept quiet for the next mile, until she started to sneeze. "Your car is musty. Turn right here."

They pulled into the short drive, which led to Anna's cottage. Now, she was concerned she'd done the wrong thing. Her best guess was that the woman was a drug addict and out of cash. The confusing part was her clothes were too posh.

"Do you do drugs?" Anna asked, nonchalantly.

Jessica shot her a glance. "Sorry?"

"Drugs. Are you an addict?"

"No..." Jessica's tone was more confused than offended.

"Good. Okay, we're here."

The Saab crawled into a farmyard, which was a mixture of grass, mud, cobbles, and concrete and large enough for a dozen vehicles. Dilapidated stables stood at the far end, with the exception of the last unit where the weatherboard cladding had been freshly stained black. Opposite was Anna's two-storey period farmhouse.

Anna directed Jessica to park next to her rarely used Ford Fiesta. She hated driving in England. The roads were so much narrower than those in the States. And, despite all her trips to the mainland, she was petrified of ending up in one of the deep ditches that ran along most country roads.

"Thanks for doing this," Jessica said as they approached the house.

"That's okay. I'm paying forward, I suppose. Not that I really like the expression. People shouldn't expect anything in return when they help someone." She paused, wondering what her motivations were. "I'm just hoping for better luck."

"I think you have to make your own luck," Jessica muttered.

"I wonder how."

When Jessica half smiled, Anna noticed the human being behind the desperado. She opened the front door, allowing the stranger into her home.

# Chapter Four

ANNA WASN'T SURE how to handle Jessica, so she decided to jump in with both feet as she always did, ignoring any potential embarrassment. "I'll find you something dry to wear."

Jessica was frantically searching through her pockets. After she'd pulled out a slip of paper, she looked up to make eye contact. Anna found it hard not to stare. One of Jessica's irises was a blue-grey, while the other looked as if the Milky Way had been imprinted in layers of greens and blues. "Wow, your eyes are different!"

Jessica's brow creased for a moment. "Oh. Um, yes. It's called heterochromia."

"I've seen eyes like yours in cats or dogs, but not people."

"It's rare."

Anna kept staring. Jessica had beautiful eyes. *I guess she won't mug me and steal my broken boiler.*

Anna took the phone from its charging station and put it in Jessica's hand. "You can make your call in the lounge. It'll be warmer in there. I'll get you a dry top." She pointed towards the lounge and was surprised to see tears in Jessica's eyes. "Are you okay?"

Jessica nodded.

"I won't be a minute."

*Towel, top, tea.* Anna started down the hall and then spun around. She darted back into the kitchen to flick the kettle on, before heading upstairs. She found two hooded sweatshirts that had hardly been worn. Even after ten years, the letters MSU, standing for Michigan State University, still looked brand new. She grabbed one of the hoodies and a T-shirt for Jessica to change into.

In the lounge, she placed the tops and a towel onto the sofa. Jessica stood by the fire, still in her wet sweater.

"Some clothes," Anna said.

Jessica pulled off her sweater. All she had on underneath was a white bra.

Anna looked away as Jessica pulled on the T-shirt. "Did you make your call?"

"Yes. But my friend didn't answer. Is it okay if I try again in a bit?"

"Of course. It's not a problem. Would you like tea or coffee?"

"A tea, please, Anna." Jessica picked up the towel.

Anna headed back into the kitchen and made tea. She didn't like the stuff herself and hadn't been able to adjust to the nation's beverage from ice tea back in the States.

"Are you hungry?" she called into the other room. "There's some leftover flapjacks I can heat up."

Jessica, now standing in the doorway, was sporting the sweatshirt and towel-drying her hair. "Um, yes, please. If it's not too much trouble."

"No trouble." Anna gave a reassuring smile. "I'm sorry it's so cold—the boiler is broken. My ex-husband was the one who always got it going again. You can go sit by the fire. You look freezing. Call your friend and leave a message. You can leave my number. It's on the receiver." *God, I'm ordering her around like she's a teenager.* "Sorry, I'm being a bit bossy."

A half smile played on Jessica's lips for a moment. "It's okay. It's your house."

"Not according to the bank, but, really, I've only had my daughter's company for a while, and I guess I'm used to—" *Do I boss Abbie around all the time?* "Well, telling her what to do. How do you take your tea?"

Again, a pause.

"With milk? Sugar?" Anna asked.

"With milk, please."

The dark-haired woman with the multi-coloured eyes must have been exhausted, and she also appeared confused. Anna passed the cup of tea to Jessica. "Go on through to the lounge."

Five minutes later, Anna quietly placed the food she had heated up on the coffee table. But it was too late. Jessica had fallen asleep by the fire. She took a woollen blanket from where it was folded over one arm of the sofa and draped it over the woman.

HOURS HAD PASSED, and it was now two in the afternoon. Anna's texts and calls were being ignored by Abbie. Anna debated going to look for her, when Abbie pushed through the front door. She decided to let the disobedience go for the sake of harmony between them.

"Why's there a dead woman in our living room?" Abbie asked after peering into the lounge.

"She's not dead."

"Is she undead?" Abbie grinned.

"Yes, a zombie guest. I just dug her up from the monastery's graveyard."

"Zombies don't eat flapjacks. There's a plate of them beside her."

"You're absolutely right, honey. I tried, but she wouldn't eat them." She hooked an arm around Abbie's shoulder and gripped the back of her head. "That's why I need your brain!"

Laughing, Abbie twisted out of her grasp. "Give her yours. You won't miss it!"

"Very funny. For that and not answering your phone and being late, no Mini Eggs."

"I'm not late. It's after lunch." Abbie darted around the kitchen table, lifting plates, paper, and bags, searching.

"It's after two." Anna reached for the cookie jar a second after Abbie pulled out the pack of chocolate Mini Eggs. Anna lunged for her as she ducked, slid under the table and jackrabbited out the other side.

Anna raced around the table to catch her and pulled the pack out of her hand. "Look. I'll do a deal." She panted. "You help me with the stable, and—"

"Mum!"

"Wait. I'm not done. And, I also need your brain for my zombie. Then you can have the eggs."

"No deal!" Abbie snatched the pack from Anna's grasp and raced down the hall and upstairs.

Anna sighed and turned to see Jessica leaning on the doorframe of the lounge with the breakfast plate in her hand.

"Oh, you're awake."

"Zombie?" Jessica smirked.

Anna blushed. "It was a joke." She took the plate from Jessica. "You've eaten some of the cold flapjacks, so I guess you're not undead."

"I was..."

Anna felt the need to break from Jessica's gaze. It was as if Jessica could see into her soul. The connection was scary and exciting at the same time. She turned away. "Any news from your friend?"

"No. I'll try again in a bit. If that's all right?"

"Yes, it's fine."

"Can I help in any way while I'm waiting?" Jessica asked. "You said something about a stable to your daughter?"

Anna crossed her arms. She didn't know this woman. "You never explained why you ended up here. I mean, on Lindisfarne."

"It's a long story."

"Are you running from a bad boyfriend, maybe?"

Jessica shook her head.

Anna uncrossed her arms and sighed. "All right." She pushed her hair around one of her ears and reached for a pair of work gloves from the kitchen table. "I'm clearing out an old stable." She passed the gloves to Jessica. "I'll find you a coat to wear. Abbie can answer the phone if your friend calls."

JESSICA WALKED A few paces behind, wearing an old Barbour coat and the gloves Anna had given her. Her wound rubbed against the glove when she flexed her fingers, and she wondered if it would start to bleed again.

"I have four chickens around somewhere." Anna scanned the courtyard. "There's one." She pointed to a fluffy auburn hen, scratching at a small patch of grass by a downpipe. "Their coop is behind the barn in a treehouse. I get three or four eggs a day at this time of year."

Anna stopped at a stone-built stable block, which consisted of four separate stalls set out in a row along the northwest side of the farmyard. At one end, a beam in the

remove all the tiles, replace the beam, and then reuse the tiles for the roof.”

“I would like to do that. John had ordered the building supplies, but I can’t afford someone to do the work.”

“John?”

“My ex-husband. We divorced two months ago.”

“I’m sorry.”

“It is what it is. I’m not sure it was for the best. But I think that’s what you’re supposed to say.”

The conversation stopped as they entered the farmhouse.

Jessica removed her gloves. “It’s a simple job; I can—”

“God!” Anna shrieked, taking Jessica’s hand. It was covered in blood from where her cut had opened up. “Come to the sink!” Anna flipped on the hot water tap and cursed when the water didn’t warm up. “Keep it under. Sorry it’s cold. You should’ve told me you needed a bandage. What’s wrong with you?”

In truth, Jessica had ignored the wound. However, she could see now it was more serious than she thought; a thick flap of skin was torn above her first knuckle.

“What’s going on?” Abbie’s voice came from behind them.

“Fetch the first aid kit. It’s in the bathroom under the sink.”

“Why? Who’s hurt?”

“Just get the kit!” Anna snapped.

Jessica glanced at Anna, seeing intense frustration and, perhaps fear, in her features. *This isn’t just about my hand.* “It’s not too bad. I’m... I mean, I was a first aider at work. It’s nothing to worry about.”

“I can see it is!” Anna’s voice was edged with annoyance. The wound, disturbed by the flow of water, coloured it crimson. "There's a lot of germs in the stables. I should've bandaged this before."

Abbie appeared with the first aid kit and slammed it down on the counter without a word. She stormed back upstairs.

"I can't get her to help me with anything," Anna muttered to herself. "Sit!"

Jessica did what she was told, feeling like a schoolkid in detention. She said nothing while Anna applied antiseptic, then a pad and gauze, before taping it secure.

"I'm sorry to be a nuisance," Jessica said, inspecting the expertly applied bandage.

"Then be more vocal and say if you're hurt!" Anna stepped away, sighed and leaned against the kitchen counter, tucking her hands into the pockets of her jeans. "Do you want to try your friend again?" Her tone was softer now.

"I left a message, but I don't think she's going to call. She's my ex. We didn't exactly stay friends after splitting-up."

"Oh, I see." Anna's mouth parted slightly and crease lines formed on her forehead.

"I should go." Jessica stood. "Thanks for all you've done. I was wondering if I could borrow—"

"You're joking, right?" Anna cut in.

Jessica's chest tightened. She knew she'd badly outstayed her welcome. "Okay. Well, thanks for everything." She turned towards the door but remembered her sweater was in the lounge. She headed there and collected it from where it hung on the back of a chair near the fire. She spun around and bumped into Anna, whose fingers encircled her wrist.

"Look, let's have a reality check." Anna spoke quickly, her American accent pronounced and her words clipped. "First, you have no money and no gas, by what I could read on your dash. I can lend you some money, but there are no gas stations on the island."

Jessica's throat tightened, and tears welled up. She swallowed and blinked, trying to banish them as Anna continued.

"But most of all, the tide is now on the way in. So you need to stay. Unless your car is amphibious and runs on air."

To her embarrassment, Jessica's tears started to fall, and she wiped them away with the palm of her hand.

Anna looked back at her with shock in her eyes and, to Jessica's surprise, pulled her into a hug. "Hey, it's okay. You can stay the night. But I'm afraid you'll have to sleep on the sofa. The guest room is a bit of a mess."

"I—"

"You're staying. There really is no choice." Anna gently released her.

"Thank you," Jessica mumbled.

"Now, you can help with dinner, if you like. Assuming, of course, I can get Abbie to come back down again. It's pizza night." Anna put another log on the fire. "We'll have to eat in here."

Back in the kitchen, Jessica crossed her arms. "You mean homemade?"

Anna smiled. "You can be in charge of the base." She took Jessica's hand and led her to a clear section of counter. "Do you know how to make pizza dough?"

Jessica frowned. "I don't even know where to start."

Anna turned on a radio next to the sink. A '90s pop song filled the kitchen.

A flour-splattered cookbook was opened and slid in front of Jessica. Anna flicked through the pages, before pressing her finger onto a recipe. "Just follow this." She opened the cupboard above her. "All you need is in here. I'll do the kneading since you have a bad hand. Okay?"

"I'm not sure—"

"Just follow the recipe." Anna tapped the open page. "You'll be fine. And I'm right here, so ask if you need help. I'll make the sauce."

"Anna, you're being way too kind to me." The words tumbled out of Jessica's mouth, unfiltered.

Anna stared at her with her piercing blue eyes. "Don't be silly." She squeezed Jessica's shoulder.

*She touches a lot. She's way too trusting.*

"Mix the salt with the flour in a sieve, then add the yeast." Anna turned away to start her own preparations.

Once the pizzas were cooked and laid out on chopping boards, Jessica looked around for something to slice them. There was a wooden block for knives, but its slots were empty, except for a paring knife.

"Do you have something to cut the pizzas with?" Jessica asked when Anna reappeared.

"I took the pizza wheel through." Anna picked up one of the boards and gestured to Jessica to carry the other two.

The lounge was small but cosy. A cast-iron stove stood in an inglenook fireplace, and its flames lit the lounge. Two sofas ran at right angles to the fireplace and were separated by a small oak coffee table. In the centre of the wall opposite the inglenook was a TV, awkwardly positioned on a bookcase.

Jessica was starving and devoured the meal without tasting it.

After the meal, Abbie sat next to her dozing mum. Her big eyes glanced from her phone to the television. She was a clone of Anna. The same features, eyes, and hair. Anna had explained to Abbie that Jessica was a guest for tonight and the girl hadn't asked any questions. What Jessica couldn't get her head around was Abbie looked to be fourteen, while

Anna seemed to be in her late twenties. *She would've had to give birth when she was in her early teens.*

When Jessica took the plates into the kitchen and washed up, the phone rang. She answered it quickly so Anna wouldn't be woken.

"Jessica?" Chris was on the line.

"Yes."

"How are you doing?"

"Fine. Do you know what happened?"

"Not really... But. Well, everything, unfortunately, points to your laptop's IP address and MAC address. They all show you had accessed the systems prior to the failed test."

"What! How?"

"I don't know."

"Spoofed maybe?"

"It's pretty hard to do. But also, there are audit logs showing you created the fault that screwed our customer systems... Did you do it?"

"Of course not. Why would I?"

"Money. And you wanted to quit. That's what people are saying."

"So, you think I'm guilty as well?" Jessica spoke through gritted teeth. Chris had worked with her for many years. She'd thought they were friends.

There was a pause on the line before Chris replied. "The police have been asking me if I know where you are. I said no. I can get into real trouble now."

"Okay, then. I guess I'm on my own."

"Hold on a second, I'm on your side, because, in truth, you're not that dumb. I mean, you're not stupid enough to leave your fingerprints all over this train wreck if you were involved."

Jessica took a breath, calming down. "So, any ideas?"

"Just one." His words hung for a second. "Where's your laptop? It seemed to disappear after you were dismissed."

"Why do you want it?"

"It's a long shot. But I can't say now."

"Check with Brian. He handed it in."

"Okay. I need to go. I'll keep working on this. Talk soon."

"Wait—" But Chris had already disconnected. She needed to ask him more questions, but at least it appeared he believed she was innocent.

She went back into the lounge to find Abbie had disappeared. Anna was still scrunched up in the corner of the sofa, asleep. Her hair had fallen away from her face, and one arm was across her lap. Jessica studied her for a moment, watching her chest rise and fall with each slow breath. A pang of guilt for the intrusion caused her to look away. After composing herself, she reached forward and gently shook Anna's shoulder.

Anna blinked, stretched, and slowly uncurled like a woodland creature.

"I thought you might want to sleep in your bed," Jessica said, taking a backwards step.

Their eyes met, and Anna stared as if seeking the answer to a question. It was an intimate instant Jessica stole from those unguarded sleepy eyes.

Anna stretched. "I must've dozed off. I'll get you some bedding." With that, she stepped out of the room.

# Chapter Five

JESSICA SWUNG HER legs off the sofa and sat up. It was a new day, but her problems were foremost on her mind. She'd spend the night trying to work out what she would do this morning, and as rays of dawn sunlight reflected on dust particles, she knew she'd been fantasising. Megan wouldn't call. There was nowhere for her to go. She'd have to turn herself in and hope Chris would find something to prove her innocence.

"It's a nice day. Not windy and it's sunny," Anna said when Jessica entered the kitchen. Anna poured a cup of coffee and handed it to her.

"Thanks. Is it possible to get to the mainland now?"

"Yes." The toaster popped, and Anna fetched the slices. She was dressed in smart black slacks and a white blouse with her hair up in a tight ponytail. It looked like she was ready for a business meeting, except it was Sunday. "The toast is for you." Anna passed over the plate.

"You didn't need to."

"You have to eat." Anna's words were frayed. She seemed nervous. "There's some jelly if you want—jam, I mean, strawberry jam." An open jar and a butter knife were placed by the toast.

Anna leaned against the kitchen counter and crossed her arms.

Jessica wasn't hungry. A dull nagging sat behind the more immediate anxiety of going to prison. She should think about getting a lawyer. It'd have to be the next thing she did. Megan hadn't called. *It's time to leave and turn myself in. There's something else, though... Something's really bugging me, beyond this whole work thing. What the hell is it?*

"I'd—" Jessica started to say but stopped when Anna spoke at the same moment. "Sorry, go ahead," she offered.

"I've been thinking." Anna's arms tightened further into themselves. "A farmer on the mainland employs volunteers to help with his camping business. I'd like to try the same here. There'd be no pay, just meals and a room, so I'm..." She hesitated.

Jessica came to her rescue. "You're wondering if I would be interested."

"Yes, I am. You did great work in the stables. So, if you need to stay a few days and help out it would be great for me."

"That's very kind." This beautiful stranger was offering a reprieve. "But, I don't want to intrude." It was the wrong word, and her tone had been too formal. Her emotions were bouncing around like a trawler in a tempest. "My ex isn't going to call. And I just need a bit of time. Another friend, he's trying to help sort things out."

"What things?"

Jessica swallowed a sigh. She couldn't talk about her predicament. Anna would surely send her away or call the police. "I had a problem at work. If Chris, my colleague, resolves it, I'll be able to go home."

"What problem?" Anna's brows scrunched together, and her blue eyes stayed locked on Jessica like a heat-seeking missile.

Jessica shuffled backwards. She didn't want to answer.

Anna uncrossed her arms. "It doesn't matter. I've made a decision to trust you because I think you need help and because any help you give me with the stables is welcome." She picked up her coffee. After a sip, Anna added, "Do you know anything about ponies?"

"No, I grew up in North London. There, a pony was £25."

Anna half smiled, but her expression showed confusion. "They cost a lot more than that."

A blanket padded into the kitchen. Abbie's face popped out and then her arms. She hugged Anna for a second. "Isn't the heating fixed yet? It's freezing," Abbie complained.

"Not yet. I'll make you some breakfast."

"Why are you all dressed up?" Abbie asked.

"Because I need to do something today."

Anna, reverently, picked up a watch, checked the time, and deposited it into the pocket of her slacks.

"But where are you going?" Abbie persisted.

"The bank."

"It's Sunday. They're shut."

"I'm going to the blood bank. Jessica needs food." Anna attacked Abbie, tickling her side.

The teen laughed and darted out of reach. "Zombie vampires don't exist."

"Nor will you, if you keep asking me questions."

"Maybe I don't already, and I'm just a ghost."

Anna stopped dead in her tracks. The colour faded from her cheeks. It appeared she was about to topple over. Jessica darted forward and put an arm around Anna's waist to support her. "Are you all right?"

A few seconds passed. Their noses were an inch from touching. Anna blinked, before using the tips of her fingers to push Jessica away. "Fine." She straightened her blouse and cleared her throat.

Abbie, watching, showed little concern.

*Is this something that happens a lot?*

"I thought you might faint," Jessica said.

Anna ignored her and went back to the counter. Her hands visibly shook as she shoved two slices of bread into the toaster then spoke over her shoulder, "Abbie, after breakfast, show Jessica how to feed and exercise Daisy. She'll be helping around the farm for a few days." When Abbie didn't answer she spun around. "All right?" she snapped at Abbie, who was heading into the lounge.

"Okay!" Abbie screeched back.


IT WAS HARD to tell if Daisy enjoyed the attention. *At least the horse's ears are not back.* They were inside Daisy's stable, where the pony stood still while being brushed down. Jessica had quickly learned most of the ins and outs of how to groom Daisy from Abbie.

"Do you look after Daisy a lot?" Jessica asked Abbie.

"My mum mostly does it. I'm at boarding school in the week."

"Oh. That must be expensive."

Abbie shook her head. She was in the process of fitting Daisy's bridle. "It's free because there's no school for children of my age on the island. The tides mean we can't get there and back easily."

"I see."

"Can you lift the saddle onto her back?" Abbie added, "I can do it. It's just that I have to get the steps."

"Sure." The saddle was sitting astride the stable door, and Jessica stretched to put it into position. Jessica had always thought ponies were small, but this one was taller than her. "Are you sure Daisy isn't a horse?"

"She's not." Abbie laughed. "Horses are fourteen-and-a-bit hands or more. Anything under is called a pony."

"If you have really small hands, won't that make her a horse?"

"No. A hand isn't a person's hand anymore. Like a foot isn't a king's foot anymore. It's a standard size. I don't remember how much, though." She ducked to fasten the saddle's girth.

It was clear Abbie knew exactly what she was doing, and Jessica resisted the temptation to assist as she really didn't know anything about horses. *Pony. It's— She's a pony.*

Once the stirrups were adjusted, Abbie opened the stable door and led the Daisy over to a set of portable steps in the courtyard.

A thought occurred to Jessica. She realised the bigger implications from what Anna had said about trusting her. It wasn't simply about her farm and pony. It included Abbie. *It must have been a huge decision. She doesn't even know me.*

Abbie used the steps so she could get her foot into the stirrup and then pulled herself into the saddle.

"Your helmet." Jessica passed it up.

Abbie laughed again. "It's called a riding hat."

When Abbie was ready, she nudged the pony forward, before twisting back to glance at Jessica. "Come on, I'll show you where the paddock is."

With Jessica walking beside as Abbie rode, they skirted around the farm buildings and passed through a small grove of mature oak trees. The path then continued along a hawthorn hedge and ended at a fenced-off field. Here, the land dipped gently. To the east, its lush green grass seemed to disappear into the sea. On the ground at intervals, low jumps were set out.

"Can you open the gate, please?" Abbie asked.

Jessica unlatched the galvanised five-bar gate and closed it behind her. She perched herself on top and watched as Abbie urged Daisy into a canter, the rider and pony travelling in repeating circuits of the field.

The view was spectacular. Light played on the distant waves, creating a blanket of green-blue studded with sparkling white jewels and, to her right, half a mile or so away, the castle of Lindisfarne stood on a rocky pinnacle. A light breeze blew, mixing the smells of the meadow with salty sea air. Jessica filled her lungs and let her mind go blank, feeling the sun warm her face. She couldn't remember the last time she'd felt the sun on her skin.

An hour might have passed before a sudden yank on the leg of her jeans jettisoned her off the gate. She thudded onto the damp grass.

Raising herself on all fours, she came face to face with a white beard, pink nose, and, finally, two bulbous eyes.

"What the hell!"

The goat bleated or perhaps belched back at her.

Jessica clambered to her feet, just as Abbie rode beside her and dismounted.

"Are you okay?" Abbie took hold of the goat's collar and tried to pull it away, but the animal wasn't moving. It seemed rather interested in Jessica's sweater and was trying to get a bite of it. "This is Kermit. He won't hurt you."

"His teeth might." Jessica gathered herself and retreated from the creature. "Is it yours?"

Abbie nodded. "Yeah. He mostly keeps Daisy company. Ponies aren't good by themselves, and Mum found Kermit in an animal sanctuary. He wasn't wanted since he's a bit of a loner. Except, he seems to like Daisy."

"I see. And you called him Kermit?"

"Yeah, Kermit the goat." Abbie laughed, and Jessica couldn't help wonder if Anna laughed like that. "Well, he's not green, and he's a wether. And, he has eyes like Kermit's. I named him when I was little."

"A wether?"

"Not really a boy goat anymore. My mum says, if he could talk, he'd be high-pitched like Kermit."

"Oh." Jessica laughed.

"Your hand is bleeding."

The bandage Anna had fitted was loose. Jessica pulled it back over her cut.

"We can go back. I'll untack Daisy and bring her back in the field."

"Sure."

They made slow progress on the return trip—the pony kept dipping its head every few feet, trying to graze. Behind them, in front, and then behind again, Kermit ambled, before disappearing through a gap in the hedgerow.

"Should we go find him?" Jessica asked.

"No. He knows his way around. He's kind of the goat king of the island."

Jessica laughed. "Let me get this straight, he's Kermit the Goat King of Holy Island."

"Yup. Exactly!" Anna laughed with her.

"Have you lived here long?" Jessica asked when the stables could be seen peeking through the branches of the oak trees near the farm.

"Yeah, since I was ten."

"How old are you now?"

"Fourteen."

"And you're from the States originally?"

Abbie nodded.

"Is your father there?"

"I don't know. Mum doesn't talk about him. She just says he left when I was two. I had a stepdad for a bit, but Mum got divorced."

The girl's expression had darkened, so Jessica decided it was prudent to stop prying.

Once Daisy's saddle and bridle were removed, a lead rope was fitted, and Abbie took the animal back to the field as Jessica went inside to reapply her bandage. She tried to make a few calls, but no one answered. Megan was a lost cause, and she knew it would be at least Monday before Chris made any progress.

"I've got homework to do," Abbie told her, zipping back upstairs.

It was still only 11:30 a.m. Grabbing a pair of gloves, Jessica headed out to the stall she'd worked on with Anna the previous day. The collapsed side of the roof wasn't visible from the farmyard. She'd spent many of her teen years doing DIY with her father, so she had a pretty good idea what needed to be done to repair the roof. Having collected an old ladder she'd seen lying against the back of the building, she got to work.

IT WAS LATE afternoon when Anna got home. She spotted Jessica pushing the wheelbarrow by the stable and waved before heading inside. After telling Abbie to focus on her homework and not her damn phone, she changed, cleaned out the downstairs spare room, and started dinner. During the day, she'd formulated a plan.

Linda, the owner of the coffee shop, had been happy with her trial and offered her a full-time position. She had arranged to start Monday afternoon, giving her enough time to take Jessica to the clinic about her hand. There was no medical centre on Holy Island, so they would need to drive fifteen miles to one in a small village on the mainland.

She planned to work for Linda during the week while Jessica, or whoever, looked after the animals and did jobs around the farm. Although she didn't like Abbie having to go to boarding school, it meant she could work full time during the weekdays without feeling guilty. It still bothered her that she was not focusing on her own business, but she couldn't see another way around it. Hopefully, by the start of summer season, there'd be enough money to buy another pony. *It's simply a matter of getting some forward momentum.*

While waiting for the roast, Anna dug out her laptop from under a pile of unfiled paperwork and set it up on the kitchen table. She wanted to update her website and add a paragraph about needing a volunteer in exchange for lodging and meals.

Thirty minutes later, Anna saw red. She couldn't get the text to format correctly and, even after ignoring that problem, when she tried to publish the update, an incomprehensible error message appeared. "Fucking awesome!" she cursed, just as her guest came through the door.

Jessica shuddered to a quick stop. "Have I done something wrong?"

Anna slipped out of her chair and touched Jessica's shoulder. "No, it's not you. I'm trying to update my website, and it's all going wrong." She tried to conceal her frustration. She wondered how much of her daily stress she showed in front of Abbie. *Too much, no doubt.*

At the kitchen counter, she prepared runner beans. "So, what have you been doing today?" Anna glanced back to see Jessica busy at her laptop.

"Abbie showed me a lot of horse things. Pony, I mean. Grooming and then we took Daisy to the paddock. Then Kermit, the Goat King of Holy Island, tried to eat me."

Anna burst out laughing at this and spun around. "I should've warned you about him. He likes denim and wool."

"Well, after that, I did some more work on the stables." Jessica smiled and turned back to the screen.

"You can use the spare bedroom," Anna added after a moment. "It has its own bathroom, but it's the colder end of the house."

"It'll be great, Anna. Thanks so much for letting me stay."

"Do you think you can look after the animals during the week? I've taken a job at a coffee shop in the town."

"I'm not sure how long I need to stay. But of course, I can while I'm here."

"Okay." Anna had expected this response, and it was why she wanted the website updated. She needed someone who would be around for longer. "Abbie boards at school, so she's not around weekdays, otherwise, I'd get her to help more."

Jessica nodded. "She told me a bit about that. It must be hard for you."

"It is. Things didn't quite work out the way I wanted them to." She sighed and turned to see Jessica looking back at her with concern. "I'll take Abbie to school first thing in the morning as the tides are that way round at the moment. So you'll need to start then and feed Daisy and Kermit."

"Sure. Do you have any other animals?"

"Just the chickens. Kermit doesn't need much looking after."

Jessica twisted the laptop towards Anna. "Is this okay?"

Anna placed a hand on the top of Jessica's shoulder and leaned over. The addition she'd attempted to the website was now perfectly formatted. Better than that, Jessica had improved the layout. "Wow, that was quick! It looks great."

"Okay to publish it?" Jessica turned towards her.

"Yes, please." Anna only then realised Jessica's body trembled slightly, where her fingers had drifted to touch the bare skin of her neck. She blushed and moved away.

"Okay it's done, but it might—"

Anna grabbed Jessica's wrist, where it rested on the table "What the hell is it with you and bleeding?" The bandage on Jessica's hand was dark with dried blood, which was also crusted at the base of her thumb and over her wrist.

"I fell and knocked it," Jessica stammered, seemingly shocked by Anna's reaction.

Anna yanked Jessica out of the chair and over to the sink. She knew she was overreacting, but it was so hard to control her fear. As she cleaned the wound again, she took deep breaths. "I'll take you to the clinic in the morning. You need stitches."

"I'm sorry I upset you," Jessica said.

Anna sighed. "No. It's me. John used to say I'm messed up. And I superimpose."

"Superimpose what?"

"My past onto the present—"

"That doesn't sound right. You're not messed up. And the past is always in the present. Even here, you see it when you look out the window. It founds and informs us."

Anna smiled while binding Jessica's hand. When it was done, she absentmindedly brushed the top of Jessica's fingers. *She has artist's hands.* The thought, and dealing with the wound, helped her fear to subside. And, if she admitted it, being close to Jessica was rather comforting.

*Perhaps that's why I'm too—I don't know, familiar with her. I've just been alone for too long. Screw John. No, it was a mistake to have ever screwed him at all. It wasn't any fun anyway. Why's she looking at me? I must look a mess... God, those eyes... Who the hell has different coloured eyes?*

Anna glanced up when Jessica's fingers closed around hers.

"You all right?" Jessica asked.

"Fine," Anna said, louder than she intended. She bit her lip and squinted at Jessica. "Okay. I'm okay. Let me show you your room."

AT DINNER, JESSICA watched with curiosity as Anna struggled to carve slices off the roast with a paring knife. By the pained expression on her face, she wasn't comfortable with the task.

"Let me," Jessica offered. She expected Anna to refuse and was surprised when she handed over the blade.

"Thanks," Anna mouthed and sat.

"You don't have any proper knives?" Jessica asked.

When Anna didn't answer, Abbie piped up. "Mum hates them."

"Abbie," Anna snapped.

"What? You don't like them. You have nightmares—"

"That's enough. I don't want to talk about this!"

There was a moment of silence as Jessica served the sliced beef.

"Well, you do," Abbie muttered, before tucking into her meal.

Jessica glanced between the two of them. It was clear a secret had been shared Anna had meant to stay hidden.

# Chapter Six

ON MONDAY, JESSICA was driven to a clinic on the mainland. Somehow, they had managed to survive. Anna's driving was scary. She couldn't keep the car in its lane and had sped along as if she was in a go-kart that only had a stop and go-very-fast button.

At the clinic, Jessica had her wound cleaned and sutured. She received a prescription for antibiotics, but she knew she couldn't go to a pharmacy without any money, so it remained hidden in the pocket of her jeans.

For the rest of the week, Jessica took care of the animals and worked on the roof of the stable. She had managed to remove all the tiles and stacked them, ready for refitting. Repairing the roof was the least she could do for Anna. The work allowed her to think about her life; where she was on its journey and how empty it felt. A judicial prison sentence didn't scare her as much as perpetual solitude.

Behind the stable block was a polytunnel half filled with straw bales. It held the sun's heat, and Jessica sat under its canopy while considering how to carry out the next stage of the build. Kermit had teleported out of nowhere; Jessica was convinced he was actually an alien with advanced tech. His oddly shaped head and domical eyes supported the theory.

Kermit butted her knees. She'd discovered the way to avoid having her clothes eaten was to feed him carrots. At first, this would satisfy him, and he would wander off. However, the goat now had a new behavioural problem.

Kermit would frequently ram into her whenever he wanted another carrot.

To escape him, Jessica ducked out of the tunnel and climbed her ladder, which was positioned inside the end stall. At the roof's apex, she considered how to raise the new rafters to replace the rotten ones she'd removed. It was a two-person job, and she didn't want to bother Anna, who came home exhausted, made dinner, and went to bed. Jessica felt guilty about not cooking, but Anna always insisted she do it, saying it was part of their arrangement.

Jessica hauled herself up and sat on the peak of the gable while enjoying a view of the whole island. Clouds raced overhead, and the sun appeared and disappeared at a moment's notice. The wind caused her hair to whip around her cheeks. She took a black hairband off her wrist and used it to bind a ponytail.

Something nudged her feet, and instinctively her hand darted out to grip the roof's ridge.

Kermit was balancing on the ladder; all four of his hooves on a rung.

"What the hell? Get down!"

Kermit did the opposite, leaping from his spot to the roof's cap. He wandered along its length, turned, and came back again. He butted Jessica in the shoulder so she almost fell twenty feet to the ground. "Get down, you nutcase frog goat!"

Descending the ladder a few steps, she tried to grab onto the goat's collar, unsure how the animal would negotiate the drop. But, when she tried, Kermit backed away. "Stupid animal!"

She glanced around, seeing a tractor and farmer in the field opposite. "Anna's going to kill me," she cursed. She navigated the final rungs and raced over to where she'd seen the tractor.

"Hey!" Jessica panted. "Can you help me? My goat's stuck on the roof."

The portly, weatherworn farmer looked at her. His lips transformed into a smile of amusement.

"Just there." Jessica pointed. Against the clay tiles, Kermit could be seen standing as if he was a goat-shaped weathervane.

"He's climbed higher things than that. I wouldn't worry."

"You know him?"

"Everyone does here. Kermit thinks he owns the place."

"So he'll get down by himself?"

"He's a goat." The farmer laughed loudly. "He climbs everything and eats anything, especially tourists. Shouldn't be here really. On the island, I mean, but he's Abbie's goat and a bit of a legend. He'll get down."

"I see... Thanks."

Jessica turned to leave when the farmer asked a question. "You're visiting? Since Saturday?"

"Yes," she said, concerned how he knew when she arrived on Lindisfarne.

"Mrs Meyer doesn't get many visitors. Suspect she needs a bit of help around the place. But I suppose it must be Miss by now."

*Shit.* Jessica had forgotten what small communities were like in England—busybodies who never got their facts first-hand.

"Can you help me with something else?" she asked, wanting to redirect the conversation, but also noticing the young man who had jumped down from the cab of the tractor.

The older farmer laughed. "That depends what it is."

"Just some heavy lifting. It won't take more than a few minutes."

"Of course, dear, my lad can help. And by the way, I'm Iain Foster." He didn't offer his hand and instead turned to his right and shouted, "David," without realising his son was standing to his left.

THAT EVENING, JESSICA was pleased with her progress. The crossbeams had been fitted with David's help. They had also managed to tack on the under-sheathing and made a start on the laths the tiles would rest on. It was only Wednesday, and she hoped the roof would be finished by the end of the week.

Anna seemed stressed at dinner, so Jessica said little. She wanted to know a lot more about her but felt she couldn't get into a deep conversation. It would lead to questions as to why she was on the run and, right now, she had to stall for time while waiting for news from Chris. If she were lucky, he'd find something to prove she couldn't have been the saboteur.

"Are you going to show me what you've been doing in the stables?" Anna asked.

"Can I show you in a few days? It'll be done by then."

"Oh, I see, it's a secret." Anna stood close by as Jessica loaded the last of the plates into the dishwasher.

"I just want it to be done before I show you."

"You're a perfectionist."

"Why do you say that?"

"Look, you've spaced all the glasses out evenly, even reorganising what's already in it. I've never seen anyone pay such attention to a dishwasher."

Jessica laughed. "Well, I guess I might be one. I never really understood why it's a sin to be a perfectionist."

"It shouldn't be. It's just the way the world works. People who cut corners win. They get crap results, but they win. And, mostly, people only think about themselves and winning. They don't realise we all end up in the same place." Anna's tone was harsh, and a scowl spoiled her delicate features.

"What same place?" Jessica was curious where she was going with this.

"Dead. We end up dead." Anna combed her fingers through her hair and sighed. "Sorry. I'm grumpy today."

Jessica touched her shoulder. "It's fine. Even grumpy, you're pretty amazing."

"Oh." Through a squint, Anna blinked. She tucked a strand of hair around her ear and said nothing. Clearly, she was uncomfortable with the comment.

Annoyed with herself, Jessica was about to apologise when Anna spoke.

"Do you want to go for a walk?"

"Sure, that would be nice." This was the first time Anna had asked her to go anywhere.

"I'm not sure I'll be good company. But here, put this on." Anna handed Jessica a lilac puffer jacket while she slipped on a burgundy all-weather coat. "We'll walk up to the castle and back."

The sun hovered above the hills of the mainland, casting shadows along the prominent features of the island. The wind was unusually still as they walked in silence, strolling through the empty lanes of the village. The soles of their shoes echoed between the dry-stone walls and old-worldly buildings.

Their shoulders brushed a few times, despite Jessica's attempts to keep a small separation between them. She didn't think Anna purposefully bumped into her, but it seemed every time she stopped concentrating on her stride, they were shoulder to shoulder.

"It's very quiet here. Kind of spooky. I'm used to London," Jessica said.

"Is that where you lived?"

Jessica grimaced. She'd said one thing, and they were already digging into her personal situation. This wasn't Anna's fault—Jessica's circumstances would be difficult to avoid touching on.

Anna didn't press her for an answer. "I don't think of it as spooky," Anna said. "I grew up on a farm in the States. Well, before my father became ill. There were few houses around us but not many."

"You had horses there?"

"Yes. We had a few on the farm and would take them to shows with my mother and sister. But really, my sister was the horse nut. I just tagged along."

"Do you still have family in the States?"

"Just my mum."

"What about in England?"

"I have a friend in London and my ex-husband lives there. But I guess I shouldn't list him." Anna flicked a hand towards a gap in a stone wall. "Let's go through here."

A minute later, they stood in the shadows of a ruined priory. Only shells of walls, towers, and windows remained. A dark green carpet of short-cropped grass covered the ground.

Jessica tried to read the knee-high plaque telling of its history, but Anna had disappeared, and she wanted to catch up. What she did read was a reminder from her school days—the priory was said to be the birthplace of Christianity in Britain, some fifteen centuries ago.

Searching for Anna amongst the ruins, Jessica stuttered to a stop when she saw her. Anna stood in an elongated trapezoid of light where a glassless window permitted the sunlight to make landfall. Her hair glowed, giving the illusion of a halo.

Approaching, Jessica moved into Anna's dais. "You look like an angel standing in the sunlight," Jessica said, her emotional brain dumping out the words before she'd a chance to filter them.

Anna flashed an unguarded smile that melted Jessica's heart and sent her pulse racing. "Just trying to keep warm. But that's a nice thing to say... Let's carry on."

They continued along the coast beyond Lindisfarne Priory, not quite reaching the path up to the castle.

"Time to go back. I'm cold," Anna said and then surprised Jessica by taking her arm. "Do you know how long you will stay?"

"I'm not sure really. But I hope my problems will be sorted in a week or two."

"You can stay as long as you need. It's nice to have grown-up company. And not be walking alone with everyone ignoring me."

Jessica understood this. In London, with so many people around, it gave the impression you weren't alone. But, in reality, you might as well not exist. The lyrics of a song she had written fifteen years ago popped in her head.

> *To walk with such purpose, so secure in your fortress,*
> *My open arms are useless, as you won't take notice.*
> *No one notices,*
> *I'm somebody else.*
> *I'm somebody else.*

*Alone in a darkening, my lifeblood dwells.*
*My faint hope expelled, above an electric rail to farewell,*
*Not even a farewell,*
*I'm somebody else.*
*I'm somebody else.*

It hadn't been a happy time for her and Jessica was thankful she'd decided to leap on the tube train when it rattled into Baker Street station, instead of jumping just before it.

Anna's melodic voice drew her back to the present. "I keep thinking about getting a dog, so I have someone to walk with. I guess you'll do for now." Anna glanced her way and squeezed her arm. It was a subtle gesture that seemed to say, *I know where you've been.*

"So, I'm a dog now?" Jessica smirked.

"It's better than being a zombie."

"True. Being your dog would have amazing fringe benefits."

"Well, you're not sleeping on my bed, if that's what you're thinking."

"Oddly, that was my first thought."

Anna bumped shoulders with Jessica. "Are you flirting with me?"

"Maybe a little bit." It amazed her how easily their conversation flowed when they did talk. It encouraged Jessica to drop her guard and be playful. The strange thing about Anna was she didn't seem straight. In fact, the opposite. Jessica had met straight women who experimented and broke hearts. Anna was just being herself. *Maybe she's bi?* Jessica stomped on the thought. *What the hell am I thinking? I'm wanted by the police!*

"What type of dog would you get?" Jessica asked, manoeuvring to safer ground.

"I'm not sure, but I need to get another pony first."

"If you bought a really big dog you could use it as a pony."

"Now there's an idea." Anna laughed.

"And if you let Abbie name it, it would end up being called Rex the pony."

"More likely, Felix the pony." Anna chuckled.

"Oh, I see." Jessica smiled. "Felix, the huge dog with a cat's name who is being used as a pony."

"Exactly!" Anna howled. "You know, you're the first person I've met in England who understands our sense of humour."

"It's not hard to understand warped."

"Hey." Anna nudged her with an elbow. "Careful, or you'll be sleeping in the stables. But I like your dog pony idea. So, I still might feed you."

"I'd be okay with that." Jessica smiled.

In the twilight, Jessica explored Anna's profile. Her immensely kissable ruby lips, pale skin, and perfect jawline. She was stunning.

Behind long lashes, blue irises flashed her way, and, at that moment, Jessica meant what she'd said last.

JESSICA HAD BEEN woken by a woman's voice mumbling in distress. The room was pitch-black, and the absence of light scared her. She listened, sitting up on the edge of her bed. But there was only silence. It was possible she'd dreamed it. It took a moment before she was able to establish where and when she was. It was the early hours of Friday, and she was in Anna's spare room located in the single-storey wing of the house.

Floorboards creaked. A minute later, she heard glass smash on the floor. Jessica donned a pair of slippers and darted out of her room, dressed in a black T-shirt and sweatpants Anna had lent her.

In the kitchen, wearing a pink robe, Anna was using a dustpan and brush to sweep up broken shards.

"Are you all right?" Jessica asked.

Anna turned and gasped, dropping the dustpan. Her hand reached up and gripped the table's edge to steady herself.

"Sorry, Anna, did I scare you?"

"Just a bit."

Jessica bent down to pick up the brush and pan. "You've got bare feet. Let me do this."

Anna nodded, straightening as her fingers clenched the top of her robe together. Deep shadows under her eyes showed her fatigue.

"What were you getting?"

"Just water. I was going to take an aspirin."

"I'll get you another. Now, out, please."

"Okay." Anna tiptoed into the lounge.

A wave of concern flashed through Jessica, tightening her chest. *She doesn't look well.* As she swept, she tried to understand this emotion. She liked Anna. She was easy to like: assertive, gregarious, beautiful and kind. But she couldn't remember ever feeling such a rush of empathy for someone before. Gut-wrenching guilt, yes, but not this.

In the lounge, Jessica passed a glass of water to Anna and sat beside her. "You can't sleep?"

Anna shook her head.

Jessica watched as Anna swallowed two pills with shaking hands that caused the water to slosh in the glass. "What's keeping you awake?"

"Nothing new. I should take my sleeping pills, but it's too early, late, whatever, to take them now."

Jessica shuffled beside her and put an arm around her waist. "I heard you talking in your sleep. Nightmares?"

Anna nodded. "Trauma when I was young. Never really got over it. But it seems to be worse now."

"Do you know why?"

Anna nodded and put her hand over Jessica's. "It's kind of you to try to help, but I don't want to talk about it, or think about it, if that's okay. To me, it's better to forget than try to remember."

"Sure." Anna looked as if she was on her last legs. "Maybe try to go to bed again."

"I need to be up in two hours, so—" Anna ran her hand over her eyes. "I may as well stay up now."

"Come here." Jessica knew sometimes the obvious solution was the best one. She gathered Anna and leaned back. "Put your feet up."

Anna shifted, tucking her feet onto the sofa, as Jessica flipped a tartan woollen blanket over them both.

"This okay?" Jessica asked.

"Yes," Anna muttered. A few minutes passed. Jessica listened as Anna's rapid heart rate slowed and her breathing synched with hers.

"You know what bothers me about you?" Anna said softly.

"No," Jessica whispered. She withdrew her fingers from where they were stroking Anna's hair.

"Nothing. And that's unusual." Anna let out a sigh of contentment. "Keep going with the hair thing. It's...well, really nice."

# Chapter Seven

"HEY, EARTH TO Anna," Linda said. "Too much milk."

Anna re-entered the troposphere, noticing the milk she was pouring was overflowing the customer's coffee cup.

She checked her watch. It was mid-morning, and Priory's Cup was quiet with one customer sipping a latte and another waiting patiently.

After redoing the order, Anna asked Linda if she could make a quick call.

"Of course, honey. We're not exactly packed at the moment." Linda was mostly reasonable, but she tended to snap at some of the younger staff during peak times. Anna wondered what she would be like when the tourist season was in full swing. She inwardly tensed at the thought. The knowledge that she had agreed to only work until the start of the summer holidays helped her to endure the day. But the job wasn't the problem. Today, the problem was a beautiful, mysterious Englishwoman who had set up residence in her brain and, to Anna's shock, in other places she didn't think possible.

In the kitchen situated through a door behind the counter, she dug out her cell. *Mobile, I mean mobile.*

She made a call to her friend in London. "Hi, Sarah, it's Anna."

"Hey, Anna! How's you, awesome girl?"

"Fine," she lied. "It's all totally fine... Is it okay to talk?"

"Yeah, it's calm. I'm just between venues, so, go ahead."

Sarah was an old friend of Anna's from her high school days in Michigan. She had made use of her dual citizenship to move to London and get a job at a music and live-events agency.

"You know how we'd planned for the first week of June—well, I was wondering if we could make it sooner?" Anna hoped she didn't sound too desperate.

"It's possible. I'd have to check my calendar. Is there a problem?"

"No, but it'd be useful if you could." Anna touched the tip of her nose to see if it had grown. She wasn't used to this lying thing. For most of the morning, she had been regressing back to her teen years, trying to remember if she'd ever felt this way about other women when she was younger. She could find no point at which the thought, *I'd really like to kiss her,* had popped into her head. And, perhaps worse, Anna certainly had never felt attracted to men in the way she was to Jessica.

"Okay. So, when should I visit?" There was an edge of suspicion in Sarah's slow delivery.

"How about tomorrow?" Anna asked, as sweetly as she could.

"Like tomorrow, this Saturday? Swear down. I know it's your birthday on Tuesday, but are you that desperate for a present?"

"No, don't be silly. It's just... It's not the sort of thing I can talk about on the phone. I'm at work."

"Work?"

"Yeah. I had to take a job in a coffee shop to make some extra money before the holidays start. But if you can't make it tomorrow, it's okay. I'll—"

"Annamaria, what's going on?"

"Sexuality crisis. Can you make tomorrow or not?" Anna raced the words out.

Sarah's gasp bounced over the cellular network and echoed in Anna's ears. "Um, when you say sexuality, what do you mean?"

"Sarah, I can't discuss this now," Anna whispered into the phone. Her cheeks flushed. She regretted calling her friend. "Let's keep the original date. Everything is perfect."

"Allow it. I can tell you're lying. If you want me to try this weekend, I'll try. Let me see what I can swap."

"Thanks so much, Sarah."

"I can't promise it's doable. I'll send a text in a bit."

"Thanks." Anna ended the call, hoping the redness in her cheeks would be put down to steam from the coffee machine.

JESSICA HAD TO admit completing the roof was easier with David around. The young man had turned up in the morning, offering to help again. By dinner time, they had replaced all the tiles, using the originals and some spares Anna's ex must have ordered at some point.

Astride the roof's peak, she was cementing ridge tiles in place while David hefted them up the ladder and shifted them to where they were needed.

"Just a couple more," Jessica told him. Her arms ached, and she could barely lift the trowel as she gathered more cement from her bucket to finish the last two tiles as they were dropped into place.

Jessica scanned her surroundings. A few clouds, as white as cotton, drifted by. She envied their freedom. The roof was done, and perhaps Chris would call with the news that would help her get home. But did she want her old life anymore? *It would be nice to stay here.* She shook her head. *Are you a fucking idiot? First, it's unlikely Chris will find anything. So, guess what—you're going to jail! And second, Anna lives in a different world. Create as many fantasies as you want, they will never become real. Stop being delusional.*

She sighed. She'd been daydreaming about Anna with every placed tile and Jessica had started to believe her fabricated happy-ever-after bullshit.

"So, are you coming tonight?" David asked. He stood atop the ladder waiting for Jessica to descend from her elevated perch.

"That's like the billionth time you've asked me. Oddly, the answer is still the same." It sounded harsh even to her own ears. He had done a lot of work for her.

"Is that a yes? It'll be fun. There's an indie band playing, doing covers."

She had to hand it to David, he was persistent, but she wasn't going on a date—except with Anna, if she asked. *Get real, there is a better chance of Kermit asking you.*

"Look, David, it's very kind, but to repeat, first, I'm not into guys. That means, so it's perfectly clear, I only date women. Second, this one is also important, you must be ten years younger than me. And last, I have no money to go out."

"I'll buy your drinks. It'll be fun. Besides, I'm thinking you've just not met the right guy."

Kermit and David had a lot in common. Both stubborn beyond stupidity. "It doesn't work like that. Can you please move? I want to get down."

Back on the ground, she walked away from the stable and inspected the completed roof. When David followed, she almost checked her pockets for a carrot. "Looks good. Thanks for your help, David."

"No worries. It got me out of helping with the pigs on my brother's farm."

Jessica decided not to dig deeper; she didn't want to know how he'd escaped his duties since it was clear his main objective had been to ask her out.

"So, see you at nine at the Anchor?" David persisted.

"Give it a rest. There must be other girls you can ask out."

"Should I ask Anna?"

A twinge of annoyance prickled her. "No. Anna's—"

She was about to lay into him when she guessed what had fired her anger. *Jealousy?* Jessica rubbed her temple. *It's none of my business.*

David's mobile rang. He pulled it out and answered. "Yes, Dad... Just coming home. Was helping Jessica with her roof... Yeah, Yeah, I'll get them."

He turned back to her. "So then, I'll see you there at nine. I've got to go." He jogged in the direction of his tractor that was parked in the next field.

"No!" she yelled after him.

Back inside the house, Jessica went upstairs to shower. With the boiler broken, another thing Jessica meant to look at, the only available hot water was from an electrically heated shower unit in Anna's en suite bathroom.

It was getting late, and Anna still hadn't come home. Now showered and dressed, she used Anna's computer to try to work out what the error codes on the front of the boiler meant. She had tracked down its manual online but couldn't concentrate. She was sitting in Anna's house when Anna should've been home hours ago.

"She said she'd be back at her usual time," Jessica mumbled to herself.

She glanced at the clock on the cooker for the umpteenth time, then again and again. 19:01... 19:14... 19:26.

She tried Anna's mobile number, taken from on a Post-it stuck to the fridge. When there was no answer, she stood up, grabbed the MSU sweatshirt Anna had left for her, and clawed it on in a hurry.

Jessica paused. *I'm overreacting. She's just late. Maybe it's taking longer to collect Abbie from her friend's house?* She frowned. *Anna's always on time and always says exactly what she's doing.* She didn't think anything was wrong, but the sinking sensation in her stomach meant she couldn't sit around and wait.

"To hell with this." Snatching up the house keys, she darted out and locked the door.

Marching down the lane, she headed into the village, hoping to find the coffee shop where Anna worked.

The first café showed no signs of life. The second, the Oasis Café in Chare Ends, was equally as dark, except for an illuminated green box, housing a public defibrillator. Distressed and unsure which direction to head in next, she stopped a passerby who directed her to a third.

Peering in through a misted window of the Priory's Cup coffee shop, she could see movement in the back of the café. She knocked on the glass. A moment later, a middle-aged woman appeared and unlocked the door.

"Yes?" the woman asked. She wore a water-soaked apron over a flowery dress and yellow kitchen gloves.

"Is Anna here?"

"She'll be out in a moment."

*Anna's not under any obligation to tell me if she's going to be late. What am I doing here?* She gripped her wrist then crossed her arms and waited opposite the café. She needed a plausible reason why'd she'd come looking for Anna.

INSIDE THE CAFÉ, Linda turned to Anna. "I'll finish the rest," Linda said. "Thanks so much for helping at short notice."

Anna smiled and was inwardly relieved. When Linda had asked her to stay late to help with the cleaning in advance of a food hygiene inspection, she'd wanted to say no, but decided she wasn't in a position to turn down extra work.

She collected her coat and stepped into the café proper, before leaving through the main door. She was surprised to see a pensive Jessica leaning against the wall opposite.

"Hi, I didn't expect you. Is something wrong?" Anna asked.

"No... No. I tried to call. I was wondering where you were."

"Oh... Linda needed me to stay late." A warm rush filled Anna's centre. It was nice to have someone care about her whereabouts. But it did seem strange. Jessica was like two different people. Most of the time, she was confident and capable, but now, she was vulnerable and afraid, the same as when they'd first met. "You've got no coat," Anna started to unzip her jacket. "Here, put on mine."

"I'm good. And sorry. You must feel like I'm bloody stalking you now."

Jessica was definitely not herself. Anna closed the distance between them and caressed Jessica's cheek. "What's wrong?"

"Nothing. I'm being foolish."

"Tell me."

"It's just, as you know...you're really all I've got. I was concerned."

Anna kissed Jessica's cheek. It had taken quite a dose of willpower not to kiss her lips. "I'll make sure I tell you next time. Okay?"

"You don't need to." Jessica glanced away, her eyes staring off into the distance before returning. "Like I said, I'm being stupid... It hasn't helped that Chris hasn't called."

"Chris is your work colleague, right?"

"Yes."

Anna took Jessica's arm, as she had the other night, and they started down the street. "Even if I can't help, it might be good for you to talk about your problem at work."

"I..." Jessica sighed. "God, Anna. It's complicated, and... It's best if I don't."

"Sure. I won't force you."

Jessica squeezed Anna's arm in hers.

"Come on, let's get Abbie, then we can head back," Anna said. "And tell me if you're too cold." But Anna knew she wouldn't.


AFTER COLLECTING ABBIE from her friend's house, to Anna's frustration, she ended up arguing with her all the way back to the farm.

"Abbie, I'm not going out. I'm tired, and I don't want to spend money in a pub listening to some crappy band."

"Mum! Please! They're called The 8-Balls. And they're doing covers of my favourite group! We're going," Abbie insisted.

"Sorry, honey. No."

"You never take me anywhere. All my friends go to gigs, and I'm stuck here!"

"You're not all your friends."

"Well, I'm going."

Anna stopped, turned, and grabbed Abbie's arm. "You're fourteen. You can't go to a pub on a Friday night. That's final!"

"Katy's going!"

"Tough!" Anna let go of Abbie and started walking again. She glanced at Jessica, who returned a concerned smile, but said nothing until she was beside her.

"David asked me to go with him to the gig as well."

"David?" Anna glanced at Jessica.

"He's the son of the farmer who owns the land next to yours."

Anna remembered seeing him, but she had never met him properly. "He must be about twelve."

Jessica laughed. "I think twenty, but his maturity might be around that."

"He doesn't know you're a lesbian?"

"I told him," Jessica half smiled. "You know, when I turned him down, he wanted to know if he should ask you."

"Seriously?"

"I said you'd be happy to go," Jessica joked.

"Oh, my God, you didn't say that, did you?"

Jessica laughed. "No." After a moment, she added, "I had been wondering if you might want to come with me. But, you're right, it's late, and I'm monetarily challenged."

Anna almost tripped up. She recovered quickly and pretended nothing had happened. However, a kaleidoscope of butterflies had taken off inside her stomach. She wasn't sure what to say. She couldn't back out of telling Abbie no. She couldn't say yes to Jessica without admitting something was going on beyond a simple friendship. She wasn't even sure she had admitted to herself what her feelings towards Jessica actually meant. *Why is this a problem? Because it is!*

She was trying to squash her imagination from spinning a romantic candlelit table for two when they arrived in the courtyard to find a blue car parked next to the house.

A woman raced over. She had a fauxhawk haircut and wore ripped navy jeans and a black bomber jacket. "Anna! There you are! I've been trying to call for the last hour."

"Sarah," Anna shouted in surprise. The two women hugged and kissed cheeks. "I wasn't expecting you until tomorrow!"

"I know. Well, the only flight I could get to Edinburgh was this afternoon. So, I pulled in a lot of favours, jumped on the plane, and got a rental car at the airport. I didn't want you to pick me up with your scary driving. And I only just made it over that stupid tidal thing of yours with water up to my fucking doors. Talk about isolated. Your end is in the middle of nowhere. And what's it with you and phones?"

"I'm sorry my cell died." Anna smiled. "It's great to see you! I can't believe you made it."

"Well, you said there was a problem about your sex—"

"Later!" Anna shrieked and glanced back to Jessica who was standing to one side with a puzzled expression.

"O-kay," Sarah stared at Anna, before giving Jessica the once-over.

Anna bit her lip, hoping Sarah wouldn't read her thoughts. She always could, though. "This is Jessica, she's staying with me for a bit and helping around the farm."

"Hi." Sarah held out her hand, and Jessica shook it. "Do I know you from somewhere?"

"I don't think so," Jessica said.

Sarah turned back to Anna, after giving Jessica another glance. "Deeping it. So you're into this peng woman?" she asked, tipping her head towards Jessica.

Anna knew *peng* meant beautiful; Abbie had been teaching her slang words when explaining the lyrics of her favourite songs. She playfully hit Sarah's shoulder. "Stop with the London slang. No one understands it. You're not even British."

"I bloody am." Sarah laughed. "I was born here."

"You moved to the States when you were one. It hardly counts." Anna hugged her friend again. It was good to see her. Sarah's family were originally from Jamaica, having immigrated to Britain, but after Sarah was born, her father's job was relocated to the States. They had gone to high school together and become friends. Sarah was one of the few who had always stayed in touch and the only person who had helped her through her sister's death.

Sarah shrugged and glanced at Abbie. "Hiya, Abbie. You've grown a lot since I last saw you. Almost taller them me. Let's see." Sarah stood beside the teen. There was about two inches difference. "By Sunday, you'll be bigger."

Abbie laughed at this.

Sarah collected her bag from her rental car, and they went inside. But, before Anna could take off her coat, Sarah piped up. "Annamaria, I'm bear hungry and need a big glass of wine. Let's go out for dinner, my treat."

"Bear hungry? You want to eat a bear?" Anna asked.

"Very hungry," Jessica answered.

"You must have a pub on this Alcatraz?" Sarah said.

"Yes!" Abbie shouted. "The Anchor pub has good food!"

Anna gave Abbie her hardest cold stare, which she knew wasn't up to much.

"Good, we'll go there," Sarah said.

"Cool beans!" Abbie said.

"It would save cooking," Jessica chimed in.

Anna was a few sentences behind the conversation. She'd only just twigged that Jessica understood Sarah's slang. *Shit! "You're into this peng woman?" Maybe Jessica didn't hear. She didn't say anything.*

"Let's go, Mum," Abbie said.

Anna rolled her eyes. "That's right, everyone gang up on the dumb blonde American." She feigned insult while grinning broadly. It was nice to have company; she couldn't remember when she'd last felt this warm inside. She thought she might cry. Instead, she pulled Abbie into a hug and kissed her temple. "Okay, you win, Miss I-always-get-my-way."

"Yes!" Abbie punched the air. "Victory again! I need to change," she said, before hurtling upstairs.

# Chapter Eight

THE ANCHOR, A small establishment at the centre of Holy Island, didn't smell as Jessica expected. Her memories of pubs were before the smoking ban when they were dominated by the overpowering stink of cigarette smoke. This one smelled of stale beer and body odour. For more than ten years, she'd avoided pubs completely, but tonight was an exception made for Anna and Abbie's sake. Abbie was desperate to see the band and, if they stayed at home, she knew Anna would insist on cooking. Also, Sarah had offered to pay. The reasons for going didn't really pave over the big crack from her past—the dreadful evening in Enfield when her dreams were shattered.

The place was a carbon copy of most old-worldly pubs in England. Enlarged Victorian picture postcards of how the village used to be were dotted along the walls, tankards hung on hooks above the bar, coins from many generations had been pushed into splits in the oak beams and a strand of tinsel, undoubtedly left over from Christmas, weaved around a set of trophies on a shelf near the dartboard.

Abbie waved to a girl her age and made a beeline towards her. The rest of the group followed. Jessica was introduced to Abbie's friend, Katy, and her mother, Beth. They managed to squeeze onto a bench at the same table. Abbie sat next to Katy, then Sarah, Anna and, finally, Jessica was on the end.

From where they were, Jessica had a clear view of the band prepping at the other end of the bar. She tried to hold onto the reasons for coming, but the vibe of the place felt wrong. The pangs of guilt and fear had started to surface when she entered and now were growing stronger. It was also bugging her that she had no way to pay for anything.

"I'm sorry, but I think I'll go back," Jessica whispered to Anna.

Before she could stand up, Anna put her hand on the top of her thigh.

"Why?" Anna asked.

"No money and—"

"You made it," David interrupted, slipping beside Jessica and turning to her. "You can join us if you want," he said and pointed to a table closer to the band, where two other clean-cut males and an underdressed young woman sat surrounded by empty glasses and beer bottles.

Jessica felt Anna's fingers tighten possessively around her thigh.

David noticed the others and offered a "Hello."

"You're Mr Foster's son?" Anna asked.

"That I am. It's the first time I've seen you here."

"Yes. I don't go out that often."

David turned to Jessica. "Do you want to meet my friends?"

Jessica was about to say, "No," when Anna forcefully answered for her. "We're together."

"Okay, no problem," David said, with an easy smile. He got up and went to the bar as his mates yelled drink orders across the room.

"Sorry, I shouldn't have answered for you." Anna's cheeks had turned crimson.

"It's okay. He's doesn't seem to understand my 'no' anyway. Yours worked."

"I'm glad." With her free hand, Anna retrieved the menu from the centre of the table. She opened it and slid it under Jessica's nose. "Don't worry about money. I'll cover you."

Jessica was pretty sure Anna didn't know what she had just done. In the space of thirty seconds, she had put her at ease around her lack of funds and had chased off the overly friendly puppy. She'd also helped calm her fears of the pub by staying close.

Finding Anna's hand where it rested on her thigh, she entwined their fingers. It wasn't so much that Jessica was desperate to hold her hand, although that was part of it. The sensation of Anna's touch on her leg had become intense, and she needed a less arousing connection. She tried to concentrate on the menu, very aware of Anna studying her.

After choosing the cheapest thing on the menu, Jessica turned to Anna. When their eyes met, Anna looked bewildered. She pursued her lips and double blinked, then shook her head as if a thought had got stuck.

Sarah was saying something to them both that Jessica hadn't heard.

"Hello. This is English I'm speaking," Sarah said, waving at them.

"Sorry," Anna responded.

"I'll order. What would you like to eat?" Sarah asked.

"The lasagne."

"Jessica?"

"The same for me, please."

"Got it." Sarah headed to the bar.

"You seemed worried when you came in here. Is everything okay?"

"I'm just not good in pubs."

"Why?"

Jessica leaned into Anna without thinking. Her head brushed Anna's. "Sorry," she said and corrected her sitting position. "They remind me of—" She sighed. "A not so great night, years ago." The memory of the horrific evening was fighting its way forward in her mind.

"What happened?"

Anna's thumb was brushing over the top of hers in a surprisingly tender motion.

"It doesn't matter," Jessica said.

"When will they start?" Abbie asked, thankfully interrupting any possible follow-up from Anna.

"Any minute now, I think," Anna answered, slowly, shifting her attention.

Jessica let out a slow breath, relieved she was not going to be questioned further. *Why are there so many things not to talk about all of a sudden?* The thought triggered the jarring reminder she was still wanted by the police. Her past, present, and future were all converging into dark oblivion. Jessica would've become the black hole at its centre if it wasn't for the reassuring hand of a beautiful American. At that moment, she felt the need to do something special for Anna and Abbie. Even if it was to be her last gesture. If Chris had no positive news tomorrow, it would be time to turn herself in.

"So why did you want to see the band?" Anna asked Abbie.

"I don't want to see them," Abbie said in a tone stereotypically projected at dimwits. "They're going to do covers of The Underfex."

"They aren't The Underfex?"

"No, Mum, they're The 8-Balls. I told you that."

"So who is The Underfex?"

"Mum, you know them! Their songs are on all the time."

Anna shook her head.

Abbie let out an exasperated sigh. "Like this." She sang the chorus to a song and Katy joined in.

"Oh, yes, I do like them."

Abbie rolled her eyes and went back to her phone.

Leaning towards Jessica, Anna whispered, "It doesn't look like they'll be any good. They're arguing."

The guitarist had his hand over the microphone and was yelling at the bass player. None of them looked to be older than nineteen. They sported the latest boy band haircuts and wore grubby, ripped jeans.

Sarah returned with a tray of drinks and a stack of crisp packets. "Bad news, they're not doing food. Good news, they'll bring over baskets of chips and sandwiches." Sarah sat and placed a glass of white wine in front of Anna, then Diet Cokes for the girls and Jessica, before reaching for her own drink.

"What do you live on out here? It's the edge of civilization," Sarah said.

Anna shrugged. "Chips and wine, mostly." She opened a packet of crisps, offering one to Sarah.

Sarah laughed. "Swear down."

Just then, the band started to play, and no one could be heard over the racket.

"God, they're shit," Sarah yelled.

Jessica frowned. They were ear-bleedingly bad.

Anna released her hand and checked on her daughter. Abbie's face had transformed from excited anticipation to abject disappointment. She'd been filming on her phone, but now lowered it. It looked like she was about to cry.

A new lyric was injected into the rendition by the lead guitarist, "I told you! You're out of tune, asshole!" He then took off his guitar and stormed out of the pub. The others stopped playing and, after a moment, the keyboardist said into his mic. "We're having a technical issue." He then raced after the guitarist, only to return a few minutes later without him and announced, "Sorry, everyone. Looks like that's it."

"Why does bad stuff always happen to me?" Abbie complained, before retreating to her screen.

"It's nothing to do with you, Abbie," Anna tried to soothe. "They're just bad."

Anna's shoulders had dropped, and lines of concern marked her forehead. She put an arm around Abbie and whispered something into her ear.

Jessica closed her eyes. She could rectify this, but she hadn't played in a long time. She'd heard the songs before and knew they would be easy to pick up by ear. *No... I can't be up there... This might be the last thing you do for them... Do it.*

Jessica gathered what strength she could find and stood. She fought the tension squeezing her insides, knowing once she started, the fear would be suppressed by the distraction of playing.


*WHAT ON EARTH?* Anna thought as she regarded Jessica interacting with the young band members. *What is she doing?* There was a lot of nodding of heads, and then the keyboardist followed her to the amps where they changed some settings.

Abbie and Katy were watching with the expectations of a dog at a dinner table.

"What's she's up to?" Anna asked.

It was intended as a rhetorical question, but Sarah answered. "I guess she's going to join in. If she does, they'll have to rename the band to The 6-Balls."

Jessica hadn't said anything about being a musician. In fact, from what she had said, it had sounded as if she worked in an office. However, there she was, adjusting one of the tuners on the bass guitarist's instrument. After he plucked a note, Jessica gave him the thumbs-up and removed her sweatshirt. She lifted the electric guitar's strap over her head and spent a moment tuning the strings.

"Abbie, can you come here a second with your phone?" Jessica asked into the microphone.

Abbie leapt up and raced over, skirting around an incoming barmaid with a tray of sandwiches and chips.

Anna put her elbows on the table and rested her chin in her palms. She had been worried for Jessica who appeared nervous on the stage, unsure of herself, perhaps even trembling. After she had lifted on the guitar, her manner had changed. The sharp edges to Jessica's features had dissipated. She no longer looked like a canary captured in a cage.

The tight black T-shirt Anna had lent her was a size too small, accenting Jessica's hips and impossibly perfect breasts. Anna couldn't stop staring, and a sensation of desire grew from within her; it was a warmth she'd never felt before. Flushed, Anna bundled up her hair in one hand and lifted it away from her overheating neck and face.

At that point, Jessica glanced her way and smiled.

*Awesome, she has a sixth sense, knowing when I'm... I'm what? Lusting after her? Extra awesome.*

"She must be able to play," Sarah said, after devouring half of a cheese sandwich.

"I guess so," Anna said, fanning herself with her hand.

Jessica seemed to be practising riffs as Abbie held her phone for her to hear.

"She's your sexuality confusion, right?"

"Shh." Anna squeezed Sarah's arm. "And yes," she whispered. "For some reason, I'm drawn to her like a moth to a flame... Maybe, not a flame, a light."

"And you think you're gay now?" Sarah said close to her ear.

"I don't know."

"She's beautiful." Sarah laughed. "I'd be gay for her."

"Jesus, Sarah. Please. Let's talk about this later, okay?"

"Why not now?"

"Because my daughter's best friend is sitting right beside you," Anna said through gritted teeth, while gently elbowing Sarah in the ribs.

Sarah took a slug of wine. "Yeah, okay. It's calm."

At near light speed, Abbie dropped back into her seat. "Jessica's going to play 'Northern Lights' and 'Winter Girl,'" she announced. Her chirrupy excitement had returned.

"Cool," Katy chimed in.

Abbie was on her screen again. Something Anna had no patience for. She couldn't understand why teens spent so much time staring at their phones. In fact, she hated it. She hated what it did to Abbie—how upset she would get, how angry; all because of some Snapchat that had turned into a dis. "Abbie, put your phone down and eat some food."

"In a minute, Mum. I need to film this."

Anna was about to tackle her daughter's defiance when the band began to play.

First the drums, keyboard, and then the bass kicked in, but it came to a halt when Jessica said, "Stop." Next, she spoke off-mic to them all.

"What's happening?" Anna asked Sarah. She figured, since Sarah was in the music business, she would know something.

Sarah was unable to respond straight away with several chips stuffed into her mouth. "Their timing—" She swallowed. "Their timing is bad. I'm not surprised the guitarist fucked off."

"Sarah, don't swear. The kids."

"Oops, sorry. Not used to children being around."

The band began again and, as their instruments blended together, the difference from when they first played without Jessica was incredible. The volume was lower, and the distortion that had sent Anna's fillings rattling was now absent. They no longer sounded like a cat dying in a corrugated outhouse. Instead, an indie group now had a progressive voice and groove.

Jessica had begun to play.

"Whoa," Sarah said.

"She's great," Anna muttered.

They flicked a glance at each other.

Four bars later, when Jessica began to sing, Anna's jaw dropped. A surge of emotion travelled through her from her chest to her head. "Heck," she muttered.

Jessica's timbre was so unique. Light and gentle but edged with soulful melismata that moved between each word.

"This is lit!" Sarah said.

Anna was gobsmacked, unable to respond. Her body was doing things she had no control over. She found it impossible to believe the dishevelled stranger, who'd appeared out of nowhere a week ago, had such stupefying amounts of talent. She even felt a bit embarrassed. Had Jessica been messing around with her all this time? *I don't understand.* The music started to replace her thoughts, causing tension and uncertainty to ebb. She listened and glanced to Abbie, who was singing along, while still filming.

This gave Anna a moment to wonder why Jessica affected her to such an extent. *I like her. That's all. She's nice to be around. No big deal. And don't forget she said she'll leave soon.* A thought occurred to Anna. She might have a crush on her. Maybe this was because, with Jessica, everything worked. Her plan was coming together because Jessica was part of it. Her days were better and her nights— *Stop.* She needed to end the preoccupation of wanting to kiss her and— *Stop!*

Anna surveyed the bar. The audience, and even the staff, were mesmerised. Beyond David's table, there was a group of older blokes overtly ogling Jessica. A surge of anger hit Anna, and she wanted to go over and slap them. Instead, she moved her focus back to the stage and the spine-tingling music.

"I know I've heard her before," Sarah said next to Anna's ear.

Jessica did a circular motion with her hand. "Repeat. Abbie, come up, please. I need help with the singing."

Abbie shot a quick glance to her mum, and Anna nodded.

"Go. You know the words. You have an awesome voice," Anna reassured her.

Abbie quickly passed her phone to Katy. "Keep filming!"

"Sure." Katy seemed relieved she hadn't been asked to join in.

A few seconds later, Jessica and Abbie sang the chorus together.

*I listened, so we can share our eyes*
*You touched, and we found our ride*
*To somewhere under an Unst sky*
*Where the northern lights bound our lives*

*My girl, you loved my low-rise denim*
*We kissed, until I felt unthreatened*
*Now somewhere above an Unst sky*
*Where the northern lights became our heaven*

As they transitioned into the verse, Jessica slid notes across the frets of the guitar, bending strings and cascading through a sequence of harmonics. She seemed able to perform the complex manoeuvres while singing in perfect pitch to the melody.

"That's really hard to do," Sarah said. "She's good. Really good."

"Apparently so..." Anna mumbled and wiped away tears of raw emotion.

When the song ended, Abbie returned to the table, and the band moved onto *Winter Girl*. Seeing her daughter singing her heart out with Jessica was the most magical moment of her life. She could say that with absolute certainty. Others might have said the birth of their child, but for Anna, that wasn't something she'd experienced.

A VIBRATO ON the fifteenth fret of the B-string ended the second song. Jessica was ready to call it quits. Her hand was hurting where she had injured it changing the tyre on the Saab, and she wasn't sure if she had pulled the stitches. She twisted the volume on the Stratocaster to zero and lifted the guitar strap over her head.

"Hey, stay!" the bass guitarist shouted to her.

She shook her head. She'd just wanted to ensure Abbie got the songs she'd requested. It was fortunate Jessica had heard them before. Both were straightforward pentatonic progressions, allowing her to improvise throughout.

Off to one side, propped against the bar, she noticed the lead guitarist had returned. He came over to her, halted, and pushed his hand through his hair. "That was sick. Awesome sound."

Jessica handed him his instrument. "You have to lead, not leave, you know."

He nodded. "Yeah... A bad day." He took the guitar from Jessica. But rather than putting it on, he set it aside and went over to talk to the bass player.

She left them to it. But a stocky guy blocked her path.

"Come and have a drink with us." He pointed to a table where three other brooding men sat. He was half cut, and his eyes hadn't fully focused.

"No thanks." Jessica tried to duck round him, but he had stepped in front of her.

"Come on, babe. I'm Carl. One of the nice ones here. I'll look after you." He crossed his arms to exaggerate his tattooed biceps.

David appeared to the left of the man. "Carl, a drink? My round," he said.

"Go back to your silage," Carl snapped, not removing his gaze from Jessica. "He's not a nice one, babe. Come on, just a drink with me, a real man."

A flash of fear hit Jessica. She was back in Enfield fifteen years ago. First, it was the pub, and then he had followed her and—*help me*, to the Chinese restaurant. She felt trapped, her throat went dry, and her chest constricted to the point she couldn't breathe.

Suddenly, a hand grabbed her wrist, and she was yanked beyond the Neanderthal. Anna was leading her back to their table, David and two of his friends blocking Carl from pursuing. Rather than confrontation, David offered drinks again, and Carl was manoeuvred to the bar.

Now seated with the others, Jessica was still trying to calm her fears. She knew it had been a mistake to play. Terrible things always happened when she did. Anna's hand slipped into hers, holding it firmly, and it hurt—partly due to the fervency of Anna's grip, but also because it was her injured hand.

"Ignore him," Anna said softly. "We'll go in a minute." She kissed Jessica's cheek. "You were incredible. Just so awesome. You've made Abbie's life, so she says. And mine." The words and contact helped Jessica to return to the present.

David sat down as he had done earlier. "Sorry about that. Didn't think he would be here. He usually drinks in the King's Head on the mainland. He's all right sober; best avoided after a few."

Jessica wanted to say, "It's okay," but it wasn't. She whispered to Anna, "Can we go?"

"Of course." There was concern in Anna's blue eyes. "All right," she announced to the table, "it's getting late and too late for you to be here, Abbie."

"Yes. Time to go," Beth added, handing Katy her coat. "That was amazing," Beth told Jessica, before saying goodbye to the group.

Jessica didn't respond. She was tired, weary beyond words. It wasn't all the effort on the roof that had exhausted her, but the encounter with Carl had brought forward terrible memories from her past. She needed to get out of the pub. It was like this every time she played. Something would be tainted and the world a worse place for it. At least, that's how it felt to her.

"Let's go," Anna said. Her tone was decisive and urgent. David darted up, allowing Jessica to stand, and Anna slid out after them in a hurry.

They were outside before Jessica registered that David had said goodbye.

As they walked, for the third night in a row, Anna hooked her arm into Jessica's and led them home.

# Chapter Nine

THE HOUSE WAS cold, and Anna considered lighting a fire. She slumped onto the sofa beside Sarah, deciding the wood burner wouldn't make much difference this late in the evening. Besides, she was running low on logs and, like everything else, they cost money she couldn't afford to spend. The bankruptcy timebomb was ticking. She had to make the pony trekking business viable while knowing one extra pony wouldn't be enough. The stress of the financial facts was too much, so she relegated them to the back of her mind. *Am I fabricating the romantic attraction to hide from my money worries?*

She gathered herself. Sarah was ready to talk and sat to attention. Anna poured two glasses of wine from a bottle John had left behind. He had been the connoisseur, and she still had a case of his preferred Rioja. But Anna didn't feel like a heart-to-heart. She was concerned about her mysterious lodger. As soon as they got in, Jessica had gone straight to her room without saying a word.

Anna tucked her feet under her bum. "I'm sorry it's cold. Heating's broken. I could light the fire?"

"Forget that. Spill your guts. What's going on?"

Anna picked up her glass and watched tears of dark wine slip along its inside, informing her it was high in alcohol. She didn't even like red wine, but there was nothing else in the house. "You're in my room tonight," she said.

Sarah's mouth curled down. "Okay, but you're deflecting. Why? What's upset you?"

Anna sighed. "I don't know. I guess I'm annoyed. That guy in the pub really rattled Jessica."

"You get them everywhere. It can't just be that bothering you."

"No." Anna took a gulp of her wine.

"So, what is it then?"

"More or less everything. There's no hot water. I'm broke and about to lose the house. I can't see the business working with the stables in ruins. I'm upset about always fighting with Abbie, and I've not yet spoken to her about my sister. I'm worried about Jessica, who goes from superstar to lost soul in an instant. I'm as lonely as hell. And to top it all off, he's out—"

"Stop... He's out? When?" Sarah's round features had become more angular as she donned a rare serious expression, narrowing her lips into a hard line.

Anna wrapped her arms tightly around herself. "A month or so ago."

"I see." Sarah put down her wine, shuffled up beside Anna and put an arm around her. "And that's why you're trying to stick it out here, on this island in the middle of nowhere, rather than going back to the States?"

"It's the main reason. I have plenty of others, if they're needed."

Sarah shook her head. "No. That last one is good enough."

Her friend's response surprised her. She'd thought, like her mum, Sarah would dismiss her fears as nonsense.

"For the other things, we'll have to talk through each problem and work something out." Sarah continued, "On the money side, I'm not sure how much I can help. My cards are maxed out. But if I can, I will."

"Sarah, no money. I just need someone to talk to. That's all."

"Okay. So, let's start with the reason you called me up then. When did you meet Jessica?"

It was getting late. Anna didn't want to delve into serious stuff. However, when she'd asked, Sarah had come up at a moment's notice to see her.

Sarah gave a sympathetic smile. "You're my best friend, Anna, but you do love avoiding things. It's kinda why you always have that long list of woes. The list gets longer and longer and, in the end, you drown in it. Sooo, let's deal with at least one of them now. Jessica."

In the faint light of the lounge, Sarah's understanding eyes were encouraging Anna to collect her thoughts and speak. "She just turned up. Like a lost puppy. Wet and hurt. She's running from something. She's not told me what it is exactly. It seemed like the only person who could help her was her ex-girlfriend who lives in Edinburgh. That's where she was trying to get to. But she's not returned Jessica's calls. So, I said she could stay if she helped out."

"And is she helping out?"

"Yeah. She's looking after the animals while I earn extra money at a coffee shop in the village." Anna paused. She hadn't yet gone to see what work Jessica had been doing on the stables.

"And you like her?"

Anna raised her shoulders and let them drop. "You know how with some people, you click with them straight away. It's like that but more so. It's like she already knows me and I her. When I'm with her, I feel normal."

"I'm not understanding." Sarah's eyes widened, and her mouth parted slightly. A second passed. "Come on, girl, explain."

"I'm not sure I can. I guess it's as if most of my life I've been driving in a car with everything in the wrong position, difficult and uncomfortable... With Jessica, the mirrors are big and easy to see out of, the windscreen is clear, the steering wheel is at the right position, and the seat is perfect, heated even."

Sarah burst out laughing. "Heated seats. Oh my God, what are you talking about?" She was in hysterics.

Anna rolled her eyes and waited for Sarah to recover.

"Well, if she helps with your driving, she's a miracle worker." Sarah chuckled and slapped Anna's thigh.

"That's not what I meant. I'm saying I'd like to kiss—" *God, the wine is talking!* Anna ripped out its larynx. She twisted the ends of her hair into a single braid and stuck it in her mouth. "I'm just drawn to her. More than I have been with anyone." Realising what she was doing, a teenager's nervous habit, she flicked the strand of hair away. "Please, don't make me explain in detail."

Sarah grinned. "You mean you want to have sex with her?"

"Sarah!" Anna's mouth stayed open for a few seconds. She'd not thought that far ahead. "I never said that." *What the heck did you think came after kissing?*

"Calm down." Sarah's tone had become serious. "But you believe you might be gay?"

"I have no idea," Anna stammered. "I don't remember feeling like this before. Not even as a teen."

Sarah bobbed her head from side to side. "Well, those years were taken from you. Maybe you're having them now? Finding out who you are."

"I doubt it. I was married to a guy for four years, for Christ's sake. But I've not thought about—" Anna lowered her voice conspiratorially "—women like this before."

"Well, you were never happy with John. Or anyone before that. Except maybe Trolly-Tom."

Anna hit Sarah's shoulder with the palm of her hand. "Trolly-Tom. You've got to be joking. The guy followed me around for all of tenth grade. He told everyone I was his girlfriend. Yuck."

"But he's a good example of how you procrastinate. You never told him you didn't like him."

"So?"

Sarah took a sip of her wine. "I'm saying you're not good at dealing with things head-on."

"I'm not sure that's true."

"Come on, you leave everything until it becomes serious. So, with this sexuality thing, are you sure you haven't been blanking it for years?"

Anna stuffed a strand of hair in her mouth again. "Look, I know John was a mistake. I didn't want to be alone. I wanted to feel safe while trying to bring up Abbie... I remember asking myself in the bathroom before we got married, *Do I love him?* The answer was *no, but it'll be okay.* And, for the record, I'm not taking the blame for him having an affair."

Sarah shook her head and half-smiled. "Whoa. That's a lot for me to absorb. You got married when you didn't love him? Hell, Annamaria, promise me you won't do that again."

Anna shrugged.

"And promise me you won't be dumb about who you're attracted to. Just know it and accept it."

"Well, when I know, I'll announce it in the local paper." Anna stuck out her tongue.

"I'm taking notes." Sarah tapped her head, stretched, and yawned. Her eyelids were now half closed. "So how long have you known Jessica?"

"A week."

Sarah's eyes zapped open. "Swear down! A week. Fuck, Anna. Stop. A week?" She sat up with her brows fused together.

"Yes, ages really. Do you think it's about time I asked her to marry me?"

Sarah twisted her body at an angle and leaned away from Anna, before staring at her side on. "Jokes, right?"

For the briefest moment of insanity, Anna thought *what if it wasn't?*

BEING BEYOND TIRED at 02:00 a.m. wasn't a bundle of kittens. Anna had given her room to Sarah and, with Jessica in the guest room, she had two choices. She could try to squeeze in with Abbie. This was impractical given Abbie had a single bed. Or she could sleep on the sofa. The sofa should have been a perfect solution, but, at the moment, the lounge was scaring all reason out of her.

She didn't like being so close to the front door, and shadows cast by moonlight on moving trees seemed to dance across the kitchen towards the lounge. From where she was stretched out, she watched them as they crept in her direction, carrying long carving knives.

She made an executive decision—perhaps answering some of the criticisms Sarah had raised against her about not dealing with things head on. She stood up and scurried down the hall, glancing back to see if the shadows had followed her.

"Jessica?" Anna knocked. She looked behind again, seeing a figure in the kitchen. She knew nothing was there. However, the coats hanging in the hall had morphed into a man with a blade held beside his leg. She opened the guest room door and darted in.

Under the duvet, Jessica was asleep, facing her. Anna covered the distance in one step and touched her shoulder.

Jessica raised her head. "Anna?" she muttered.

"Can I get in with you? Sarah's in my bed. I tried to sleep on the sofa, but I'm weirded out now." She said everything in a blur and didn't wait for an answer before diving over the top of Jessica and slipping under the duvet. She wriggled back-to-back with her. "Sorry. I was seeing things in the kitchen." Her words travelled on panting breaths.

"Like what?" Jessica asked gently.

"I'll go; I'm being crazy. This is embarrassing." Anna started to push herself up.

Jessica flipped and put an arm around Anna, threading her fingers with hers. "Stay. I've got you."

Anna felt Jessica's breath on the back of her neck and curled their entwined hands against her chest. "Thanks," she whispered. Her breathing was now under control, and she started to relax. With Jessica pushed up against her, she was warm and felt cared for; a feeling she didn't want to go away.

"Do you want to tell me about it?"

After hearing her sing, Anna recognised some of Jessica's mezzo-soprano timbre in her words. She tugged their hands tighter between her breasts. "Not right now. I just want to enjoy you holding me... I feel safe here with you. Not sure what I'll do when you leave."

A kiss touched Anna's exposed shoulder and a surge of heat pulsed away her fear. She waited, imagining a flurry of kisses along her neck and heading to her lips. But none followed. Thoughts spun through her mind. *I could roll over and kiss her, touch her. I could ask her to make love to me— that would be weird. Very weird. Odder than you jumping into her bed?* "We fit together, somehow." The words slipped out of Anna's lips as an axiom.

Another kiss on her shoulder and squeeze of her fingers. "We do. Sleep now, beautiful."


THE MORNING CHORUS woke Jessica. Bleary-eyed, she glanced over to the digital clock which read 05:16 a.m. The dull light of dawn lit the bedroom, and the din of the birds made Jessica look up to ensure they weren't building nests on top of the wardrobe. Her other senses kicked in, and she felt the pressure of Anna's body against her. With her head buried in Jessica's neck, Anna's arm hugged Jessica below her breasts. Blonde hair tickled Jessica's face. Raising her left hand, she stroked Anna's hair, flattening it and eliciting a small contented sigh from the sleeping woman.

For the next two hours, she did not dare move, not wishing to wake Anna and break their enveloped closeness. It was excruciating. She was filled with a need to touch her. However, her overwhelming desire, as she watched the light cast on the opposite wall slowly brighten and creep along the surface, was to protect her. She closed her eyes and fell asleep to Anna's soft snores against her chest.

At 10:14 a.m. the clock berated Jessica, telling her she was a useless slob and must get up. Alone, she missed the warmth that had been beside her. It was more than missing her. It was if she had been on a secret island, an Eden laden with delights, to only have taken a wrong turn and, in the blink of an eye, she was in a foreboding underground car park with flickering fluorescent lights and no exit in sight.

She crawled from beneath the duvet and pulled off the T-shirt she had slept in. The cold room caused goose bumps to form on her bare skin. She'd have to skip showering since the morning was almost over. It wouldn't matter anyway. She couldn't stay, she knew the place she was destined for.

It would be cruel to allow Anna to become more dependent on her. They had a connection, but the Eden couldn't be explored further. Jessica's future was inevitably prison, and she was being selfish, taking advantage of Anna's openness and kindness. She needed to face the music.

Dressed in the clothes she'd arrived in, Jessica walked through the house to find it empty. The kitchen had not yet been tidied from breakfast, and dirty plates, open jam jars, and toast skeletons were left on the table. *I'll clean it up later.* She hesitated, realising there was no later. She was leaving.

Outside, the sky was blue, devoid of clouds, and the air was warmer than in the house. To her right, the old Saab was parked in front of the double doors to Anna's stone barn. She headed across the courtyard to a small, planked door at the end of the outbuildings. Behind it, there was a room that must have been an outhouse in the days before indoor plumbing. But now, it was where Anna kept her lawnmower. Jessica had remembered a fuel can of petrol was stored there. Her plan was simple: put the petrol in the car and drive off before there was any chance of goodbyes and possible tears. She knew she would cry.

The hinges on the weathered door squeaked when it was pulled open. Jessica reached down for a green petrol container perched on top of a mower. She grabbed the can, took it to her car, and poured half into the tank.

After returning the petrol container, she looked across the courtyard; Kermit was now standing on the Saab's bonnet. She froze when a woman's scream echoed around the farm.

# Chapter Ten

JESSICA RACED TOWARDS the origin of the scream. It sounded like Anna and had come from behind the stables. She couldn't tell what it meant and ran at full speed; an instinctive need blocked out all other thoughts.

When she rounded the corner of the building, Sarah was higher up the gentle incline that rose in the direction of Anna's paddock. She had her arms crossed and wore a puzzled expression, which was highlighted by a smile. Below, Anna stood on a bale of straw. It must have been dragged a few feet outside of the polytunnel. Her arms were waving wildly towards the roof. Catching her breath, Jessica approached carefully, unsure of the situation.

"Are you all right?" Jessica asked, looking up to Anna on her bale.

Anna spun around and jumped down. She wrapped Jessica in a bone-crushing hug.

"I thought you'd been hurt—" Jessica's words had been squeezed out of her and then stifled by a kiss. Time slowed as a hand slipped delicately onto her neck. Anna's lips, hot and wet, pressed hard against hers before easing off much too soon. The tip of a nose brushed along the side of her own and eyelashes fluttered against her cheek as Anna slowly released her.

"I can't believe what you've done!" Anna slid her fingers along Jessica's arm to her wrist and then to her hand. She gripped it fiercely. Jessica winced; it was her cut hand. She was still recovering from the kiss when Kermit's horns bumped her, causing her to fall into Anna, and the pair tumbled over the bale of straw into the polytunnel.

"Shit!" Jessica said, pushing herself up on her elbows. She had landed on top of Anna, whose arms were about her waist. "Are you all right?"

"Fine," Anna said with a laugh.

About to roll off, Jessica found she couldn't. She was truly stuck, trapped by Anna's deep blue eyes, by her hands that clung tightly to the sides of her sweater and by Anna's red lips, which Jessica was desperate to taste again. This woman had the ability to flip her world upside down, and now, all thoughts of leaving had been banished. Her mind turned to mush, and she let herself be captured. She closed her eyes as their lips made contact again.

This time the kiss was firmer, and there was a sense of urgency causing her to tremble from her core. Anna's need seemed more desperate than her own and Jessica felt her hands slip under her jumper and T-shirt to touch the bare skin of her back. The kiss deepened, and their lips opened slightly. Anna's tongue sought out Jessica's. They shared the intimacy for a long moment until the need for air tore them apart. For an instant, Anna drew Jessica's lower lip into hers, before it was pulled away.

"I... I've wanted to...wow." Anna's words were carried on rapid breaths.

Jessica didn't know what to say. The kiss had been mind-blowing, and she had no brain cells left to respond.

"You... You fixed the roof," Anna said, her breathing still ragged. Anna's fingertips slid gently along her back before the pressure of her palms drew her in for another kiss. In the heated tangle that followed, they rolled to one side, bumping into the bale.

Jessica freed herself first, needing to get a grip on what was happening. As much as she enjoyed their heat, their connection, she knew it wasn't right when a few minutes ago she'd been planning to leave.

She glanced up to see Sarah leaning over the bale.

"I was going to ask if you're okay. But I can see you are." Sarah smirked and quickly spun around. "I'll catch up to Abbie and leave you two to have a roll in the hay," she said over her shoulder with a laugh.

Anna's hand, against Jessica's cheek, forced her to turn her head and look into those beautiful blue irises again. "I was—I mean, I'm being a bit forward. It's just you changed everything." Anna grinned. "I don't know how you did it, but you repaired the stables. Not one stall, but the whole damn thing!" Her words wavered ecstatically. "How the hell did you do that?"

Jessica double blinked. She'd never been kissed like that before. She hadn't felt so stripped bare and enveloped in affection at the same time.

"We need to stop," she blurted out.

"Okay." Anna's eyes narrowed. She rolled and jerked up to stand. "I'm sorry. I shouldn't have done that. It won't happen again." Her tone was formal, as if she was explaining to a police officer why she'd been speeding.

Jessica jumped to her feet and grabbed Anna's wrist before she could walk away. She desperately reeled her in and gathered her into her arms. They stayed motionless for almost a minute. Jessica had her eyes shut and her cheek against Anna's. It was impossible to say something that wouldn't sting. She loosened on her hold on Anna. "Things are complicated, and I... Hell—"

"It's okay. I get it." Anna's expression had lightened, but her lips were still pursed. "I'll try to be better behaved."

Jessica scrunched her brow. For the first time in a very long time, she needed someone more then she could bear. She tipped her head, pressing her forehead against Anna's, and cupped Anna's jaw with her hand. "You don't need to. You're already perfect."

"God, I'm far from that." At her hips, Jessica could feel Anna was twisting the folds of her sweater in her hands. "Anyway, I'm not the one who rebuilds a whole stable block in a week. I still can't believe you did that."

"David helped as well. And you already had the supplies, I just—"

"There's no just about it. It's a miracle... You're a miracle."

From the house came the distant sound of the phone.

"That could be my work friend," Jessica said.

More ringing, then it stopped.

"You should stay and see if they call again." Anna moved out of Jessica's arms. "I should catch up to the others."

Anna turned and headed up the hill towards the field beyond.

When the phone rang again, Jessica was already in the house. "Hello," she answered.

"Jessica?"

"Yes."

"Hi, it's Chris. Sorry for not calling back sooner. I didn't have much to report until this morning."

"That's okay. What've you found out?" Holding the cordless handset to her ear, she paced between the kitchen and the lounge.

Chris spent the first ten minutes recapping everything Jessica already knew. She tried not to show her frustration by yelling at him to get on with it.

"You said you were working on appraisals," Chris continued. "So, I checked the audit logs. It has you logging in around eight a.m. and off at the end of the day."

"Yes, that's right. So?"

"No one had access to your laptop when you weren't using it?"

"No, Chris, I always keep it locked and with me."

"Okay, well, when I checked the authentication logs for the appraisal system, your connection had a different IP address from the previous day and the one you would normally be allocated."

"Why's that odd?"

"Because that's not how our network is set up. The IP address you get is associated with your device. You'll always get the same one."

"Okay. So why would it be different?"

"You're sure it was your laptop?"

"Yes, the case has a dent in a corner. No one swapped it. What are you getting at? Wait—" Jessica tapped the phone against her temple and took a few steps, before returning it to her ear. "If my IP address is recorded on the sabotaged systems, then it must have been my laptop." She took a second. "So, what was I using? Just part of it?"

"Exactly. I think they cloned your hard drive and swapped out the internals. If they used your components in another laptop when it connected to the network, the hardware would identify itself as yours. The one you were using only had the original casing and different internals. That's why there were anomalies in the appraisal system logs."

Jessica rubbed her eyes. This seemed a long shot. "I guess that's possible. But why not simply steal it?"

"They wanted it to look like you and not get caught. And, once you know what you're doing, it only takes fourteen minutes to swap things out. I tried it myself."

"Okay, but they still need all my login details."

"Doesn't matter. If they cloned your hard drive, they just need one password. The login when you open the lid. That's easy to get by looking over your shoulder and watching key presses. Once signed in, the data will be decrypted, and other passwords are cached on the disc."

Jessica sighed. It seemed pretty far-fetched.

"What's wrong, Jessica? You don't think I'm right?"

"I think it's possible, but I don't remember anyone having access to take it apart. And even if it was true, who'd believe it? It's beyond a jury's understanding."

"That's why I wanted to get hold of your laptop. You can tell if it's been tampered with because two of the screws are under a warranty label. I've asked the police if I can look at it. I've not heard back yet."

"They don't suspect you're helping me?"

"I've been assisting them with the investigation. I said I needed it to check if other servers had been affected."

"Don't get yourself in trouble for me."

"No worries yet, Jessica. Try to remember if someone had access to your kit for more than fifteen minutes? It must've happened sometime before you started work that day. And I think you need to get a lawyer involved, a smart one. I'm not sure there's much more I can do. All right?"

"Yeah... Thanks, Chris, for all you've done."

"I'll call you in a couple of days."

The call ended, and Jessica returned the handset to its charging station. What Chris had told her was a possibility, but only if someone had physical access to her laptop. She didn't think it was likely scenario, but it could explain how she had been framed.

She rubbed her temples and sighed, still unsure what to do. She'd have to wait. But she suspected the police would catch up to her. Britain had cameras everywhere. Sooner or later they would link her to her brother, his car, and then to her journey north. She wasn't sure how many cameras there were in Northumberland, but she felt she'd made the right decision to stick to the back roads.

Once outside, her thoughts drifted to the kiss. Her mind backtracked further while her legs propelled her towards the black Saab. She had intended to leave without saying a word.

She leaned against the driver's door, needing to work out what to do next. An odd clanking on flexing metal caused her to turn. Then a stink of musty cloth and grass caused her nostrils to flare. Kermit had jumped up onto the bonnet. The goat folded his muddy hooves under his bulbous belly and lay down. She glanced at him, noticing he was chewing on a scrap of blue fabric. Some poor soul had recently lost the rear pocket of their designer jeans.

She tried to formulate a plan of how to get a lawyer involved and when would be a good time to turn herself in. *Should I wait for Chris's next call? God, what am I going to do about Anna?*

The dots wouldn't connect. Her mind was filled with the sensations of Anna's kiss, flipping her stomach upside down. Suddenly, she understood why. *Apparently, I've been too stupid to see that I'm—* She couldn't bend this new realisation into something more convenient and rational. *I'm falling for Anna and now...*

"I'm so fucked," she told Kermit.

The goat didn't offer insight, continuing to grind his teeth on the patch of denim. A moment later, he farted.

*Great.* Jessica attempted to waft the smell away. *Damn that roof. I shouldn't have fixed it... She wouldn't have kissed me then. And, damn you, farting goat! What the hell am I supposed to do?*

ANNA AND SARAH lounged against the galvanised gate while Abbie exercised Daisy in circuits around the paddock. The day was exceptionally warm with a gentle breeze. The sky was clear and the sun, given free rein, had raised the temperature a good ten degrees.

"So?" Sarah asked.

Anna had been waiting for the question. However, knowing something was coming hadn't automatically meant she was ready for it. "So, what?"

Sarah laughed. "You know what."

Anna crossed her arms and turned to watch Abbie press her pony towards the hurdles again. The pony approached and slowed to a near stop, before stepping over the low bar, one hoof at a time. Anna couldn't help but smile at her daughter's audible curses of frustration. Although Abbie persisted in trying to get Daisy to jump, Anna had long since admitted defeat and given the pony the name Daisy because of her bovine jumping technique.

"Own up, kiddo," Sarah insisted.

"Okay, okay. Yes, and yes," Anna said, without moving her attention from her daughter and the pony-cow.

"Does that mean your sexuality confusion is sorted?"

Anna scrunched up her face in anguish.

Sarah laughed. "You don't need to answer. It's pretty obvious."

"Look, it was one kiss. I was excited about the roof being done. Stop going on about it!"

"I've hardly said a thing."

"You were about to," Anna snapped.

"So, you're not going to tell me why you're all red and have straw in your hair?"

"Definitely not." Anna quickly brushed her fingers through her hair.

"You know the I've-just-made-out look suits you."

Anna spun on Sarah and pointed a finger in her direction. "Anyway, it's your fault for saying I'm not proactive."

"Calm. Blame accepted." Sarah chuckled. "Especially if I've gotten something off your list of woes."

Anna rolled her eyes. "It's likely added to it," she muttered, stepping away from the gate. She called across the field to Abbie, "How about a picnic?"

Abbie smartly turned the horse, and it trotted over to where they stood. "Sure. Where?" Abbie asked.

Anna took hold of Daisy's bridle. "I thought Coves Haven beach?"

Abbie eyed her mother with suspicion. "Why? You've never wanted to go there before."

"Do we have to argue about this as well?"

"I'm not arguing. It's just strange."

"It's not strange. It's called getting some fresh air."

"All the air here is fresh."

"Not if you're near Kermit."

Abbie laughed and dismounted. "Can Katy come?"

"If her mum agrees. Let's unsaddle Daisy. We'll leave her to graze." Anna undid the girth while Abbie took hold of the bridle.

Sarah joined them. "I don't really do beaches."

"It's hardly a beach. It's a strip of sand with rock pools. It'll be too cold to do anything except eat a few sandwiches."

"Do you know what happens when sand and sandwiches mix?"

"It'll be fine."

Anna dragged the saddle off Daisy's back and walked past to place it on top of the gate. Abbie removed Daisy's bridle, and the pony immediately dipped her head to graze on the emerald grass.

"Let's head back and find Jessica," Anna told Sarah.

Her friend bumped their shoulders and winked. "You mean your girlfriend."

Anna's cheeks flushed. She glanced to her daughter, who was a few feet away. Abbie showed no reaction to Sarah's remark.

"You know, you get way too much pleasure out of embarrassing me," Anna whispered, as they headed back to the farmhouse.

"As I said before, know it and accept it."

Although annoyed with Sarah and worried what Abbie was thinking, Anna really liked hearing the words "your girlfriend." They sounded right.

# Chapter Eleven

MONEY WAS ONE problem Mike didn't have after being released from prison. He opened the door of the fridge and pulled out a bottle of Coors Light. He twisted off the cap and downed a third of the beer, before settling on the sofa. He had inherited the one-storey Michigan home along with twenty thousand dollars from his mother.

He placed the beer on the coffee table as Fox News blared on the TV. He picked up a brown envelope, ripped off one edge, and shook it until two passports fell out. Mike flicked through the worn one first. The fifteen-year-old passport had been resurrected. On the photo ID page, his father's picture had been replaced with his own and the date of birth adjusted. The expiry date had also been changed. As long as it wasn't checked too thoroughly at immigration control, he'd be able to use it. However, to be on the safe side, he'd have to carefully select his route to and from the UK.

He dropped it and picked up the second.

This passport had been his mother's, but now, instead of a seventy-four-year-old woman, a blonde girl looked back at him. The picture had been lifted from the web. It was of his daughter, who he hadn't seen in twelve years. And, thanks to the feckless social media platform she used, he knew where she lived. He'd even managed to make a fake account and, pretending to be a teenage girl, he'd got one of Abbie's friends to add him. As a friend of a friend, he could see most of her posts. Using the details he'd discovered, he had persuaded Abbie to add his fake identity directly and from there get her phone number. Something he suspected would come in useful.

Finding someone with access to DHS systems had been the most difficult part and the bulk of the cost for the forgeries. He'd taken the word of a dark web anonymous hacker that the secure database records for the passports had also been modified to match.

He'd take Abbie back and punish Anna for surviving and sending him to prison.


ANNA WALKED AHEAD, stopping every now and then to allow the others to catch up. Perhaps the picnic had been a bad idea. It seemed like she was the only one who wanted to go on the walk to the unused strip of sand on the eastern shore. But she needed a way to get Jessica to let her guard down. The miracle worker always seemed more relaxed when they were outside. She wanted to know more about her and wanted to ask her questions to help her understand herself.

"You walk too fast," Sarah said when she drew near.

"What are you complaining about? I'm carrying all the food."

"Only because your A-type Gemini-ness wouldn't let anyone else carry it for you."

"Geminis aren't A-types."

"Then your birthday must be wrong." Sarah extended a hand. "Let me carry the pack now."

Anna shook her head. "No need, we're here." She pointed along a narrow path of sand cutting between shoulder-high mounds of tawny coastal grasses.

Behind Abbie and Katy, Jessica trailed with downcast eyes; she was lost in her own world. Anna wished she hadn't kissed her. It seemed to create a wedge between them. *I take that back. I'd do it again... I just hope she isn't upset about it. Is she upset? It's so hard to tell. She's not said a word.* She wanted the trip to the beach and a picnic to re-establish their connection, but the plan seemed to be failing. She let the backpack slide off her shoulders and handed it to Sarah. "Find a spot with the kids, I'll catch up."

"Whoa, a concession," Sarah joked, took the backpack, and started down the path with Abbie and Katy following.

"You okay?" Anna asked when Jessica reached her.

Jessica gave a quick nod. They stood staring at each other, then Jessica surprised her by taking her arm. "Is the beach much further?" she asked as they navigated the narrow space with sand slipping under their shoes.

"No. Almost there." Anna glanced at her. "Um, can we forget about the kiss and start again?" she said with a waver in her words.

Jessica smiled. "I don't want to forget about it. It was heart-stopping."

There was silence for the next dozen strides.

"I'm glad it wasn't just me thinking that, since I've never kissed a woman before. Not like that anyway. Sorry, I—"

Jessica spun her around into her arms. "You have nothing to be sorry about, ever. Not to me." The strength of her conviction made tears pool in Anna's eyes.

"What's happening between us?" Anna said in a whisper, allowing her tears to fall.

"God, Anna." Jessica pulled her into a tight hug. "Whatever you want."

JESSICA TOOK A bite of the sandwich Anna had passed to her. They sat together on a small towel spread on the beach. It might have been the sound of the slow-breaking waves washing onto the pristine coast, or the invigorating sea air that had cleared Jessica's mind.

It wasn't until Jessica started to eat she remembered she'd gone without breakfast, and the cheese and tomato roll tasted divine, even with a peppering of sand.

She slipped her arm around Anna's waist, and Anna, in turn, leaned against her.

The pair watched Sarah, Abbie, and Katy as they challenged the gods of the sea. They were in an epic battle with the waves, going as close as they dared when the water receded, then running backwards when a new wave broke onto the shore. The duel would only end one way: wet shoes, socks, and jeans. The sea can be cruel.

"I can see why you like it here," Jessica said, between the girls' screeches when they misjudged the speed and size of an incoming roller that soaked their shoes as they raced away from the cold salty water.

Anna turned and smiled. "On a day like today, yes. But many days aren't like today. They are windy, cold or it's grey or it does nothing but rain. You know, I suspect if you were here, I'd like those days as well." She lifted Jessica's bandaged hand and softly caressed her palm and fingers.

Jessica squeezed Anna closer to her, knowing she needed to say something. She couldn't keep Anna in the dark. They were becoming way too close. "I'd love to spend more time here. But I've got to get clear of my problems in London. If I don't, it's not fair on you."

"I've guessed that. But, you've not explained why?"

Jessica's heart raced, and a dull headache began to pulse. *Tell her, it's not right to lead her on.* "I...I'm wanted by the police."

"Oh."

Anna tensed and withdrew, letting go of her hand. After a few seconds, she asked, "What for?"

"Fraud, but I've done nothing wrong. Someone framed me. I know you have no way of believing me. But it's true. I'd hoped my friend at work would uncover what had happened."

"I see." Anna's voice had lost its wistfulness. "What kind of fraud?"

"They think I intentionally caused a quality issue. It resulted in the company losing half of its value on the stock market. They think I did it to make money from shares I own in a competing firm, but it's not true. Chris has an idea that someone sabotaged my laptop. He's trying to investigate it."

Anna was quiet for a long time, forcing Jessica to look away and shift on the towel so they weren't touching.

Out to the east, a band of dark clouds gathered on the horizon. The waves were getting bigger, and the wind had picked up. At least seven waves crashed and retreated before Anna said anything. "If you're innocent, why'd you run from the police?"

"I guess I was scared. I knew no one would believe me. I have no way to prove it wasn't me. Not to a jury anyway. But—" Jessica paused, trying to find the words to say how she felt. "I think there's something else as well."

"Like what?"

"I can't be there anymore. Be what I was... I can't face it, the stress of it. Having to fight all the time just to breathe when everyone wants to destroy you because of what and who you are and what you have achieved. I was never good at dealing with the bad sides of people." Jessica wiped away a tear on the sleeve of her jumper.

Anna let out a slow sigh. "Well, thanks for telling me. To be honest, I thought when we first met that it was likely to be something a lot worse."

"And you still helped me?"

"I admit I debated it. But you convinced me."

"How?"

"You have the most special eyes I've ever seen. You know, they must mean something."

"It's just heterochromia."

"No. That's a label. It's a sign. I'm sure of it."

Jessica was concerned. *She shouldn't think I'm special because of my eyes.*

"Anna, you've been so kind to me, but the police will track my car and find out I'm here. I was thinking of leaving. I mean, I don't want you and Abbie to get mixed up in this."

The battle between the weak humans and the sea continued, with both Abbie's and Katy's jeans now wet up to their knees. The girls' ear-piercing screams, whenever a wave broke, could have awakened Neptune himself. Sarah, standing between them and holding their hands, had managed to stay dry.

Anna wrapped her arms around Jessica's neck and looked straight at her. "Listen carefully, Jess. I care about you. There's something special happening to me because of you."

Jessica started to speak when Anna's fingers touched her lips.

"I'm not ready to give you up. Miracles happen when you're around. And I believe you. We'll get this resolved. So, no leaving me in the night, okay... I couldn't cope with that. Now, all you need to say is 'Yes, Anna.'"

Tears rolled down Jessica's cheeks. When Anna lifted her fingers away, Jessica repeated, "Yes, Anna."

Loud squeals of laughter punctuated with swearing caused them both to look seaward. Sarah had fallen over and was on her hands and knees in the foam of a retreating breaker. "This is your fault, farm girl!" Sarah yelled in Anna's direction.

Abbie and Katy's boisterous hysterics were contagious, and Anna stifled a laugh by covering her mouth.

Jessica was concerned Sarah might get washed out to sea and rose to her feet, darting quickly over to help. By the time she got there, Sarah was already up and sloshing her way to the shore. The front of her shirt drooped with the weight of the absorbed seawater, while her jeans were soaked through.

Overtaking Jessica, Anna went to help her friend, but then stopped short on seeing how drenched she was. "Mer-thing, return to the sea from whence you came," Anna ordered in a commanding tone as she gestured with a slashing motion of her arm towards the waves.

"Can I keep her as a pet?" Abbie asked, laughing as if her brain might explode.

Anna appeared to be considering the question, putting a hand on her chin. "Very well, child. The pond may be big enough."

Abbie was the closest, and Sarah lunged towards her. "Come here for your hug!"

"No way!" Abbie turned tail with Katy following, leaving a spray of sand from the treads of their trainers as they blasted along the beach.

Sarah changed direction, targeting Anna with outspread arms. "You get the hug then."

"No, you don't." Anna backed away and tore after the girls.

Jessica smiled, forgetting the seriousness of what she'd been discussing moments before. She handed their only towel to the mer-thing. "You better dry off."

Sarah smiled back and took it. "For the record, I hate beaches."

Jessica nodded. "You can have my sweater." She pulled it off and offered it.

"That's kind of you, but you'll be cold in only a T-shirt."

"I'm not wet. I'll be fine."

Sarah didn't argue. She quickly unbuttoned her soaked shirt, dried off, and slipped on Jessica's sweater. "That's really kind. I knew I liked you."

Katy and Abbie were now trying to escape Anna, who insisted she was going to sacrifice them to appease the sea gods.

Abbie whipped behind Jessica, using her as a buffer.

"No, you don't. And, don't use my girlfriend to protect you," Anna said.

Abbie chuckled, while spinning circles around Jessica.

*My girlfriend.* The words caused a flutter. It wasn't so much her use of the term. But more that Anna had said it in front of everyone. A strong emotion, a sense of belonging, overcame her.

"Abbie, get Jess!" Anna attacked while Abbie pushed on Jessica's back. They were both attempting to shove her in the direction of a big wave that had crashed onto the beach

They wrestled her towards the sea while Katy and Sarah hung back.

"You're going in!" Anna insisted.

"I'm not!" Jessica tried to twist away. "Sarah, some help, please! I gave you my sweater!"

"Nope," Sarah yelled back. "There's a mer-thing code against intervening."

The wave washed over their ankles and all three, spurred on by the icy water, spun around and raced to safety.

"Thanks for soaking my feet." Jessica threw a strand of seaweed towards Abbie's hair.

Abbie ducked out of its way, laughing.

Sarah had her hands on her hips. "Now that you've gotten that out of your system, can we go back?"

Anna nodded. "You guys go and get dry. I want to show Jessica the castle." She turned to her. "If you're okay doing that with wet feet?"

Jessica shrugged. "Sure."

The group separated. Jessica and Anna headed along the coast southward to where Lindisfarne Castle stood above the land. The wind had swelled to a strong breeze, and the sky was darkening as angry clouds swept in from the east.

"ABOUT THE GIRLFRIEND thing," Anna said. They walked in the same stride and Jessica seemed to relax as they continued along the footpath. "I couldn't think of another way to describe you to Abbie." *I couldn't have just called her a friend. If Abbie caught us holding hands or, heaven forbid, kissing. What on earth would she think? Stop, you know you wanted to see how everyone would react... God, I'm so contriving.*

"I don't mind. We've shared a lot already. I understand the sentiment, and it's sweet."

"Phew, I was starting to doubt myself."

Anna needed to find out more about this woman who had suddenly become very important to her. Beyond what she was discovering about herself, when Jessica was around, magical things happened that were changing her life for the better.

"So, how do you know how to fix roofs?" Anna asked.

"My father was a builder. I used to spend a lot of time with him. I was always a bit of a tomboy. And, really, it was a way to avoid mixing with my peers."

"You didn't like them?"

"I didn't understand them."

Anna could easily imagine Jessica being a bit of a loner. "So, where did you grow up? Family?"

Jessica glanced at her. "I was born in Yorkshire but grew up in Enfield. My parents moved there for work. But I only have my brother now."

"I'm sorry."

"It's not your fault."

Silence persisted until Jessica took her hand. "Continue with the interrogation, Supreme Inquisitor."

Anna smiled at this. "Okay. When did you know you were gay?"

Jessica laughed. "Oh my God, you skipped quite a few questions there."

"You don't need to answer. I was just curious."

"I'm teasing. It's okay. Well, I guess when Myra Bedi moved in a few doors down. I was fifteen."

"I see, um so, how did you know that you...?" Anna was unsure how to ask the next question, and her cheeks flushed. She wanted to understand how people found out they were gay and how she'd missed this glaring fact about herself. Because, after the kiss this morning and how she felt about Jessica, she knew who she was. In some ways, this was comforting as it explained the discord she had felt in her past relationship. But, on the other hand, it was terrifying; uncharted territory that she had no idea how to navigate.

"Did you want to ask how I knew I was a lesbian?"

Anna nodded. "Yeah. That."

"I just knew. But, I guess, if you want something more concrete, I was the prince and Myra, a few doors down, was the princess in my fantasies. I didn't have to make it that way. It was what I felt and dreamed. Before that, I didn't think of anyone."

"So what happened?"

Jessica sighed and tightened her fingers around Anna's. "Let's just say it wasn't a Disney ending."

Anna knew she was dipping into the fragile, anxious Jessica. "Your turn," she said with a smile.

"Sorry?"

"Your turn to grill me."

"Oh."

"Go on, ask me anything."

"All right. Why are you so beautiful? On the inside and outside."

"I'm sure I'm not." Anna knew she must now be beet red.

"You're stunning. Sometimes I can't believe you're standing next to me. It's like I'm gate-crashing a Pre-Raphaelite painting."

Anna hesitated; no one had ever said something so flattering. "I...don't... Hey! Those are not really questions. And you're embarrassing me."

Jessica frowned. "You're right. They're facts, and I didn't mean to embarrass you."

Anna took her arm, in place of her hand, and curled herself around it. She pressed her head against Jessica's shoulder as they walked. "Jess..."

"Yes?"

"You know, when you say things like that, I end up completely yours?" Anna waited for a response. She hadn't meant to put her on the spot, but she knew she had. One answer would mean Jessica wasn't interested in her, another would mean she was. She cursed herself for being so indirectly direct.

Halting, Jessica turned towards Anna, gathered her and kissed her. The noise of the wind stopped, the cold piercing through her clothes was replaced with heat, and her heart ached.

Once their lips were no longer pressed to each other's, Anna stayed captivated by Jessica's unique eyes. "You don't need to gate-crash," she said.

"I don't understand."

"In that painting... You have an invitation." Anna didn't want to explain further. But she was pretty sure she had just spelled it out in burnt umber and titanium white. She was pushing her emotions to the edge, her desires, her wants, and she wasn't sure if she had painted a fantasy in the sand. "I'm sorry; I'm being weird again."

Jessica laughed. "I love your weird."

"Well, you're the first." Anna gave a half smile.

They walked on. The castle was another ten minutes away, but the light had dimmed, and the temperature had dropped. She was concerned how cold Jessica must be wearing only a T-shirt.

"Looks like a storm." Anna pointed out to sea where squalls of rain were hammering the whitecaps. "I think we better go back." A rumble of thunder caused the pair to turn, and they quickened their pace.

# Chapter Twelve

JESSICA COULDN'T TELL how late it was in the gloom. The heavy rain had soaked their clothes and made it hard to see. By the time they reached the paddock, the heart of the storm was almost over their small island.

Daisy was in some kind of pony frenzy, charging from one side of the paddock to the other, shaking her mane and snorting.

"Damn it," Anna yelled above the din from the storm, while running towards the gate. "Abbie hasn't brought her in! She is so irresponsible. Even the saddle is still there, getting ruined!"

At the gate, Anna snatched up the bridle and raced to the centre of the field, but kept it hidden behind her back. The pony was galloping at full speed from the far corner towards her.

Unsure what to do, Jessica hesitated. She was still standing by the gate when Daisy collided with Anna and knocked her over.

Jessica watched in horror as the pony continued forward, the front hooves missing Anna's head by a fraction where she lay curled up in a ball. She gasped when Daisy trod on Anna's left leg.

"Anna!" Jessica sped to where she lay. She bent and placed her palm onto Anna's shoulder. "Darling, are you okay?" Anna didn't answer, and Jessica tried to remain calm and focused. Fighting back the fear, her first aid training kicked in—*DR ABC. Danger first.* Daisy was still out there and could charge back at any moment. Jessica scanned the field and located the pony at the far end. "Anna?"

Anna uncurled her arms from about her head and struggled to speak. "Winded, give me a sec," she said, panting.

The rain had plastered Anna's hair to her face, making it hard for Jessica to see her expression. "Stay still." Jessica double-checked where Daisy was, but when she glanced back to Anna, she was already on her feet.

"Where are you hurt?" Concern knotted her stomach.

"Jess, it's okay. Just my leg." She pushed her away. "Where is she?"

"There." Jessica pointed, before reaching down to pick up the bridle. The pony snorted as it cantered along the top fence.

"Let's get out of here," Jessica insisted.

"No. We need to get her stabled. She'll hurt herself if she decides to jump over the fence. She could break a leg. If she does, then that's it for her."

"She's too spooked."

Anna hadn't moved from where she stood. "Hell, I'd try to get her into the horse trailer, but John had the hitch on his car."

"We need to leave her. It's too dangerous with the lightning."

With the next crash of thunder, the pony reared and galloped in their direction. Anna headed towards Daisy to cut her off, but this time with a noticeable limp.

"Stop!" Jessica yanked Anna's arm, preventing her from getting too close, as the pony sped by, a few feet away.

Spinning on her, Anna glowered.

"I want you safe," Jessica said vehemently. Their faces were inches apart, and she watched as Anna's scowl slowly relaxed.

The rumbles of thunder were now less than thirty seconds after flashes of light that lit the sky above the North Sea.

"The Saab has a tow bar," Jessica blurted out, only now remembering this.

"It does? Okay! Get the trailer. I'll stay here and keep track of Daisy."

Jessica wiped the rain out of her eyes. "Don't stay in the field."

"I'll keep clear of Daisy. I promise." Anna took her elbow. "I'll be okay. Don't be long."

"I won't." Jessica turned and rushed back to the gate. She scrambled over it, rather than opening it, in case Daisy charged. Rainwater splashed up her already soaked jeans when she dropped down the other side. Without looking back, she kept going until she reached the farm.

She bolted through the front door and snatched up the keys to the Saab from a bowl on the kitchen counter.

"What's going on?" Abbie asked, her voice filled with angst.

"Where's Sarah?"

"Asleep on the sofa."

Jessica didn't have time to wake her, so she grabbed two all-weather coats from the hooks by the door and darted outside.

The Saab started on the first attempt. She turned on the headlights, knocked it into reverse, and backed up towards the trailer, which sat on a slight slope in the corner of the yard. With a spin of the tyres on the drenched ground, she aligned the car with the trailer. She shoved open the door and raced around to attach the two together.

She'd done this a couple of times before with an old trailer her father had used for building supplies, but it had been a while. There were a handbrake and a turn handle. She released the handbrake, only to have the trailer lurch forward. The hitch collided with the rear of the Saab, denting it above the bumper.

"Shit." She ratcheted up the trailer's brake and jumped back into the car. She inched it forward to try again. This time, she slowly eased the handbrake off, guiding the hitch towards the ball on the tow bar. Once it was in position, they slotted together with an affirming clunk.

She was starting to pull away when the passenger door was yanked open, and Abbie hopped inside.

"Stay here!" Jessica said.

"Where's Mum?" Abbie demanded.

"She's waiting for me to bring the trailer."

"Why?"

"To collect Daisy. She's spooked by the thunder."

"Oh—I forgot about her." She winced. "Mum will be mad."

Jessica tensed; she to needed hurry. "Abbie, stay in the house." Abbie would be safer indoors; the convertible would offer no protection against the lightning.

"I'm coming."

Apparently, Abbie was as strong-willed as her mother, and there wasn't time to argue.

"All right. Keep your hands on your lap and away from the body of the car."

"Why?"

"Lightning."

The car stuttered towards the gap in the stone wall which led to a lane she guessed headed to the field.

"This seat is wet." Abbie raised a cupped hand to catch a stream of water that was pouring from the gap in the convertible's roof. "Your car leaks."

*God, she's sitting in water. This has to be fast.*

"Is this the way to the paddock?" Jessica asked.

"Yeah."

The trailer's left wheel hit the edge of the wall, and she had to reverse to attempt the tight turn again.

Lightning flashed.

"Nine...ten...eleven—" Abbie stopped counting when the thunder sounded. "Two miles. It's five seconds for each mile. And the odds of being hit by lightning in your lifetime are one in three thousand."

"Good to know," Jessica muttered, between gritted teeth. *I should've made her go back.*

They bumped along the muddy lane with the lightning providing better visibility than the car's 1980s headlights.

Abbie continued to count from each strike; she was now stopping at eight.

It had seemed like hours, but only a few minutes had passed when they arrived at the field. Anna opened the gate for them, and Jessica stopped, winding down the window.

Anna glanced over to Abbie and back again. "Drive in, do a circle, and drive back out. Park the trailer so it's blocking the gate. We'll send Daisy towards it then force her in."

"Got it." Jessica passed a coat through the window.

Anna slipped it on and then leaned into the car. "Abbie, you shouldn't be here."

Abbie shot back, "I'm helping!"

A second passed before Anna responded. "Get out then."

Abbie opened the door and slammed it closed.

Keeping the speed steady, Jessica performed a U-turn in the thick grass. She could see Daisy at the top of the field, running along the fence and back again. After completing the manoeuvre, she parked the trailer so it was halfway through the entrance to the paddock. She stepped out and put on the other coat she'd brought. Not that it would do much good. She was already drenched from earlier, but at least it would keep her warm—she was chilled to the bone.

"Over here," Anna yelled to her daughter in the gloom. They were moving the jumps to create a makeshift corral.

Counting the gap between the thunder and lightning, Jessica only reached six.

The pins holding the rear of the horsebox in place slid out with ease, and Jessica yanked the tailgate towards her. She needed to use all her strength to stop it slamming down to the ground. Once lowered, it formed a ramp into the interior.

"Jess, stand by the horsebox," Anna yelled. She moved slowly away, all her weight shifting to one leg as she took each step. "Abbie, you stay behind the jumps. Keep your arms spread wide. I'll go chase her down."

"Wait!" Jessica quickly caught up to Anna and snatched her arm. "You stay by the trailer. You're hurt. I'll fetch Daisy."

Anna stared at her as another flash of lightning zapped across the sky. The air felt as if it buzzed with electricity. "No. I'll go."

"Anna, you're limping. Besides, I don't know how to get her into the box."

Anna sighed. "All right then. Be careful."

The wind had blown her hood off for the third time, and Jessica allowed it to flap about her shoulders. She wanted to get this bloody pony stowed away as quickly as possible and get Anna and Abbie out of the storm. She knew the animal was important to Anna and Abbie, but she was also desperate to know the extent to which Anna had been hurt.

For the briefest moment, she wondered where Kermit was. *That ugly goat will be okay. He probably summoned the storm because I haven't given him a carrot today.*

Jessica approached Daisy, who had stopped to look at her. The pony snorted and charged her but then changed course. Jessica held her arms out and marched towards the animal, blocking her path. The pony whinnied, reared, and galloped down the field. Jessica tore after her. *Jesus, she can run when she wants to.*

Daisy continued in the same direction, racing alongside the jumps Anna had set up at intervals to steer the pony towards the trailer. Just when it appeared Daisy would simply run right inside, she slowed and reared.

Anna approached from the right. "Abbie, there!" She pointed to the same position on the left.

Panting, Jessica was about to ask what to do, when Anna called to her. "Jess, now walk slowly towards her."

Another flash and deep rumble caused Daisy to lurch into the box. All three of them quickly raised the ramp and latched her inside.

"Thank God! I thought that was going to be a lot harder."

Abbie quickly collected the saddle. She was carrying it back when a jagged bolt of electricity arched across the sky. It hit a point at the top of Lindisfarne Castle.

The hairs on Jessica's arm stood up. "Let's go! That was bloody close." She was no longer hiding her worry. The odds of being hit by lightning, standing by two large chunks of metal at the centre of a thunderstorm, were definitely lower than one in three thousand.

It hadn't taken long to get Daisy into her stable. The pony had calmed down after being confined to the interior of the horsebox. They left the car and trailer where it was, heading to the house. Jessica took Anna's arm to support her as she struggled through the sodden yard.

Once inside, they stripped off their coats. Jessica glanced into the lounge to see Sarah still sprawled out on the sofa. She was hoping to lead Anna in that direction and get her to sit down.

"Mum, what's wrong?" Abbie's voice wavered.

"Just got bumped by Daisy. It's nothing. Why don't you get ready for bed?"

The worried frown on Abbie's face changed to anger in an instant. She spun around and headed down the hall.

"Did you eat?" Anna called after her. There was no reply. Anna repeated the question, this time louder.

"Sarah made pasta," Abbie yelled back.

"Did Katy get home all right?"

"What do you think?" Abbie muttered, turning the corner to the stairs.

Jessica wondered why Abbie was backchatting her mum. *She's stressed and not sure how to deal with it. Anna hasn't explained that it's not her fault.*

"She's in a foul mood," Anna said.

"She's upset," Jessica offered. "You should talk to her." She put an arm around Anna's waist.

Anna sighed. "I will, but not now."

A minute passed with nothing said. Jessica felt the need to break the silence. "You need to get changed. You're soaked." She moved strands of wet hair away from Anna's face.

"So are you." Anna's fingers brushed Jessica's cheek. "I'm surprised we didn't become X-ray skeletons out there."

"Me too. How's your leg?"

"It hurts if I put weight on it. Help me upstairs?"

In the master bedroom, a single lamp flickered when the lightning flashed. Anna stood with her weight on one leg with an arm outstretched against the door of an oversized pine wardrobe. She unbuttoned her jeans with her free hand and tried to pull them off. The wet fabric stuck to her skin and was held fast by her swollen thigh.

"Let me help." Jessica knelt beside her and eased the jeans down.

"Careful," Anna whimpered.

Once the jeans were below her knees, an angry stain of purple and blue was visible, covering most of Anna's upper thigh. "Hell... No wonder you're limping."

Anna put her hand on Jessica's shoulder for support as she gingerly stepped out of her jeans.

Jessica explored the damaged area with her fingertips. She glanced up to see Anna watching. Her blue eyes were almost a sea-green when mixed with the incandescent light of the bedroom.

"You were amazing tonight, well, not just tonight..." Anna's voice trailed off into a whisper. "I don't know what would've happened without you."

"It wasn't only me."

"You need to accept your awesomeness."

Jessica stood. She wasn't used to compliments. Sure, she had received them at work. But there, they mostly were superficial and, at the worst, passive-aggressive sarcasm. Out of habit, she changed the subject. "Are you going to shower?"

Anna nodded.

Jessica took hold of the hem of Anna's tank top and pulled it up over her head.

Anna laughed. "I could've done that."

Jessica leaned towards Anna. Her hands slid around the soft skin of her waist. She had expected to only lightly kiss her before going downstairs. At least, that's what her head had been telling her to do, but her passion, charged by the atmosphere in the room, desired more.

The sound of the rain provided a backdrop and depth was added by rumbles of thunder as the storm progressed inland. When their lips touched, it was different from earlier in the day. It felt like there was more at stake. They kissed deeply, with frantic need. And, after separating, they both were breathless.

"I should get changed," Jessica said, her own legs feeling wobbly. "And...and sort out dinner."

"You should." Anna tipped her head to one side while biting her lip. She slowly moved away. Her fingers were caressing Jessica's forearm, and that simple contact made her hesitate. At that moment, she felt a deep connection with Anna, as if she was something precious she had lost and then found. Her eyes dropped to the curves of Anna's breasts.

She noticed the scars.

There was one three inches wide, just above Anna's left breast, and another half-hidden by the band of her bra. Jessica wanted to ask how Anna had got them, but now wasn't the time.

She quickly moved her gaze to Anna's eyes. "You need help to the bathroom?"

"I'll be all right. But I might need some ice and painkillers."

"Okay." Jessica turned while she still could. The image of Anna's perfect but scarred body was hard to break away from. Something terrible had happened to her. She watched as Anna hobbled towards the bathroom. "You're sure you don't need help?"

"I'm fine, but Sarah might need to stay on the sofa tonight," Anna called back. "I'm not sure I can make it back downstairs."

"I'll bring you something to eat," Jessica offered, but Anna had already disappeared into the bathroom.

Jessica stood at the threshold of the door for a moment. An overwhelming need to protect and look after Anna consumed her. She needed to understand what had happened to Anna. How she'd been hurt. The scars on her body, an injury from her past, must be part of what was plaguing her at night. She would do what she could for her.

Jessica slowly descended the stairs, gathering her thoughts and feelings, trying to condense them into meaningful fruits she could pick, keep or discard.

A sense of déjà vu caused a tremor to race up her spine. The last time she'd felt like this was with Myra. Was the universe taunting her again? Showing her a utopia she need only reach for, but when she did, as with Myra, would an axe slam down and slice off her hands?

*God, please don't let this end like it did with her. I can't do that again.*

# Chapter Thirteen

JESSICA COULDN'T FIND any ice, so she grabbed a bag of frozen peas. She had just closed the fridge when the lights went out.

"Shit." She remembered seeing a torch in Anna's junk drawer and felt her way around the table to the sideboard.

"Abbie! Jessica!" Anna's frightened voice called.

In the dark, Jessica raced upstairs and was about to open the door to Anna's bedroom when a LED light flashed, and a hand snatched at her wrist.

"Wait. You have to be careful," Abbie said, then shouted through the bedroom door, "Mum. It's me and Jessica."

"Is anyone else with you?" Anna asked, terror ripping apart the syllables.

"No, Mum, just us." Abbie turned to Jessica. "Open the door but be careful. She might have her hammer."

"What?" Jessica tried to read Abbie's face, but she could only see her outline in the diffused light from her phone.

"She has a hammer under her bed. When she's scared, she gets it out. She almost hit me with it by mistake."

"God." Jessica opened the door and stepped in. "Anna. It's me."

Standing in the corner beside the bed, Anna's form was revealed by Abbie's phone. She was wet from the shower and wrapped in a towel. In her right hand, she held a claw hammer in a defensive position away from her chest.

Without hesitation, Jessica went to her. She took the hammer from her hand and threw it onto the bed. She wrapped Anna into a hug and held her. "Honey, it's only a power cut."

Jessica could feel the woman's frantic breathing. "We need to check if he's here," Anna muttered.

"Mum, no one else is here." Abbie rubbed her arm.

"You're safe," Jessica soothed.

"I'm...sorry, sorry... Where's Sarah?"

"I'm here," Sarah's voice came from behind. She also had her phone with her, and its light flashed around the room.

For a moment, all that could be heard was Anna's slowing pants. "Sorry, panicked."

Jessica released Anna and turned to her friend, "Can you sit with her? I'll find some candles."

"Of course," Sarah said, before letting out a gasp. "Fucking shitholes. Did you just do that?" Sarah's phone was shining on Anna's black and blue thigh.

Anna shook her head. "Daisy stepped on me. My fault."

"God, girl. Sit down for fuck's sake."

"Sarah, your language," Anna said in a whisper.

"Mum, it's okay." Abbie collected the hammer and shoved it under the bed.

"Can you help me find the candles, Abbie?" Jessica asked.

"Yeah."

After collecting candlesticks from the lounge, they placed them together on the farmhouse table and lit the candles. "Your mum hasn't eaten, so I'm going to make something. I guess it'll have to be a sandwich. Do you want anything?"

Abbie shook her head.

"Does your mum get scared a lot?" she asked while grabbing ham, lettuce, tomatoes, and butter from the lifeless interior of the fridge.

"Not always, just at night. But I'm at school most nights."

"Do you know what scares her?" Jessica asked as nonchalantly as she could. However, in the candlelight, she could see Abbie's frown turn into a scowl and then, to Jessica's astonishment, her expression shifted to utter sadness and tears broke loose.

"Oh, honey!" Jessica pulled the girl into a hug.

"She has nightmares. I don't know what she's afraid of. I try to help," Abbie sobbed.

"Sweetheart, it's okay," Jessica wasn't sure what else to say. Unable to explain what Anna's fears were, she wondered if it was some form of post-traumatic stress related to the scars on her chest. Whatever it was, it was clearly taking a toll on her daughter.

"I just forgot about Daisy... I was video editing with Katy. Mum's all over the place. I don't know what's wrong with her." She sobbed between each word.

Jessica held her, allowing Abbie to release pent-up emotions, perhaps for the first time. Taking hold of the girl's shoulders, she leaned back and looked into her puffy, red eyes.

"Listen, princess. It's not your fault. It truly isn't. None of it."

Abbie wiped away her tears on the sleeves of her Ariana Grande hoodie.

"Everything will be all right. I'll help." Jessica promised, hoping to hell she could honour the vow. "Okay?"

"Yeah."

The frozen peas were still on the counter, and Jessica handed them to Abbie. "Here, take these to your mum."

Abbie looked down at the bag. "You know you need to cook them, right?"

Jessica laughed, causing Abbie to quirk a smile. "It's for her leg. I can't find any ice."

"Oh."

"And take a candle."

Abbie nodded, wiped her eyes again and picked up a candlestick. It created flickering shadows as she travelled down the hall.

*She's like Florence Nightingale...with a bag of frozen peas.* Jessica sighed. *There's so much I need to do here.*


TO THE RIGHT of Anna's bed, the candle on the chest of drawers emitted a soft orange light, illuminating the room. Anna was propped by three pillows. A bag of thawing peas wrapped in a towel was pressed to her leg. She poked the last corner of the sandwich Jessica had made for her into her mouth. The paralysing fear from earlier had subsided. Jessica had eventually brought her back down to reality with reassuring words and the comfort of her presence. It had taken an hour before she accepted he wasn't there. Then another hour passed while she considered her behaviour. She felt embarrassed by her reaction to the blackout, especially when it had been in front of everyone.

She glanced down at Jessica asleep beside her. A flutter of affection caused her to bend down and kiss Jessica's hair. Jessica's long, lean body lay stretched out beside her. She wore a pair of striped pyjama shorts and an oversized white T-shirt. Her chestnut hair partly concealed her face. Anna couldn't resist sweeping some of those strands away from her cheek. *Who made you so perfect?*

Jessica's smile, when she chose to share it, would light up the air around her. Her amazing different coloured eyes were something she could stare into all day. *And, God, she can sing.* Anna sighed. She definitely had a crush on this woman. *It would be hard for any sane person not to want her.* She reminded herself she was unhinged. At least that's what John used to tell her.

When Jessica had pulled off her shirt earlier that evening, she had expected they would make love. Jessica's eyes had been so dark and sultry. *She's not like that. She takes nothing and has done so much for us. Who is a sleeping Jessica for? Not for me...*

A tear ran down her cheek as she dared to accept what was right in front of her. She shifted under the crisp white duvet cover, careful not to bump her injured leg, and snuggled against Jessica's back. A soft murmur came from Jessica when Anna brushed her fingers over the impossibly soft skin of her abdomen. She hadn't meant to touch her, but Jessica's T-shirt had shimmied up.

"I'm going to need you to make love to me soon," Anna said in her softest whisper, daring her declaration to be heard. She kissed the base of Jessica's neck and then pressed her cheek against the same spot.

"Would now be okay?" Jessica whispered and slowly turned her body to face her.

"I thought...you were asleep." Anna stammered.

"It's hard to sleep beside someone so stunning." Jessica's lips were a hair's breadth away.

Anna hesitated for a moment. Her heart raced out of control. "Thanks... And, well, yes to your question," she finally said, almost mouthing the words.

Jessica kissed the tip of Anna's nose. "You're sure? Your leg?"

Jessica's hips started to rock, causing her thigh to bump firmly against Anna's centre. "My God—" Stifling her own voice, for fear she would wake someone, Anna bit down on her lip, shocked by how close she was; she'd been focusing so much on Jessica. The thought they might come together surged her closer to her summit.

She desperately kissed Jessica, wanting to keep her mouth on hers as she tried to pleasure Jess before her own crescendo, but it was too late. Her body arched, and she bucked. Her tongue twisted around Jessica's as she rode out the waves, still forcing her fingers to continue their motion.

"Anna," Jessica whispered into Anna's mouth. She trembled against her, as another pulse of release weaved through Anna's entire body.

The room went silent apart from the rain outside the open window. Anna allowed her breathing to sync with her lover's as they slowed together. She kissed her again, but this time a tender lingering kiss, leaving three words stuck in Anna's mouth. She wanted to say them. They were impatient to be spoken. But she knew they might not be true, even if they felt like they were at this moment.

The candlelight faded, as the flame exhausted its fuel. Anna was quiet, trying to decide how she felt. It was such a mixture of emotions she had no choice but to cry.

"What's wrong?" Jessica asked, her voice laced with concern.

"Just overwhelmed."

Jessica's arms tightened around her. "Baby, you sure?"

The words were there again, but she dared not speak them. How could she, when they had only met a week ago? "I've never had that together with someone. I mean, at the same time."

"That goes for me as well. You're incredible."

Pushing gently with her fingers, Anna directed Jessica to lie on her back. She stretched out beside her. She needed to think about what had happened between them.

Her mind raced with the regret that most of her adult life she had lived a lie. She had denied herself the pure ecstasy of such a powerful release and all the sensations she had experienced for the first time. All those things had happened with Jessica in a way that felt perfect, normal, like a real life.

Her feelings fitted into the weird, emotional Anna. The Anna who said things before she should. Who jumped to conclusions that weren't real. Who always seemed to have to backtrack miles just to take a step forward. But, with Jessica, it didn't feel like she was backtracking. It felt like she was journeying to a new world, where she didn't have to worry about being safe, treading water or simply pleasing others. But could she start again, for a third time?

*Go to sleep with the one who made you come with her to somewhere new.* She smiled at this, closed her eyes and drifted off.

# Chapter Fourteen

THE DISTINCTIVE CACKLING of a magpie woke Jessica. In the early dawn light, she climbed out of bed, needing to use the toilet. A glance at the flashing digital clock told her the power was back on.

Feeling chilled, she grabbed her T-shirt and yanked it over her head. Glancing out of the window, she could see two magpies hopping back and forth in the front garden. *Two for joy?* She bid them a good morning, before padding over the pine floorboards to the bathroom.

When she returned to bed, she sat down on its edge. Asleep on her front, Anna had her arms bent with her hands hidden in her tousled hair. Her bruised thigh was visible in the cool air. *She needs that checked out.*

Desperate to snuggle up against her, but not wanting to wake her, Jessica carefully got back under the sheets and pulled the duvet over them. After all the events of yesterday, Anna must be exhausted. Jessica slipped her hand under Anna's and was surprised when Anna's fingers curled around hers. She closed her eyes. The calls from the magpies ended abruptly with a flutter of wings.


JESSICA STIRRED TO the sound of Abbie's earnest voice from inside the bedroom.

"Mum, look!"

"Abbie, I'm fast asleep," Anna muttered.

"Just look."

"What? You woke me to watch a YouTube video... It's awesome. Now let me sleep."

"Mum, it's after nine!"

"I don't care."

"Mum— Forget it... Jess?"

Jessica pushed herself up on one elbow to look over the peak of Anna's shoulder. She quickly grabbed the edge of the duvet and drew it up to cover Anna's bare back. "Yes?"

Abbie held her iPad towards her, but it was too close for her to see. She took hold of the corner and tried to focus on the screen. "Is this the video you were editing?"

Abbie nodded. "Yeah, it's gone viral!"

"Oh." It showed the two of them singing in the pub from Friday. She smiled, pleased at Abbie's excitement and relieved she had put on her T-shirt when she'd first woken. "When did you post this?"

"Yesterday, before the storm."

Jessica read the number in the corner. "Whoa, that's quite a few views."

"There are a lot of comments about you as well. Wait."

Abbie took the iPad and, after a second, popped it back in front of Jessica. "It looks like the views are still going up. See, eight more. Will you teach me to play the guitar? I can borrow one from school."

Jessica smiled. "Sure."

"Cool beans." Abbie went quiet. "I fed Daisy. She's okay. The chickens are all okay as well."

"That's good."

"Kermit is hanging around outside the house. I think he is waiting for you."

"Great," Jessica muttered.

"Can you help me with breakfast now?" Abbie whispered.

"Umm, yeah, I suppose...Give me a second."

With that, Abbie spun around and darted out of the room.

Jessica tried to digest the fact that the video they were both in had close to thirty thousand views in less than a day. *Will the police see it and find me?* She didn't think so. But she was also tired of worrying about it. Facing the reality of things was becoming more important with each hour in Anna's company.

Anna rolled over, flopping her arm across Jessica's chest.

"Morning," Jessica whispered.

"Mm-hmm," Anna muttered before her breathing changed to slow snorts.

"Wow, aren't you two cute."

Jessica snapped her head to the right.

Sarah stood beside the bed wearing a robe and holding a towel. She also wore a big grin. "I'm going to use the shower. Okay?"

"Ah. Sure." Jessica could feel her cheeks flush. *What is this, Saturday on Oxford Street?*

Once she could hear the shower running, she took a moment to find the strength needed to leave the warm bed and the beautiful woman strewn next to her. She thought about Abbie and how she hadn't been fazed by seeing them together. Kids were so much more accepting than adults.

The door squeaked on its hinges. Jessica watched it creep open, but no one entered. There was a sudden bad odour in the air, and she wafted her hand in front of her nose. The duvet started to slide off on its own accord.

"God, what's that smell?" Anna muttered, rolling slowly to one side and pushing herself up. "Kermit! He's eating the bedding!"

Jessica jumped up and tugged at it. The goat wouldn't let go.

Anna rubbed her eyes, then leaned over the edge of the bed, searching. She came up with her top and pulled it on.

"What's he doing in here?" Anna asked, still coming to.

"I don't know, but he won't let go!"

Anna began laughing. "He's winning."

Kermit marched to the far side of the bed, causing Jessica to tumble forward onto the mattress.

"You better put these on. Not that I don't like seeing your butt." Anna chuckled and threw Jessica's pyjama shorts in her direction.

She missed.

Kermit snatched them up and started to chew.

"You threw them right at him!"

"He looked so hungry."

"Give my shorts back, devil goat!" Jessica lunged for them and gained hold, just as Kermit started to walk towards the door with them hanging from his mouth.

She managed to rip them free and inspected them to see if she could put them on. But goat spit wasn't something she wanted near her. When she turned, Anna was clasping her pyjama bottoms. She had them scrunched up in a ball, ready to throw them.

"You can wear mine... If Kermit doesn't get them first."

"No, you don't!" Jessica leapt onto the bed and pinned Anna's arm, but she adeptly swished the bottoms out of her reach.

"I'll give them to you for a kiss."

"God, you're so demanding."

"And a coffee and breakfast in bed and—"

She kissed Anna, who wrapped her free arm around Jessica's neck. The bottoms were retrieved without a struggle when the kiss deepened.

"Um, goat in the bedroom problem...need to sort it," Jessica said with her lips still pressed to Anna's. She really wanted to ignore Kermit at this point. "Sarah in the shower... And a teenager waiting for me in the kitchen."

"So, no fun then." Anna nibbled on Jessica's neck.

"Anna, I need to get dressed—" Jessica stammered.

Anna laughed and pushed Jessica away with two hands. "Go bond with your goat friend." She rolled back into her pillow, dragging the duvet over her head.

Jessica smiled. She tugged on the bottoms and stalked over to Kermit, who stood staring at her. She grabbed hold of his collar and led him out into the hall. The goat seemed content to accompany her. "A carrot for you. But you have to stay outside."

"Oh, my God!" Abbie laughed when she saw Jessica leading Kermit to the front door. "How'd he get in?"

"Window maybe? I think he's after a carrot."

"I already gave him some. They're in the bucket outside. But he wouldn't eat them."

Jessica shoved Kermit's rear to get him to leave the house, and she followed him out.

A clear sky and cold air met Jessica beyond the front door. She reached into a galvanised bucket set on a section of broken millstone to the left of the door and grabbed a carrot. They were animal feed grade, rather than from a supermarket, larger and a faded orange colour. She offered one to Kermit. He took it, munched and swallowed. Jessica presented another, but he didn't take it and instead trotted across the courtyard.

"Great. He only wants me to be the one to pamper him," Jessica muttered to herself. She shook her head in disbelief and went inside.

"Can you help me now?" Abbie asked, holding a bag of flour.

"I'd like to wash and get changed first." Jessica desperately needed a shower after all that had happened last night.

"Can you do it now?" Abbie's eyes were hopeful and determined.

"Why?"

"It's Mum's birthday. Well, it's on Tuesday, but I want to do it today while Sarah is here too."

"Oh. How old will she be?"

"Twenty-six. But she's been twenty-six for the last three years."

"I see... So, what are you making?"

Abbie picked up her iPad and started to thumb the screen.

"I want to make crêpes."

"Do you have a recipe?"

Abbie showed Jessica the iPad.

While Jessica made the batter, her thoughts dwelled on the fact that she had no money to buy Anna a birthday present. This was soon replaced by a nagging discord. *Anna must have been fifteen, maybe even fourteen when Abbie was conceived.*

ANNA LIMPED INTO the bathroom. She took two paracetamols with a gulp of water from the tap. Her leg had stiffened overnight, and she found it too painful to put any weight on it. She'd been hiding this as she suspected Jessica and Sarah would insist they take her to a hospital. She didn't want to spend Sunday morning driving to the nearest A&E and likely have to wait the rest of the day to be seen, before being told she should stay in bed and not travel or walk anywhere. She'd see the doctor at the medical centre when it was next open.

In the shower, the hot water cascaded over her. Her thigh throbbed from the heat and she shimmied to one side so that it was out of the spray. She finished washing her hair, hopped back to the toilet, and sat on the closed lid.

"How the heck am I going to work?" she muttered.

From the washbag on the cistern, she removed a pair of nail scissors. Her nails weren't long, and a few had been cut right back after being broken doing work around the farm. She had tried to keep them all a good length. John was rather particular about Anna looking her best. She clipped all her nails as short as she could. Not as an act of defiance, but due to a new practical necessity and, perhaps, to show who she truly was.

There was a knock, then Jessica's voice from the bathroom door. "Do you want breakfast in bed or are you coming down?"

"I'll come down. But I'll need help." She didn't want to be a wimp, but the stairs had been built two hundred years ago; the rises were higher than they should be, and the steps were narrow.

"Okay. I'll wait for you."

"We should take you to the hospital." Jessica insisted for the third time, once they had made it to the bottom of the stairs.

"It's too far, and there won't be anything they can do. You can take me to the clinic on Tuesday. And you can get your bandage redone."

Jessica flipped her hand in front of her, as if noticing the grubby dressing for the first time. "What's wrong with going Monday?"

"It's a bank holiday. It'll be shut."

"Oh, yes."

Once Anna was sitting at the kitchen table next to Sarah, Jessica went to help Abbie. From the sweet buttery smell and from what was on the table, she could tell they were making pancakes.

In the background, Abbie's phone played music through a small portable speaker, while in front of her was a rush placemat and a knife and fork. Anna moved the knife as far away as her reach would extend.

In the centre of the table was a ramekin of sugar and another of—she tasted it, lemon juice. There was also a bowl of sliced strawberries next to an open tin of golden syrup. Anna glanced between the three people she most cared about with a smile dancing on her lips.

"What's for breakfast?" Anna asked. "And where's my coffee?" She was being playful with her demands, but she really did need some caffeine.

"Crêpes." Abbie lifted a non-stick frying pan off the electric hob and showed Anna the contents. "Like, should I flip it now?" she asked Sarah.

"Go for it."

Anna was about to say "be careful" or "don't make a mess," but caught herself.

Abbie flicked the pan, and the crêpe dutifully flipped in situ.

Sarah clapped.

"Wow, that's awesome." Anna laughed. "How'd you learn to do that?"

"While you were in the shower, Sarah taught me."

"We sacrificed a couple of crêpes for the betterment of womankind," Sarah added.

Jessica handed Anna her favourite, chipped purple mug filled with coffee while whispering, "Happy early birthday."

Anna's emotions spiked, and she tried to keep her tears under control.

A plate containing a crêpe was placed in front of her. "You can put what you like on it. Does it look okay?" Abbie asked.

The crêpe was yellow with a brown pattern that looked like the cratered surface of the moon. *I'm not going to cry. I'm not going to cry.* It was the first time Abbie had cooked for her.

"It looks amazing," Anna managed to get out while hugging Abbie around the waist.

After Abbie returned to the stove, Jessica put an arm around Anna from behind and kissed her cheek. "Overwhelmed again?"

Anna nodded. "This is a different world to a week ago," she whispered. She glanced over to Sarah to see her studying them.

Jessica released Anna and went back to stand beside Abbie as she flipped another crêpe.

"I take back what I said about you procrastinating." Sarah kept her voice low.

Anna shrugged. "It's okay."

"I was wrong. I think you two might have something special."

Anna poured lemon juice and sprinkled sugar over her crêpe, before rolling it up. She hadn't felt embarrassed because of Sarah's compliment. In fact, it felt like an affirmation of her feelings towards Jessica.

Sarah leaned close and whispered, "By the way, I know who she is." She paused and flicked her eyes to Jessica, who was still busy at the stove. "I knew I'd seen her before. I once had to help book a lineup for a retro alt-rock festival, digging up bands from the revival in the noughties. Her name was suggested by a few people in the office. But we couldn't locate her. I wonder why she ended her music career? They said she was amazing."

"She would've been young."

"Seventeen. Google Jessica Esland. You'll find a couple performances. Really popular at the time, not mainstream, but indie when indie meant indie."

Jessica put a plate containing a crêpe in front of Sarah and sat down opposite. "They'll get cold."

Anna cut off an end with her fork and popped it into her mouth. "This is amazing," she called to Abbie.

Abbie turned. Her posture showed confidence, and she smiled. "I'll keep cooking until you say stop."

Sarah smeared jam on her crêpe. "Keep them coming, honey!"

Anna shifted her focus to Jessica. "So, you were Jessica Esland and amazing? Well, I know you're amazing. But why did you give up music?" She knew her question was out of left field, but she wanted to know.

Jessica double blinked, her smile dropped, and she wrapped her arms around herself.

"Annamaria," Sarah baulked. "You can't just ask things like that."

There was silence for a moment, except for Abbie's phone playing a song from The Underfex.

Annoyed with herself for upsetting Jessica, Anna reached across the table and took her hand. "I'm sorry. I shouldn't have asked."

"It's all right. I need to share it with you," Jessica whispered. "But it's not an ideal breakfast topic."

The next crêpe, flipped a bit too vigorously, hit the ceiling and stayed there. Slowly, it peeled off and landed on Sarah's plate.

Abbie and Anna burst out laughing.

"Skillz, gurl!" Sarah said, reaching for the jam.

"Hey, that's Jessica's." Anna took hold of Sarah's plate.

"No way, it was flipped to me."

They yanked it back and forth across the table.

"Fine then." Anna let go. "Eat it with all the cobwebs and dead flies."

Sarah studied the crêpe as if it might be possessed by an evil spirit. She shrugged and tucked in anyway.

When Anna returned her gaze to Jessica, her smile had returned. A longing sparkled in her magical eyes. Those three words popped back into Anna's head. She sighed and wished breakfast would never end.

# Chapter Fifteen

FATIGUED FROM THE events of yesterday evening, Anna limped back to the sofa in the lounge. Sarah had left a few minutes earlier and given Anna a present, telling her not to open it until her birthday.

She pushed the present to one side, turned on her laptop, and began plugging pointless numbers into a spreadsheet. The tension of her crippled finances caused her head to pound. There was no way to magically conjure up thousands of pounds.

She wondered what Jessica's plans were. She didn't want her to leave. In fact, she couldn't face the possibility of Jessica not being around.

Her thoughts went to those exquisite moments the night before. It caused a pulse of excitement to ripple through her. She put down the laptop, grabbed her mobile phone, and dialled a number she'd never planned to ring again.

"Hi, John, it's Anna."

"Hi… I wasn't expecting to hear from you… How are you doing?"

"Fine. And you?"

"Good, thanks. You caught me tasting wine. I'm in France on a short break with Heather."

She wanted to avoid any small talk. "John, this is a quick call. I have a friend who needs some legal advice. I was hoping you could spare some time to talk with her."

There was a second's pause before John answered. "Perhaps, what's the background?" His tone now included an edge of anticipation for some unknown reason.

Anna relayed as much as she dared tell about Jessica's troubles without having her permission to do so.

"I see. Interesting... Anna, I'd have to treat this as a formal appointment. And given the serious nature, it will have to be in person."

"Okay... I need you to do this as a favour. You understand. My financial situation is not ideal, and I don't think that's all my fault." She paused. "Jessica is staying with me at the moment. She's important to me, and I need your help." Anna hated saying the last few words.

John responded straight away. "Of course, I'll help." He cleared his throat, before continuing. "I'm back on Tuesday. Where do you want to meet?"

His quick agreement had taken Anna by surprise. She twisted her hair with her free hand, gathering her thoughts. "Can you come here? It's best she doesn't travel for the reasons I explained."

Another pause on the line. "Does two on Tuesday work?"

"It will have to be around eleven because of the tides."

"Okay, eleven then."

"Thanks." Anna tried to keep her emotion out of the response.

When the call ended, she felt drained. She stretched out on the sofa and turned to face its back, closing her eyes. *At least he has agreed.*

As she drifted off to sleep, her mind travelled down rat holes, leading to events in her past. Times with John, Abbie, and then her brain latched on to a darker memory. The one that haunted her most nights.

## ANN ARBOR, MICHIGAN, AUGUST 2002

Spotting Sarah, Anna made a beeline for her table. "You can't hang out here all day," Anna said through gritted teeth.

"It's not against the law to sit in a coffee shop. Besides, I like watching you work. It's so fuckin' weird."

"Shit, Sarah," Anna whispered. "Don't swear in here."

Sarah laughed and jiggled a cassette-sized device at her. "Look, I got one!"

Anna's curiosity got the better of her. "What is it?"

"An iPod."

"Wow, those are expensive."

"Hell, yeah." Sarah cupped it in her hands. "But you're my little bitch now, aren't you?" She flipped the iPod and kissed its shiny back.

"You can't make out here. Get a room."

"Only if you join us." Sarah puckered her lips and made a kissing action towards Anna.

Anna laughed. "Stop that."

"Not my fault you're cute."

"You need help."

"Exactly." Sarah chuckled.

Anna sensed a stare from the other side of the room and glanced over to see her boss giving her the hex.

"Gotta work." She turned and started to clear a nearby table.

Sarah threw a scrunched-up napkin at Anna, which bounced off her shoulder.

"You missed something." Sarah pointed to the paper ball on the floor.

Anna shook her head, trying to hide a smirk. She bent down with cups and plates in both hands and tried to pick up the napkin between two free fingers. The toe of Sarah's Reese Denim sneaker nudged her.

"Sarah!" Anna yelled, drawing the attention of other customers in the coffee shop. Embarrassed, she lowered her voice. "You'll get me fired."

"That'd be awesome because then you can give me a lift home."

Anna rolled her eyes. She'd only just gotten the job a few weeks earlier and Sarah, after discovering this, would turn up every day after she finished her summer job at a music shop, begging for a ride home.

"I've got ten minutes left." Anna headed back to the counter.

"Get me a free muffin," Sarah yelled after at her. "A blueberry one!"

An hour later, after dropping Sarah off in the opposite direction, she'd pulled into the drive of her family home on the western outskirts of Ann Arbor.

"Hey, Mom." Anna dropped her keys in a bowl on the kitchen counter.

"How was work?"

"Okay, a bit quieter than normal."

"Your pickup working out for you?"

"I love it!" And she did. It was a white 1993 Dodge Ram, with a large chrome front bumper, which, more by luck then ability, Anna hadn't yet smashed into anything.

Her mom had bought the pickup as a present after she passed her driving test three months ago. It had changed her world. She was free to go where she wanted, when she wanted, no longer needing to ask for rides. Or worse, having to borrow her mom's car, which required half an hour's discussion about the dos and don'ts of driving before she could get her hands on the keys. The slight problems of gas money and Sarah using her as a chauffeur were easily tolerable. The part-time job at a coffee shop downtown was only a fifteen-minute drive away, and she had her own money for the first time. It seemed as though the world would finally submit to her will and she could be herself.

"Annamaria, I've got to take Dad to a doctor's appointment. I should be back around six. I managed to get him ready without too much of a fight this time. The medication is at least helping with that." Her mom placed her handbag on the kitchen counter. "I better use the bathroom before we go. Can you keep an eye on him for a minute?"

"Sure… Where is he?"

"I sat him in his chair on the deck."

Anna nodded and headed across their dated 1970s kitchen. She pushed open the screen door and stepped out onto the deck. It was in need of a coat of paint, something she had promised to do before school started again in September.

A clear sky, except for a few smudges of white, and a temperature in the eighties, made for a perfect late summer day. The blue wicker lounger, where her father normally sat, was unoccupied.

"He's not here!" Anna called into the house, before scanning their expansive yard. The property was a turn of the century farm, but the land had been subdivided to the point they now only owned two acres. Her father had been a farmer, and being a lot older than her mother, he had retired a few years ago.

A small red barn sat at the end of their driveway's turning circle and, behind it, broadleaf trees obscured the neighbouring property. She spotted her father ambling in a zigzag route out of their yard.

"He's making a break for it!" Anna yelled towards the screen door as she set off after him. Before she could catch up, he rounded the edge of the barn and was no longer in sight, causing Anna to increase her pace.

Her father had Parkinson's disease. It was advanced now, and he was 1 per cent of the person he'd been. It was cruel to say that at 50 per cent, he was a kinder person. Anna chastised herself for the thought.

When she found him, he was on his back like an upturned ladybird.

"Come on, up you get." She had to use all her strength to help him to his feet. He would be a foot taller than her if he stood straight. Something he rarely did. "Are you okay?" He didn't answer but instead stared at her with a blank expression.

Then, in a rare moment of lucidity, he asked a question, although it was obvious he didn't know who he was speaking to. "When will this end?" His face was ready for a meaningful answer, ready to engage with a response that would provide enlightenment.

Anna couldn't think. She didn't know what to say. It wouldn't end. It would only get worse and worse.

"Soon." It was her first ever real lie, and it chilled her that sometimes the truth couldn't be told.

The answer appeared to satisfy him. He gave a small nod, his stature raised, as if everything was now right with the world.

She brushed him down, picked the dried leaves off his plaid shirt, and guided him back in the direction of the house.

Her mom grabbed his arm when they approached. "We're going to be late. I told you to stay in your chair." She shepherded him in the direction of their car.

Anna watched for a moment, still fazed by having to lie to her father. *I'd better check on Spot.*

She stepped off the deck and meandered to their remaining field.

When her sister was twelve, the pony had been her pride and joy. Now, at twenty-one, Emma had a two-year-old girl, and Spot was too old to ride. Emma was still with the same man she'd met at eighteen, but they hadn't married. They lived in a suburb of Detroit, and Anna rarely saw her. She'd hoped to visit more often, but her mom didn't like her going into Detroit.

Another reason she hadn't seen her recently was Emma's partner, Mike. He was always aggressive towards her and sometimes worse. She didn't like how he looked at her.

The phone rang, but by the time she had reached the house, it had stopped. A moment later, her cell beeped. She pulled the small device out of her pocket.

"Where's Mom?" Her sister's frantic voice crackled in her ear.

"Taking Dad to the doctor."

The line went quiet for a heartbeat.

"Anna, I need you to come and collect me."

"Why, what's up?"

"Please come," Emma pleaded.

"I just got home. What's wrong with your car?"

"Mike won't give me the keys." She sounded in near hysterics. "Please! He's drunk and being an asshole. I need to get out of here for a bit."

Anna's chest tightened. Emma and Mike always fought and sometimes it even came to blows.

"Okay, Emma. I'm coming."

It should have been a forty-minute drive to Emma's house, but, with the rush-hour traffic, it had taken an hour and a half.

She turned into her sister's road, driving slowly past the rundown houses. A couple were boarded up, while, in front of others, trash clung to the street's edge. In complete contrast, many were bustling, with families working on cars or sitting on their porches, drinking beer and laughing.

Anna pulled into her sister's double drive, slipped the column shifter into park, and turned off the ignition. She walked around to the rear of the house since the front door was never used.

She paused when she heard her niece wailing and Emma yelling. *Nothing new then.* But she wasn't sure. Emma's tone lacked the conviction it normally had when dealing with Mike.

She knocked on the back door. If it had been just her sister at home, she wouldn't have bothered. But Mike was always at home now, and Anna didn't want to get on his wrong side. Not that he had a right side. At least, none she'd seen.

"It's Anna," she yelled.

The house went silent, and then Mike yanked open the door.

"What the fuck are you doing here?" His words were slurred. In one hand, he held a beer while his foot propped open the door. He ogled her up and down.

"Emma!" Anna called around him.

"Anna, go home!" Emma's words came fast and urgent.

"That's right, fuck off." Mike let the hydraulic closer slap the screen door shut in front of her as he turned to go back in.

Anna hesitated, but she couldn't simply leave.

She yanked open the door and raced into the kitchen. Mike faced Emma, yelling at her. It looked like he might hit her.

"What's going on?" Anna screamed. Abbie, her two-year-old niece, was standing on the floor beside her mother, crying. When she saw Anna, the toddler wobbled over to her. Anna instinctively picked her up.

"I told you to go home." Mike launched himself towards Anna. One of his hands curled into a fist.

Then everything happened too fast.

Emma had pulled a knife out of its block on the kitchen counter. She darted between them.

Up close, Anna could see that her sister's face was swollen, her eyes red raw, with mascara smeared down her cheeks. Emma pointed the knife at Mike and waved it towards him. "You leave them alone!"

"So, bitch, you're going to stab me now?" He reached to try to catch her hand, but in his drunken state, missed. The knife pierced his forearm, causing him to reel back in shock. In an instant, his shock turned to rage, fuelled by alcoholic venom.

Anna had never seen such fury. He grabbed Emma's hand, twisting her wrist until the knife fell. He snatched up the blade and, in one motion, stabbed Emma in the chest.

Rooted to the spot, Anna tried to scream, but no sound came. She lowered her niece and darted to her sister. "No! No!"

But Emma was already on the floor with a growing pool of blood spreading under her.

"This is your fault!" Mike roared at her. He spun Anna around and pushed the blade into her ribs, then again as she fell.

Through searing pain and a sinking sensation, as if the ground was dropping out from under her, she watched Mike burst out of the house and heard his car screech down the road.

Abbie had dropped to her rear and covered her face with her arms while crying.

Anna reached into her pocket, with one hand was pressed against her chest, and dialled 911. Blood filled her mouth as she tried to speak.

"My sister... Stabbed, I... I think she's dead!" Just getting the words out was agony; fear and dread were pulling them apart. "I'm hurt too." She trembled.

"Please provide your location."

She gave the address the best she could. The phone slipped from her hand.

"Mommy," Abbie wailed, standing up and then taking unstable steps towards Emma.

"Everything will be okay," Anna said, choking.

She tried to push herself up, but the effort made her faint, and her brain flashed brown-red then white. She collapsed but managed to stay conscious. Unable to move, her eyes focused on an object inches from her nose. Anna followed the second hand of Emma's watch on her lifeless wrist; a tick for every minute. And then it stopped.


ANNA WOKE TO a soothing voice. Fingers stroked her hair and cheek.

"Sweetheart, you're okay."

She blinked to clear her eyes, forcing them to focus. A woman with different coloured irises stared back at her.

"You were having a bad dream."

"Where's Abbie?" she asked in a sudden panic, needing to know she was safe.

"In her room, doing her homework."

Anna clenched her jaw and closed her eyes tightly, trying to clear the too-vivid images.

"What time is it?"

"After five."

Propping herself up, Anna rubbed her eyes. She'd dreamed about that day so many times, and she'd become accustomed to how it affected her. But this time it had seemed more real, more threatening. Her past was seeping into the present.

"Are you all right?" Jessica asked.

Anna sighed, leaned forward, and clung to Jessica as if her life depended on it. Something told her it just might. She gave her head a quick shake, trying to vanquish the demons dancing in her skull. Thoughts became words she'd meant to keep secret.

"With you, yes."

IN A PUB, close to his hotel, John finished the dregs of his pint of IPA. He had planned to start looking for an apartment to rent but, after Anna's call, it appeared there was a possibility he hadn't expected.

Heather had given him the boot a week before, forcing him to take a room in an economy hotel in Stratford. Except there was nothing economical about hotels in London. He had made a big mistake, and he knew it. Sure, Anna was frigid and rubbish at sex, but he wanted her back. Anna's friend's problems had given him a way in, a means to justify seeing her. He lifted his phone off the bar's varnished, hardwood surface and texted the intern his firm had assigned him.

*Something's come up. Can you take my casework on Tuesday? Give me a call when you want to be briefed.*

A few seconds later, his phone buzzed with a text.

Pamela: *It should be possible. I'll call you shortly.*

# Chapter Sixteen

ADRIAN CHAPMAN GLANCED up from his desk to the detective who had entered his office.

"We have a lead, sir," the detective stated in an even tone.

"Which case?"

"Hokthorn equity fraud."

"What's the lead?"

"Last Tuesday, we spoke to Miss Cox's brother in North London—"

"I know." He turned his attention to the view from his fourth-storey office.

Routemaster buses and black cabs whizzed along the Embankment, while beyond, a river cruise boat left its jetty to head down the Thames. It was quiet for a Sunday afternoon, and his team was falling behind on closing cases. So, he had insisted they all come in. At least today, he could get things done without his boss breathing down his neck.

"Well, sir, he said he hadn't seen her. But, when we asked around, two people in the Black Horse pub across the road identified her from her photograph."

"Get on with it, please," he snapped.

"This morning, Darren Cox reported his car stolen. But there was none in his drive when we questioned him. Meaning, it had disappeared long before he reported it missing." The detective glanced down to read from his tablet. "It was a black Saab convertible, 1983. Registration H72—"

"Look at these." Adrian touched the bags under his eyes. "I'm growing old waiting to hear about this lead."

"Understood, sir. The vehicle was logged by an average speed camera heading north on the A1. That was the evening Miss Cox disappeared. After this—"

"North. I see." He scowled at the detective. "The car should be easy to find then." He waved his hands round his head as if casting a spell. "Somewhere...north."

Unfazed, the detective continued. "After this, Miss Cox was caught on CCTV at a service station near Durham. We believe she left the motorway on the A690. Using that timeframe, we're going through the camera feeds to track down her route."

Adrian sighed. "How long will that take?"

"We should have the results by the end of the day."

"Any social media alerts for Miss Cox?"

"A few hits. I'm in the process of reviewing them."

"If she's not located by the end of the week, I want to deprioritise the search. She'll turn up eventually. I need more focus on Blackmoors Bank."

"Yes, sir."

"Oh, and let that IT manager from Hokthorn, Chris something, look at Miss Cox's laptop. And make sure he's supervised." He turned back to the window. "He might find something we haven't."

SUNDAY WAS PAST sunset and, even though it was the end of May, it still was cold at night. Jessica had lit the woodstove to keep the room warm. She'd have to look at the boiler again, if only so Anna could have a warm bath. On her return to the kitchen, she finished cleaning up the dinner leftovers and made two cups of coffee.

Anna's mood had worsened as the day progressed and she had remained in the lounge, complaining her leg was stiff.

Jessica placed a cup on the table for her and sat on the sofa opposite. "Something wrong?"

Anna turned to her. "Have you seen my watch? I had it yesterday morning. But I can't find it."

"Sorry, I haven't. I can take a look."

Anna sighed. "I'm pretty sure I lost it outside. I checked the time when the storm started... It was my sister's." She blinked and wrapped her arms around herself.

Jessica stood. "I'll look for it now."

"It's okay. I searched the house already. I must have lost it in the paddock." Desolation swept across her face before she masked her emotions and changed the subject.

"I need to work out what to do with this volunteer thing," Anna said, her gaze flicking back to her laptop's screen. "I had a dozen people reply to the website. I'm kind of surprised, I didn't expect anyone to actually see it."

"They're likely searching for volunteering work in the area."

Anna nodded. "A few are creepy, but there's one or two that might work out... The thing is, when I put up the notice, I'd thought the spare room would be free. So, you'll have to give it up."

Jessica went rigid. "I see... It's probably time I left anyway." Her own words chilled her soul.

"Whoa. Hang on a sec! That wasn't what I meant. The opposite, in fact."

A few seconds passed, and Jessica allowed herself to unwind. "What did you mean then?" She took a sip from her cup, hoping the caffeine would give her some clarity.

Anna turned to face her. "I want you to sleep with me."

Jessica choked on her coffee and was forced to clear her throat. "Now?"

"No... Well, yes... I mean, it's not like we haven't most nights, and Abbie doesn't have a problem with it as far as I can tell. And I felt that, well—am I being weird again? Asking before I should... Maybe we should talk first? I mean about us. Let's do that."

Jessica let out a sigh of relief. She walked around the coffee table and dropped down beside Anna, before kissing her on the lips. "You're adorable."

"Adorkable, more like. Is that a yes? You'll share my bed, bedroom...me?" Anna batted her eyelashes at Jessica, emphasising the last word.

Jessica wasn't about to say no, but, in the context of the police finding her, this idyllic proposal was analogous to a mayfly's existence. She needed to expose the feelings stuck to her sleeve. "Anna, I'm head over heels crazy about you. You must know that. So, yes. But, I can't promise anything will last, not with the police after me. I could say a lot more...much more about how I feel about you, but I don't want to hurt you when it's likely I won't be able to stay for long. I need to really face up to things."

Anna responded straight away. It was as if she already knew what Jessica had planned to say. "I understand all that. And I've not said the things I want to say as well, for the same reasons. So, we'll need to sort out your problem."

Jessica tilted her head down and rubbed her eyes. After a moment, she turned back to Anna. "I was going to try to find a lawyer tomorrow, but I forgot it was the bank holiday."

Anna put down her laptop, twisted her body, and tipped onto Jessica so that she was pressed up against her chest. Her hair flopped over Jessica's face, and she gathered the strands, tucking them to one side.

"I have a lawyer for you, my ex-husband. He studied law at Oxford. He deals mostly with medical litigation. I've called him, and he said he'll be over Tuesday. He's really not someone I'm keen to see again, but I'm sure he can help."

Jessica blinked, and tears rolled down her cheeks.

Anna wiped them away with her fingertips. "He's in France, at the moment, with his whore-ific fiancé."

The lump in Jessica's throat made it hard to speak. She nodded, before muttering, "Thank you."

Anna smiled, but it didn't hide the concern in her eyes.

"Jess, I care about you. We'll sort this out."

Jessica tried to slip out from under Anna.

"Stay."

"I'll take a look in the paddock for your watch." Emotions overwhelmed her. She needed time to herself to think.

"Jess! It's too dark, and if it dropped out of my pocket when I fell, it'll be impossible to find. Besides, I want you here... Please, I want you close. I don't want to be alone right now."

Jessica hesitated. Anna was right. She wouldn't find it. And the fact that Anna seemed fearful again meant she couldn't leave.

Two coffee cups grew cold in the ensuing silence. A flicker from the fire travelled across the room.

"It's not me, is it? Causing your nightmares?" This was something Jessica had wanted to ask for a while now.

A woeful frown formed on Anna's face for an instant. "A bit maybe. You're bringing me to life. And, well, that comes with baggage I've been avoiding."

"I don't understand."

Anna shrugged. "It doesn't matter."

They held each other while the world stilled. It was as though they were in the eye of a storm. *If only we could stay this way.*

Jessica wasn't sure how to ask why Anna had her sister's watch. But she was pretty sure the reason was a tragic one. "Where does your sister live?"

"She doesn't."

Taken aback by the response, Jessica gaped at Anna. She'd half-guessed this to be the case, but it was the way Anna had revealed the information. It was as if Jessica had asked if her sister smoked. "I'm so sorry…" She managed. "What happened?"

"She died when I was sixteen."

"Oh, darling, that must have been really hard for you." Jessica wrapped her arms tighter around Anna.

Anna let out a sorrowful sigh. "I think of her every minute of every day."

Jessica nodded slowly. "Because you have her watch?"

"No… Because I have her daughter."

"Sorry?" Jessica needed to make sure she completely understood. "Abbie?"

"Yes." Anna put a hand over Jessica's. "Don't say anything to her. She doesn't know." She turned her head to catch Jessica's eyes, seeking reassurance.

"I won't." They looked so much alike she'd assumed Abbie was Anna's child. She now understood the age difference. Anna didn't have a daughter when she was fourteen; Abbie was her niece.

"Maybe I should tell you the whole story," Anna said in a whisper.

"Only if you want to."

"It's time I told someone other than Sarah. John knew a bit. But I never felt comfortable opening up to him."

Jessica waited for her to continue. But Anna unwrapped herself from her arms and stood. "We'll need lots of wine for this."

"I'll get it."

Jessica returned with a bottle and two glasses. It wasn't until Anna was on her third that she started to talk about what happened when she was just sixteen.

"Emma lived in Detroit with her boyfriend. I was too young and self-centred to tell her to leave him." She paused and took another gulp of the red wine. "She was five years older than me." Anna closed her eyes and leaned back.

When she spoke again, her words came tumbling out in a tempest of release. "She called me once. She needed to leave him. I'm not sure if it was forever... Mom wasn't around, so I drove over. Mike was beating her, I think. Not for the first time. I had picked up Abbie, and Mike came at me. Emma grabbed a knife and protected us." Anna was crying now. "He was drunk. He got the knife from her. He stabbed her. Then me." Her hands were pulled into the cuffs of her light blue sweater, and she used them to wipe her eyes.

Jessica remembered the scars she'd seen on Anna's torso.

"I woke up in the hospital. They told me I had lost a lot of blood, my sister was dead, and Mom had Abbie."

Wanting Anna to say everything she needed to, Jessica waited. Red eyes found and held hers. The story had connected the dots: Anna's fear of knives, her scars, her sister's watch, and learning Abbie wasn't her daughter.

"You know, what happened was horrific." Anna emptied her wine glass. "But the effect it had on our lives, especially Mom's. That was a lot worse. I'm thankful Abbie was too young to remember."

Jessica nodded slowly, trying to mellow the rage that had suddenly bubbled up. Noticing her arms were crossed tightly around herself, she made an effort to untangle them. She needed to be somewhere for Anna to hang her emotions and fears rather than reflecting them back at her.

"After," Anna continued, "it took a long time before things got back to normal. Well, they never really did. But I managed to get through high school and applied to go to Michigan State. I was there for a month before I dropped out."

"Why did you leave?"

"So many reasons. I guess first I couldn't really cope. I was still having flashbacks, but also because of my mom. She was struggling to look after two children."

"Two children? You have another brother or sister?"

"No. My dad."

Jessica blinked in confusion. "Your dad?"

"He had Parkinson's disease. There wasn't much left of him. He couldn't dress and needed help to go anywhere. A toddler really. We didn't have insurance or money to pay for private care." Anna paused and stared off towards the wood burner where the dying embers glowed faintly through the glass. "So—" she glanced back to Jessica. "After my mom had a breakdown, I dropped out, cared for Abbie, and went to work full-time as a barista. I thought I'd go back at some point. But that never happened."

*Don't pry*, Jessica told herself, but there was one question she needed to ask because she suspected it was linked to Anna's fears. "What happened to the evil fuck?" she blurted out.

"Yeah... Well, he's not someone I like thinking about." Anna gave a pensive smile.

"Of course not." Jessica kissed her temple.

Anna swivelled so she could tuck up against Jessica. "He got twenty years. But was released after fifteen. A few months ago." Anna tipped her chin up, and her anxious eyes searched Jessica's. "What if he comes here after Abbie?" Her words were desperate and pleading. She was near breaking point again.

Jessica took a deep breath. She needed to show strength and security. She adopted her voice normally reserved for talking to executives about critical issues.

"Does he have a legal right to her?"

"No. I adopted her after I married John."

"You think he'll do something vindictive?"

"Yes," she whispered without hesitation. "It's what keeps me awake at night and why I keep a hammer under my bed. And... It's why I married John. It's why I moved to the UK. It's why I live on an island surrounded by the sea. It's why I've done so many stupid things."

"None of that is stupid." She gripped Anna's shoulder. "You're a smart survivor. Don't question yourself. To me, you're pretty much perfect."

Anna ran the fingertips of both her hands along the line of Jessica's jaw. She repeated the motion while focusing on her eyes. When she stopped, she left her hands in place and inched forward to kiss Jessica deeply.

"I think I'm—" Anna muttered.

"Sorry?" Jessica mouthed when Anna didn't continue.

"Nothing... Wine speaking." Anna halted any further questions when her lips pressed firmly against Jessica's.

When they separated, they both were panting, needing to breathe.

Anna stood, took Jessica's hand, and tugged. "Let's go to our bed. I need you to touch me."

She said *our bed,* and all Jessica could do was follow.

# Chapter Seventeen

DEW COATED THE long grass of the paddock as Jessica brushed through it. She had gone with Abbie, who had been eager to ride Daisy in the morning so she'd have time later for revision.

The far corner of the field offered a view of the sea, and she could hear the waves rolling onto the shore. She kept an eye on Abbie as she took Daisy through her paces.

Anna's birthday was tomorrow, and Jessica didn't even have money to buy a card. She thought if she could find Anna's watch, cook a meal, and maybe get the hot water working, then those might at least be considered gifts of sorts. It hadn't slipped her mind how much she owed Anna for taking her in. But more than that, she couldn't shake the feeling she needed to do all she could for her.

Collecting one of the plastic uprights from the jumps, she walked to where Anna had been knocked over. She placed the standard down to mark the edge of where she would search. Taking small steps, Jessica scanned the ground. After ten minutes, she decided it was hopeless. The grass was too long and wet.

She stood and placed her hands on her hips. Abbie trotted towards her and slowed to a stop. "What are you doing?"

"Your mum thinks she lost her watch around here."

"That would be hard to find."

"Maybe, but I think I should..."

Abbie wasn't listening and pointed beyond Jessica. A black and white collie blasted past, turned to a noise that sounded like a bird call, and darted back the way it had come.

David was walking towards them. He blew a whistle, and the dog stopped in its tracks and lay down. "Stay. Fairweather." Behind him in the next field, a tractor was hitched to a trailer loaded with fencing material. His father was inspecting the weatherworn posts that ran along the field's edge.

David waved as he approached.

"Treasure hunting?" he asked. "There's supposed to be a lot of old relics in these fields, but I've never found any."

Jessica smiled. "I'm trying to find Anna's watch."

"You'll be lucky." David fumbled in the pockets of his muddy overalls. "Here." He handed Jessica a crinkled envelope.

"What's this?"

"The guitarist from the band on Friday gave it to me to give to you. Suspect it's a thank-you note. You were much better than they were." He pointed to the back of the envelope. "That's his number. He said to call them if you want to join the band."

Jessica half smiled and tucked the letter into her jeans. "I don't think it would work out."

David shrugged. "I tried to learn the guitar once. I bought an electric one on eBay and even bought lessons online. But I found it way too hard to play."

"Do you still have it? Abbie wants me to teach her."

"No." He laughed. "I put it under the wheel of the tractor and drove over it...ten times."

"Ah."

Jessica looked around David, to Mr Foster, some fifty yards away. The collie was no longer flat in the long grass but racing towards the older farmer.

David crossed his arms. "Did you see the lightning the other night?"

Something wasn't right. David's father tottered backwards and bumped into the large rear wheel of the tractor. His hand was against his chest while Fairweather barked and circled him.

Jessica took flight, running past David in the direction of the tractor.

"What's up—" David yelled after her but was soon in chase.

When they reached the fence, she ducked under the wire and towards the floundering man.

"Dad!" David yelled and bent down to him.

"My chest," he muttered, before tipping over onto the ground. The collie barked incessantly, then settled down next to him, whimpering.

"Shit!" Jessica had to push the dog away before she could start to undo his shirt "He's having a heart attack! Call 999!"

David hesitated, his face ashen, apparently unsure what to do.

"David! Call it in."

Coming to his senses, he pulled his phone out of his pocket.

Jessica leaned down, put her cheek beside Mr Foster's mouth, and watched his chest. No movement. She pushed her fingers against his neck, checking for a pulse from his carotid artery. There was none.

"Ambulance," she heard David say.

"Tell them your father has had a heart attack. That he's unconscious and has stopped breathing. Tell them I'm starting CPR." She shifted herself over the top of the elderly farmer and began chest compressions.

"David Foster. It's my dad, Iain Foster. We're a mile northwest of Lindisfarne in a field. Beside a tractor... Yes... Yes... I'll stay on."

Jessica slipped to Foster's side, tipped his chin up to make sure his tongue was not blocking his airway. She pinched his nose and gave a breath, checking his chest was rising. She did another, before returning to straddle him and begin thirty compressions.

"They're sending the air ambulance." David was visibly shaking and barely able to speak.

"How long?"

David asked on the phone. "As soon as they can. Whatever that means. They're at a traffic accident." He patted the collie who had its snout resting on Mr Foster's leg. "It'll be okay, girl." But there was no conviction in David's words.

It was taking too long. Jessica wanted to swear, but that wasn't going to help anyone. She could keep the blood flowing, but she wouldn't be able to get his heart started again. She glanced over to Abbie, who was sitting on top of Daisy on the other side of the fence with a worried expression. Jessica needed a defibrillator. The green box by the café came into her head. She had spotted it the other day when she'd searched for Anna.

"Abbie!" Jessica called. "You know the café in the village, the one with the garden?" The name had escaped her.

"The Oasis Café?" Abbie shouted, her tone puzzled.

"I think so," Jessica prayed it was the right one. "There's a defibrillator there. But it might be labelled AED."

Abbie's expression was one of puzzlement, before being replaced by a resolute tensing of her lips and brows.

"I'll fetch it," David said quickly. "I can go on the tractor."

Jessica didn't like what she was about to do, but it was the best course of action. "No, David, I need you here." She continued to count, trying not to miss out any numbers while speaking. "I won't be able to keep doing the compressions for long."

The cycle repeated, and, after two breaths, Jessica started the compressions again. "Abbie, ride to the café. Bring the defibrillator here. Fast as you can!"

"Okay!" Abbie called back and immediately tugged on the left rein before compelling the pony into a gallop with her heels.

"You'll need to call a number," Jessica yelled, but Abbie was already ripping across the paddock with clumps of grass flying from Daisy's hooves. Mr Foster's collie barked and let out a bone-chilling howl, before settling back down beside her master.

"Be careful," Jessica said to herself.

THEY WERE OUT of bread and running low on coffee. The last had given Anna the incentive to attempt to walk to the village, deciding it would be better to exercise her leg than allow it to seize up.

Her thoughts went to last night with Jessica. She shook her head. They weren't the kind of moments to relive when meandering through the holy town of Lindisfarne—they were overtly arousing. She flushed, then dampened the pangs of desire by refocusing on the throbbing pain from her damaged leg.

As she turned into Green Lane, a blur of white and brown nearly knocked her over. She watched, dumbfounded, as a Welsh part-bred cut the corner and jumped over a low stone wall into the car park on its way out of the village.

"Abbie! What the hell!" Anna tried to race after them but, after two strides, she had to stop. Her leg was burning, sending spikes of pain along her spine.

With no choice, she slowed to a pace reserved for retired tourists who seemed to have all the time in the world when, in fact, they had much less than everyone else.

A woman cut in front of her. "Anna?"

"Yes."

"I'm Cathy, one of the first aiders on the island. Abbie is your daughter, right?"

"Yes. Do you know what's going on? She just raced past me on her pony." A thought occurred to her. "Is someone hurt? Jessica?" Her body instantly drained of all warmth.

"No, it's Iain Foster. He's had a heart attack. Your daughter is taking the AED to him."

"Oh." She paused and swallowed the emotion that had threatened to undo her. "Do you know where she's going?"

"Yes, a field outside the village. She said it was near your paddock. Can you show me the way?"

"I can try."

"I called the emergency services. They said the air ambulance had already been dispatched, but we need to get there and see if we can help."

"Who else is there?"

"David Foster and Abbie said your friend, Jessica."

Cathy took long strides, stopping when Anna failed to keep pace.

"Sorry, my leg is messed up." Her inability to keep up had become an intense frustration.

"We'll take my car and try to get as close as we can." Cathy pointed a short distance along the road. "It's over there."

Walking at a painful rate, Anna followed, as Cathy told her what had happened.

"I saw a horse at the café. You don't see that every day. Perhaps a hundred years ago you might have. I managed to ask your daughter a few questions. It made more sense for her to take the AED. She would get there quicker."

Cathy unlocked her car, which was parked on a concrete drive beside a pebble-dashed cottage. She glanced at Anna. "Your daughter has a lot of nous for her age. Riding here and collecting the AED."

"I just hope she doesn't fall off. It's the first time I've seen our pony jump anything." Anna ducked into the vehicle. It was started as she shut the passenger door. They sped backwards out into the street, and Anna directed Cathy towards the bridle path that led to her paddock.

THE SOUND OF hooves caused Jessica to turn. Abbie was galloping at full steam in her direction but, this time, from the bottom of the field rather than across the adjacent paddock.

She could see Abbie held a plastic briefcase in her left hand. Abbie pulled Daisy to a stop a few yards from where Mr Foster lay, his shirt already unbuttoned, with David performing CPR. Jessica had corrected his timing more than once but was grateful he had taken over; her arms felt like jelly.

"I've got it!" Abbie yelled as she kicked her feet out of the stirrups, swung one leg over the saddle, and jumped onto the grass. Daisy released a loud whinny, before dipping her head to graze.

Taking the defibrillator from Abbie, Jessica squeezed Abbie's shoulder with her free hand. "Well done!" She spun around and then ran back to David and dropped down beside him. After she'd opened the AED, it started to issue commands in a robotic voice.

"Call emergency services," the machine demanded.

"Done that," Jessica muttered, wondering why the air ambulance still hadn't arrived. It had been at least fifteen minutes. She took in a long breath, which caught in her throat. Enough time had passed that the odds were against Mr Foster's heart starting—it might be too damaged.

"Pull the blue handle," the robotic voice insisted.

She did so, opening up a pack containing two wired pads.

"Remove clothing. Remove blue backing plastic and place the pads as shown."

David looked at her, his face drawn and fatigued. Sweat beaded on his brow.

"You're doing great, David, keep going," Jessica said. "I'll attach the pads." She shot her head around to Abbie. "Pull the dog away!"

Abbie grabbed Fairweather's collar and was able to drag the whimpering animal a few yards from her master.

Once the pads were stuck to the dead man's chest, the machine beeped for ten seconds.

"Stand clear," the AED said.

David quickly stepped away.

After five more beeps, there was a loud click, and Mr Foster's body spasmed where it lay.

"Continue CPR," the AED said without emotion.

"It hasn't worked!" David's words were filled with anguish.

Jessica moved quickly on top of Mr Foster and started the compressions again. Fairweather appeared, having broken free of Abbie's grip.

"We don't know yet. Pretty sure it always—" She got her counting in sync with the rhythm of her hands against his chest. "Always says to continue CPR."

To her left, behind David, Abbie stood with her arms crossed. "Abbie, when the helicopter comes, it will spook Daisy. Move her into the paddock. Okay?"

Abbie nodded and mounted her pony. She rode her down the field.

Jessica suddenly felt some resistance to her motion, and she stopped for a moment. Bending over Mr Foster's mouth, she felt a gentle breath against her cheek and saw his chest rise of its own accord.

"He's breathing!" She twisted her head to David, who had his hand over his mouth.

"Place the patient in recovery position," the machine interrupted.

Jessica did so and then double-checked his airways, before rising and placing a hand on David's shoulder. "Keep talking to him, reassuring him."

"Okay." David knelt beside his father.

Jessica took a few more steps away—she needed some space after what she'd just been through.

Abbie returned, coming over to stand beside her.

"You did great. I think you saved his life," Jessica told her in a whisper.

Abbie hooked her arm into Jessica's and leaned against her.

*I wonder if Anna is still at home? How am I going to find her watch? I should look at the boiler... Clean out the other stables. Oh, Abbie wanted to learn the guitar. Maybe start her on open chords—* She cut off her thoughts; she was hiding again, hiding from the seriousness of what had happened.

Fairweather started barking moments before the sound of a helicopter's rotor cut through the air, and four sets of eyes turned to watch it approach.

The next ten minutes passed without Jessica registering them. The helicopter landed in the centre of the field. Two paramedics disembarked and saw to Mr Foster while asking Jessica questions. They couldn't say how the man was, other than he was alive.

Anna and another woman, who said her name was Cathy, had arrived.

Jessica watched as the paramedics tried to stop Fairweather from boarding the helicopter, but the dog jumped past them. Seconds later, they took off with the collie, David, and his father on board.

Cathy collected the spent defibrillator, saying she would drop by tomorrow. Jessica wasn't sure why, except possibly Cathy thought she hadn't handled the incident correctly and wanted to talk about it.

"Are you all right?" Anna asked.

"Fine. You don't need to keep asking me that," Jessica said a little too forcefully.

"Okay," Anna responded without anger. "We should head back to the house. I'll make us some lunch."

Jessica didn't want to move—she was out of phase with everything. A few minutes passed as she tried to gather herself.

Approaching along the fence, Abbie led Daisy to where they stood. Anna remained close by.

Jessica made eye contact with Anna. "I hope I've done the right thing...with David's father," she whispered.

"You always do the right thing." Anna put an arm around her and hugged her.

Jessica sighed. "I don't know…"

Anna's hand slipped into hers. "Let's go."

"If it's okay, I'll come in a bit. I need to clear my head."

"Of course, it's okay."

Daisy snorted behind Anna, causing her to turn away. "Don't be long," she said over her shoulder.

Abbie helped Anna onto Daisy before they ambled away in the direction of the farm. Jessica couldn't see them as individuals. They appeared as a single unit, encapsulated in some kind of bubble. She wondered if she would ever be part of such a haven. Anna had said she had feelings for her, but fate had shown Jessica, in the most painful way, that such things were beyond what she deserved.

She ducked under the fence and entered the paddock again. She picked up one of the crossbeams used for Daisy's jumps and went to the spot where Anna had fallen during the storm. During the previous hour, clouds had swamped the sky, dimming the sunlight and making it harder to see detail on the ground.

"You couldn't just make the sun glint off it, could you! It's not like I'm asking for much. Just to find a simple watch. You can't even do that for me, can you? Holy Island, my ass… Come to think of it, when have you ever done anything for me? Except one big problem after the next. What next? Really? What fucking next?"

She released the beam she was dragging and nudged it with a kick. She dropped to her knees and started at one end. Using the beam as a straight edge, she inspected the ground inch by inch. When she'd completed one length, she rolled it forward and started again.

Hours passed, but still nothing. "It will be right at the end. Or nowhere at all. Carried off by a magpie and dropped into the bloody sea!"

Jessica continued. She didn't know why she was so angry. The events of the day seemed to have released everything that plagued her. Life was so short. The thought of going to prison and never seeing Anna and Abbie again felt like a stake through her heart. *Why am I not allowed to be happy? Is that too much to ask for? Will I die never having joy?*

She realised she hadn't been concentrating and had to backtrack. Scouring the last five lengths again, she came across a small loop of metal. She picked it up and poked off the mud. It was gold and resembled part of Anna's watch. She wiped it clean on her sweater, only to discover it was an engagement ring. A small diamond was held in its mounting. It wouldn't be worth much; the owner must have lost it decades ago, and perhaps the storm had exposed it. She tucked it into her pocket and started forward again.

Her neck was sore, and her knees were soaked by the time she reached the plastic upright she'd originally placed. She sighed. Her arms also hurt, and it took a moment before she remembered why. Performing CPR had taken its toll. She didn't want to think about Mr Foster lying there, unmoving.

*It would be better to get a metal detector. It might not even be here.* She wanted to find it for Anna or she'd have nothing to give her.

*The thought never counts.*

She picked up the plastic upright to reposition it; she'd try a few more lengths before she gave up. Jessica's brow wrinkled, and she stared down at the patch that was now exposed by the moved standard. *I fucking bet it's there.*

*That's how it works, that's how it always works. It's some kind of joke, causing me to make it harder for myself.*

A smell of rotten eggs wafted by, and she spun around to see Kermit staring at her.

"You've come to help have you, goat? By gassing me?"

Kermit stood, motionless and unblinking. Jessica turned her back on him. It wasn't the wisest of things to do, but she no longer cared if he butted her into the mud.

On her hands and knees, she checked the square foot where the standard had stood.

A minute later, a slender, black leather strap dangled from the tips of her pinched fingers. A woman's gold watch ticked behind a layer of mud. She wiped the face clean, discovering it read 6:30 p.m.

"Okay. Thank God... Maybe," she muttered, rising to her feet.

*I hope David's father is all right.*

She headed back to the farmhouse. Grim determination edged her face. *I won't give up. Not yet. No matter how fucking hard everything always is.*

"Boiler next."

# Chapter Eighteen

THE FARMHOUSE DOOR swung open as Jessica thumbed the latch.

Anna stood in front of her. "You've finally come back."

From her tone, Jessica couldn't tell if she was annoyed or pleased to see her.

"So what else have you been up to?" Anna asked. "Rescuing seamen, fighting injustice?" Anna glanced down at Jessica's jeans. "Or, by the looks of it, making mud pies?"

"Definitely mud pies. Do you want one?"

"No, but you could have them for your dinner."

Anna was still blocking the entrance and, despite the banter, Jessica sensed she was about to get a bollocking. Anna had expected her to come back for lunch hours ago.

"Can I come in?" Jessica asked.

"Not yet. I need to say something to you." Anna took a step towards Jessica and drew her into a tight hug. "I need you to promise me something. I know it won't be easy for you because you keep everything to yourself. But you mustn't." She pressed her cheek against Jessica's. "You don't have to carry everything that upsets you. I need you to share those things with me." Anna's blue eyes shone with fierce conviction. "It's important for us." She deposited a quick kiss on Jessica's lips. "You promise?"

Jessica nodded. "I'll try. I'm sorry. I guess I've spent too much time on my own."

"You're not alone anymore. Please understand that." Anna shifted to one side, so they both could enter the house. "And, you don't have to eat mud pies, I've made dinner. But you might want to shower first. How'd you get so dirty anyway?"

"Fell over," she lied. "Any news on David's father?"

"Beth phoned about an hour ago—" Anna paused. "Iain's doing all right." Her voice cracked. "And it's thanks to you. He's not completely okay. He's in the coronary care unit, but he's been speaking a few words."

Jessica let out a sigh of relief. "That's good."

"Beth and her mother are beside themselves with how grateful they are to you and Abbie."

"I just hope he gets better soon."

"I said I'd take Katy and Abbie to school tomorrow, so Beth can go to the hospital. Then I'll go to the clinic."

"You'll be able to drive?"

"My car's automatic, so I'll use my right leg. I never learned how to drive a stick shift."

Anna brushed her fingers down Jessica's jaw, before sliding them along her neck and onto her shoulder. "How are you feeling?"

Jessica hesitated, but then answered truthfully. "I don't want to have to go through that again. And... I feel out of sorts. Kind of shook up. I..." She blinked her eyes and looked down, finding it hard to explain her frame of mind. "There's too much worrying me at the moment, and it turns everything into a pool of mush."

"We'll sort it out. You've got me now, and that's not going to change." Anna kissed her. "Now go have a shower, my heroine."

Anna was on the phone when Jessica came back down, towelling her hair while wearing a robe. Abbie sat at the kitchen table with her school books spread out in front of her. Her head was low to her pen, and she furiously scribbled in an exercise book.

"I'll warm up your lasagne, won't be a sec," Anna called, with her hand over her phone.

In the lounge, Jessica perched close to the fire and finished drying her hair. She could hear Anna's conversation and wondered who she was speaking with.

"Yes, that time should work." Anna's voice changed in volume as she moved around the kitchen. "Darling, that's wrong." There were a few seconds of quiet. "No birthday presents... Unless you want to fix the central heating. The boiler's not working. You always had a knack with that thing... Okay thanks, tomorrow then."

Abbie turned up the music coming from her iPhone as Jessica entered the kitchen and sat down at the table.

"That was John. He said he would be here around noon."

Jessica nodded, but the prospect of talking to him unnerved her. She also didn't like what she'd heard during the phone call. *Darling? They're divorced. What if... What will she do if I go to prison? Get back with him?* She shook her head, just as Anna put a plate of food in front of her.

"Something wrong?" Anna asked.

"No." Jessica glanced up. She really didn't know how their relationship stood. It had no future at the moment. While Anna could plan for hers, she had only a cell to look forward to. "Thanks for the dinner." Jessica attempted a smile.

"You're welcome."

JESSICA WOKE WITH a start, remembering it was Anna's birthday. She quickly got dressed, pulling on her dirty clothes from yesterday. After grabbing a cup of coffee, she went outside. Anna wouldn't be back until midday, and she hoped to have time to fix the heating.

The error on the boiler had indicated no fuel. She suspected Anna must have checked this but, still, she went over to the rectangular oil tank in the front garden, which was hidden behind a willow screen. Tapping on its side, she could tell it was three-quarters full. She followed a line towards the house where the fuel pipe must run.

Outside the kitchen window, a flower bed had apparently been recently planted. Tall dark-green stalks with yellow and purple flowers were spread throughout. She didn't know the first thing about plants but, to her, they appeared as extra-large daisies.

She collected a shovel and dug carefully in the loose soil at the bed's border. It wasn't long before she uncovered a copper pipe ten inches down that ran towards the oil tank.

Jessica frowned. *This should be protected in a channel.* She dug further, exposing the fuel line running through the bed. At one point, there was a lateral dent in the pipe. *Anna must have made this with the shovel when planting the flowers.* Other than the crimp, there was no sign of a leak.

Pushing herself up, she fetched a pair of pliers from Anna's junk drawer in the kitchen. On her return, she pinched the pipe back into shape, hoping it wouldn't split. With the pliers tucked in her back pocket, she headed inside.

In the kitchen, she reset the heating and turned on the tap. She heard the boiler fire up and felt the water change from cold to warm and then become too hot to keep her fingers under.

"That was easier than I thought." She laughed, pleased Anna could now have a hot bath for her birthday. Jessica pulled the pliers out of her pocket to put them away and, as she did, an envelope fell out. It was the one David had given her. She picked it up and was surprised to find it contained a hundred pounds with a scrawled note.

*Thought we should give you some of the money from our gig. If you want to be part of the band, give me a call, Jay. Thanks again.*

It was the first time in weeks she'd had actual money. Even though it was a small amount, she felt the loosening of the vice-like tension that had been crushing her ribs into her lungs. She remembered Anna's watch and removed it from her jeans. She placed it on the kitchen table, before darting up to the bedroom.

After she'd slipped on clean clothes, she dashed down the stairs with the gig money in her hand.

The house keys were in the bowl beside the door. Jessica grabbed them and, once the door was locked, hurried towards the village. She'd have enough time to get Anna a card and present. *But—* Her pace slowed. *Luck like this doesn't happen to me without something going wrong.*

ANNA ARRIVED HOME at eleven, an hour early. The tide chart she'd read in the morning indicated noon would be the latest she could cross. While waiting for her appointment at the clinic, she checked the chart again, realising she'd been looking at the wrong day and the tide was due in much sooner. She raced back to the causeway, crossing it with the waves lapping the edge of the tarmac—an occurrence that seemed to happen more often than not whenever she went to the mainland.

"What a horrible birthday present," she muttered, pulling in beside a black Audi sports car. With her forehead pressed against her steering wheel, she gathered her strength. "He'd better not have a fucking present for me."

She fought to unfasten her seatbelt. The button for the buckle had broken a month before, and now it took a delicate touch to get it to disconnect. Her fifteen-year-old Ford Fiesta was definitely on its last legs. She took a deep breath and gently coaxed the belt to release her. She got out and slammed the door, instantly regretting the action; she couldn't afford any more expenses.

Inside the house, she found John sitting at the kitchen table, sipping a cup of coffee and tapping on his phone with the thumb of his right hand. On the table, a bunch of flowers was in a measuring jug filled with water.

Waves of annoyance flashed between her temples until they distilled into quiet indifference. *If he can help me in any way, dealing with him will be worth it.*

He hadn't changed much, perhaps put on a few pounds, but he still looked very much the dapper English gentleman, dressed in smart cords and a white, striped shirt without a tie. On his wrist was a Yachtmaster Rolex.

"When did you get here?" Anna asked, popping her handbag on the countertop.

"About an hour ago. Sorry, I let myself in. You still have the spare key in the tool shed." He stood. "It's good to see you again, you look—"

Anna held up her hand with her palm facing him. "Let's keep this professional. I'm glad you've come to help Jessica."

"I'll do what I can." He slipped the flowers forward, before shoving his hands into his pockets. "Happy birth—"

She frowned, trying to control her anger. "Professional, please." She thought she was over it, his affair, his lies, but the rage still gnawed at her insides. "I need a coffee. Do you want a refill?"

"Sure. Thanks." John handed over his cup. "So where is this Jessica?"

"She must be outside." Anna flicked the mixer lever forward on the sink to fill the kettle and gasped. "The water's hot!" She turned and looked at John. "The boiler's working? Did you do this?"

John approached her.

Anna saw her sister's watch on the table and snatched it up. She closed her fingers around it and held it tightly against her chest. "You found this as well?" A tear broke free, and she wiped it away. Anna's mind was racing. Dots were connecting, but she felt the wrong shape was emerging.

Before she could stop him, he wrapped her into a hug.


*SHE'S ALREADY HOME.* Jessica walked past Anna's red Ford and another car. *Hell, and her ex is here as well.* She quietly stepped into the house, tucking the carrier bag with a present and card for Anna under her arm.

To her left, she caught a glimpse of two people hugging. A tall broad-shouldered man and Anna. It had looked a bit more than a friendly hug. *Are they getting back together? Is that the real reason she asked him to come here?*

Her thoughts skipped through everything Anna had told her. Nothing had suggested this, except the phone call yesterday when she had heard Anna call him "darling." Unsure, she drifted backwards and lifted the keys to the Saab from the bowl near the door.

ANNA PUSHED JOHN away. "Back off. I don't want you to touch me!"

"Of course... I understand. I've not done things right. I shouldn't have—"

"Enough." Anna stepped away, still holding her watch close to her heart. She examined his face carefully. *Fuck... What the hell is he saying... And where's Jessica?* She swallowed.

His face was expressionless, with no sign of blushing; his hands were unnaturally at his side as if he was on stage.

"Where did you find my watch?" Anna asked.

A few seconds passed, and he remained motionless. "I didn't," he finally answered.

"The hot water?"

"Not me." John crossed his arms.

Anna grimaced; she had assumed, if only for an instant, it had been him. Why, she wasn't sure. She replayed what had happened and understood. Most people give off telltale signals that would provide clues. As a lawyer, John was a poker player of sorts, so he reacted in a way which would give him an advantage, independent of the truth.

She knew it was best to be direct when dealing with his ilk. "If I hadn't asked, would you have admitted you hadn't done those things?"

"I'm a lawyer, I never admit to anything. But course, I would have."

Anna knew his attempted joke to be a half truth. She wondered how much of her relationship with him had been misstatements that worked in his favour. The question she had now was a critical one. *Will he do the right thing for Jessica?*

"Why do you want to help me?" Anna asked without emotion.

"You asked me to come. And the case sounded intriguing. Plus, as you said, I owe you a few favours... And I suppose I wanted to see how you were doing."

She didn't like his answers. She couldn't tell which of the four were important to him and they didn't seem to be enough of a reason for him to come. She knew how he worked. He always made things out as if he was being altruistic when that was rarely the case.

She tapped her fingers slowly on the table, considering if she should send him away. *Even if I can't trust him, Jessica might get something useful from him. It'll be better to get the most out of something bad then throw it away. As long as the smell doesn't linger.* She laughed out loud, then stifled it with her hand. *When did I become a philosopher?*

He shifted from one foot to the other. "What's so funny?"

"Nothing. Sit. I'll find Jessica."

As Anna approached the front door, she noticed it was ajar. She never forgot to close it. *Did Jessica come in—God! What did she see?*

Anna ran across the farmyard. It had started to rain but, midway, she realised Jessica's Saab was not parked in its spot by the barn.

She spun around, sped back to the house, and grabbed her keys, without a word to John.

The rain thudded against the roof of her car as her trembling hands tried to key the ignition. "For Christ's sake!" She ducked down to see the exact alignment and rammed the key in.

THE CAUSEWAY HAD been consumed by the sea. Jessica turned off the engine. She wasn't sure if the tide was going out, so she waited, watching its level rise on the road sign ahead. She thought about attempting to cross, but the warning read: "DANGER! Do not proceed when—" The rest was underwater. The windscreen had started to steam up but, even through it and the heavy rain, she could tell the tide was on the way in.

The nausea, which had started when she had left Anna, had grown exponentially. Cupping her face with her hands, she tipped her head against the driver's window. *Enough is enough. Time to turn myself in.* She hadn't expected to have a future with Anna, but it was a horrible way for it to end. She thought about Myra from when she'd been a teenager. "At least it's not as bad as that. I'll have to—"

The passenger side door opened, and Anna hurled herself into the seat. Rain and a cold wind accompanied her.

"Jessica! What the hell do you think you're doing?" Anna's breathing came in fast gasps.

She didn't know what to say. Anna's face was distorted with anger but, behind it, concern showed in her blue eyes.

"You're crap at keeping promises! And if you think something is going on between me and John, you're crazy!" Anna closed her eyes. A few seconds passed, and when she spoke again, her tone was filled with sadness. "You know, I moved here because I thought the tide would help to protect me from Abbie's father. But I didn't know it would also keep the person I love from leaving me."

Jessica's eyes found Anna's. They were filled with tears.

"If you must leave, at least do it in the morning so I can say goodbye." Her words had turned to sobs. A stream of rain from the gap in the soft-top poured onto her shoulder, soaking her ivory sweater.

Reaching out, Jessica grabbed the side of Anna's jumper and yanked her desperately towards her. She tucked her head close so their cheeks were pressed against each other. "I'm sorry. I'm just messed up."

"I know. But how do I get you to understand? How...? I love you, and I need you to stay. Please." After a minute, Anna pulled away and stared at her. "So?"

Jessica let her tears fall. She tried to say the words but couldn't. It would end with too much pain. The last time she had spoken them, so many years ago, Myra had been nearly beaten to death.

"I see," Anna said, her voice trembling. She twisted in the passenger seat, pulled the latch on the door, and flung it open.

"Anna, wait!"

Anna looked over her shoulder towards Jessica.

"I love you," Jessica blurted out. Her whole body shook, and the words were almost lost in the sound of the rain.

"Then come home." Anna slammed the door closed.

# Chapter Nineteen

ANNA DROPPED DOWN onto the bed, muffling her sobs with a pillow. Jessica had become entwined into the fabric of her being in the most intimate way, and she couldn't face losing her.

"Why is it so damn hard for her to understand?" She grabbed a pillow and dragged it over her head. She knew Jessica would come back. *But will she stay? What the hell is wrong with her?* She flipped onto her back with the pillow pulled tightly against her face. *What is the point of asking bedsheets these questions!*

She thought about phoning Sarah, but what would she say to her friend? *She's leaving me because she thinks... What is Jessica thinking? She doesn't tell me anything.*

The sound of the bath being filled caught her ear, and she rolled, slipping her legs off the end of the bed. Only then did she feel the throbbing pain in her thigh. The bedroom door opened, and Jessica padded in. Without saying a word, she sat down beside Anna and put an arm around her waist.

"Why do you always try to leave?" Anna's voice trembled with sadness. She thought maybe this was being too direct. But it was her way and the part of herself she didn't want to change.

Jessica's eyes flicked down to the rug covering the planked floor. "I'm afraid."

"Of what? Prison? That's not going to happen."

"No. I thought it was that, but it's something else."

"Talk to me." Anna used two fingers to push Jessica's hair around her ears. "Tell me, or this will be a world of pain for both of us."

Jessica's eyelashes fluttered before she rubbed them with her free hand. "I think it's to do with my first relationship. And it's why I stopped playing the guitar. Something happened, and it was my fault. So, for me, every silver lining has a cloud. And it seems when I find something I love, it gets taken from me."

Anna gave Jessica her best stern stare, the one she used to encourage Abbie to admit she had eaten four cookies before dinner. "Tell me again. But replace all the somethings with the actual things. It's me, remember. I'm not some stranger in a pub."

Pressing her chin to her collarbone, Jessica started to speak. "Myra Bedi. She was the first person I came out to and told I loved. I was sixteen, playing in our local pub, and after, we went to get a Chinese takeaway a few doors down. While we were waiting for the order, a guy from the pub came in as I was kissing her, said something about needing to show us what a man was really like. I told him to fuck off, and he punched me in the jaw. When I woke, I was in an ambulance. I couldn't see Myra, and no one would tell me what had happened to her."

Anna hadn't expected this. She'd thought it would be just a broken heart. But this sounded sickening. The lack of emotion in Jessica's delivery added to her dread. It was as if she was reading a news story; she seemed to have disconnected herself from the events. Anna rubbed the back of Jessica's neck as she continued.

"It was weeks before I found out she had nearly died of internal bleeding from the beating he had given her. After that, she wouldn't see me. Her parents wouldn't open the door when I tried to visit her. She wouldn't answer any of my messages. And that was it. I never saw her again."

As much as Anna wanted Jessica to talk more about what had happened, she knew that couldn't be done. Her own experiences, and what her mother had gone through after the death of Emma, caused a big red warning light to flash. Jessica had packaged up the ordeal in a shoebox, and she was reading the label on the top. *Now's not the time to open it.*

Anna kissed her and pulled her in for a hug. "So, you're a bit broken, like me. We'll share the bits that work to make us whole. Okay?"

Jessica gave a forlorn smile. "Sure," she whispered. "I love you."

"I love you too... But I suspect the bath is overflowing, and the kitchen ceiling will collapse."

"Shit!" Jessica bolted to her feet, but Anna kept hold of her hand.

"It's okay, John's down there. We can dig him out later," Anna joked.

"I was pouring the bath for you...for your birthday." Jessica rolled her eyes and grimaced. "I got you a card. A present."

Anna stood. "You found my watch and fixed the hot water as well, don't forget."

"I'm sorry, I've made your birthday hell."

"No!" Anna put her fingers on Jessica's lips. "You said you loved me. That was hard for you to say and I can have a bath for the first time in a month!" She wrapped her arms around her shoulders and kissed her firmly. "Bath or Jessica? Bath or Jessica? Hmm? I think both." She slipped her hand into hers.

"I better go downstairs and talk to John, hadn't I? He'll be wondering what we're doing."

Anna gave a mischievous grin. "God, that would mess with his head. I like it!" She yanked Jessica down the hall towards a cloud of steam.

Crouching by the tub, Jessica turned off the taps with an inch to spare. The white bathroom was small, with a ceiling that followed the slope of the roof. Various seaside themed knickknacks hung on the walls. There was a driftwood mirror above the sink and a collection of seashells in a bowl on the windowsill.

Jessica rolled up her sleeve and pulled the plug to drain some of the water away. "John could leave," she said, replacing the plug.

"He won't. I think he's looking to get back with me, which is fucked up." Anna undid her jeans and slipped them off. "But, thinking about it, the sooner you talk to him the sooner we can get rid of him." She yanked her wet sweater over her head. "And, for the record, he hugged me without my permission." Tangled in folds of her jumper, she inched towards Jessica. "Help!"

Jessica freed a shirt button snagged in the wool of Anna's sweater. Anna undressed. In her birthday suit, she wrapped herself around Jessica and kissed her. "Thanks for my present. Awesome sauce." She slipped into the warm bath. Sighing with contentment, she reached for Jessica's wrist. "Jess, I don't trust him, obviously. But he's an expert lawyer. You'll need to decide if you want his help."


JESSICA OFFERED JOHN a coffee, which he declined. She wasn't looking forward to the discussion.

At the kitchen table, she dropped onto the stool opposite. "Where do you want me to start?"

"The beginning," he joked.

"Well, first the universe cooled. Is that too far back?" She checked her tone, reminding herself she needed his help.

He mimicked a politician's smile. "Well, we are time constrained."

*Stop messing around. You have to do this.* "I suppose I've everything to lose," she muttered.

"I didn't catch that." His head tilted to one side.

She forced herself to uncross her arms and straightened. "A month ago, we had an incident at the place where I work, Hokthorn. It's a software company." She noticed he wasn't taking notes. "Do you need the exact dates?"

"Not at this point. Just an overview."

"Well, I was woken in the early hours and told an update had gone wrong, affecting the majority of customer systems. By the time we cleaned up the mess, my company's shares had lost most of their value. The investigation concluded that I instigated the issue by doctoring a test script, but also by changing the code to break our customer systems. The Serious Fraud Office was called in. They accused me of equity fraud." Jessica let out a slow breath. "I had cashed in on Hokthorn options prior to the incident, and I still held stock in the previous company I worked for. A competitor. Their stock rose as a result of our bad update."

"I assume you didn't create the incident or know in advance it would happen?"

"No," she said dryly.

"So why did they have reason to believe you were the cause?"

Jessica rubbed her face. She didn't know if he would be technical enough to understand. "Apparently, the audit logs showed that my laptop accessed the affected systems. My IP address was recorded in the code check-ins as well."

"Okay. And where was your laptop during the times in the logs?" he asked, leaning forward.

"I was using it to work on appraisals in my office. A colleague of mine, Chris, checked the appraisal system. It showed I had used it, but a different IP address had been recorded, which would suggest a different laptop—"

"Two laptops, one yours used to cause the incident, and another you were using?"

"Yes. But, that day, I definitely had my laptop. Chris thinks someone swapped out the internals, so on the outside, it still looked like mine. But it's impossible to prove."

"A kind of identity theft?"

"More like identity swap."

"I see."

"The thing is, when it was examined later, it was back to normal, with the correct hardware."

John remained quiet and glanced at his phone before asking another question. "Who else at Hokthorn would gain?"

"Only those with shares in competitors. A few of us were headhunted from Genism Systems a couple of years ago."

"Any of them have a grudge against you?"

"A few, yes."

"I'll need their names." He recorded the names on his phone as she spoke them. "So, what exactly have you been charged with?"

"I don't know. After I was dismissed, they froze my cards and bank account. I went to my brother to borrow some money but, when I was back at my flat, I saw the police. They were in the process of breaking in. I guessed they must've had a warrant. After that, I...well, ended up here."

"All right. I wouldn't bring up the fact you saw them at your flat unless pushed to do so. As it stands, you've not been charged with anything. It's best it appears you're not avoiding arrest, but just visiting a friend. Did you know Anna before this?"

"No. I broke down on the island." She let the words stand, accepting *she* had broken down rather than the car. "I was trying to get to my ex-girlfriend in Edinburgh. She didn't return any of my calls, so Anna put me up."

"I see." He paused, staring directly at her.

"What do you think I should do?" she asked.

"I don't think there's much you can do that won't have to happen in a courtroom. It will be a matter of building a strong enough case to ensure a jury has reasonable doubt."

"I see." Jessica rubbed her eyes. "What's the likely sentence?"

John shrugged. "Could be anything from one to ten years. Depends on the amounts involved." A minute went by while he tapped on his phone. "More likely ten or more. Hokthorn lost a lot of value. And..." He paused to continue typing. "There are numerous lawsuits from big-name customers, I see."

She dropped her head into her palms. *Ten years. Not forever, but a fucking long time. Abbie will be twenty-four, Daisy dead and Kermit... Who knows, he might be immortal. Will Anna find someone else?*

"Look, Jessica. I hate to point out the obvious, but you should start acting like you're innocent... I assume you are?"

"Yes, of course!"

"Okay, give me time to do some background research, allow a week, then I think you should return to your flat in London. And call the police. Once you're charged, call me. From there, I'll start building a case to support you. But it is very important, as far as anyone is concerned, that we haven't had this conversation, and I haven't visited you." He glanced over his shoulder. "The first time we are said to have communicated has to be the call you make once you're charged. Understand?"

Tears started to fall, and Jessica dropped her head into her folded arms on the table.

A hand slipped along her back.

"It's okay, darling. I'll be with you all the way," Anna said softly into her ear, before kissing her temple.

Jessica collected her strength, cleared her throat, and straightened, focusing on John. So far, he had given away no emotions, but now there was an element of surprise edged in the lines around his eyes and mouth. "So, you'll represent me?"

"Yes," he said, after a slight hesitation.

"I don't have any money. Nothing."

"I'll pay for it," Anna cut in quickly.

He glanced from one to the other. "This is something we can discuss later. In the meantime, write down exactly what happened. Go back a few months before, years, if you need to. You should be trying to identify who would frame you, who had access to your laptop, and who would gain." He slipped a business card across the table, before turning to Anna. "I thought I could take you to the Crown for lunch?"

Jessica went rigid. *Is this part of his payment?*

"I had planned for us to eat here." Anna glanced at her and Jessica noticed the barely concealed disdain in her eyes. She also knew they hadn't been shopping for a week and there was little to eat. "I still have some of your red wine, so if you want, go into the lounge, and I'll pull some lunch together." Her words rang flat but were overlaid with an artificial charm.

John stood. "Sure. Like old times."

"Bastard," Anna said under her breath, once he'd settled on the sofa in the next room.

Jessica wrapped her arms around Anna from behind. "He's manipulative."

"For sure."

"I'll tell him to go." Jessica started to loosen her hug, but Anna tightened the coupling of their arms.

"It's a game. We need to let him think he's winning until you're safe."

"We'll find someone else."

Anna shook her head. "He's one of the best."

"I...I don't want him near you."

Anna turned in her arms. "If he gets closer than a yard, I'll get Kermit to eat his balls. Although John might like that."

"That's disgusting."

"Too much?"

Jessica nodded. "I don't want you to be indebted to him. Not for me."

"You're strange." Anna pushed a strand of hair away from Jessica's eyes. "You must know by now, I'd do anything for you. Selling my soul is definitely on the list."

Jessica laughed. "You can sell it to me."

"You can have it for free, as you're broke and beautiful." Anna kissed the line of her jaw, before following a path to her mouth.

"A trade then. Yours for mine."

"Deal. I'll put yours on eBay. Someone will want it. I might have to list it a few times, though." Anna grinned.

"You witch!" Jessica pushed Anna into the fridge, pressing her body against hers. They stared at each other for a long moment, sharing a smile.

"Speaking of witches," Anna whispered. "Go see if the chickens have laid some more eggs."

Jessica furrowed her brow. "Why?"

"Egg mayonnaise sandwiches. It's the best I can do."

HE WATCHED THE two women in the kitchen with a raised eyebrow. Anna said something he couldn't hear, but it wasn't hard to make out the words from the movement of her lips.

"I see," John muttered under his breath. He was very good at reading the smallest signals between people, a skill honed in the courtroom. But with Anna and this Jessica, he didn't have to be an expert to know what was going on. His brain raced through options, as if playing out different sequences on a chessboard, to find which move would be best.

Taking the case could be a perceived conflict of interest, since apparently his ex-wife was in a relationship with the client, but only if it was discovered he was trying to get back with her. *She never showed any attraction to women. I guess it explains her frigidity in bed.*

He could make a phone call and report Jessica's whereabouts. A quick separation. *I have to seem to be helping. This will get me in Anna's good books, then I'll let the case cave in. Unethical, but it will separate the two. I then step in and reconcile Anna's sorrow at losing her lover.* He decided he'd leave after lunch and not provoke Anna any further. *Funny how things work out.* He smiled. The case would be an easier route to repossessing her than the one he had originally envisioned.

# Chapter Twenty

"WE'RE STILL GOING?" Nadia Chandra asked. She'd recently joined the City of London Serious Fraud Office and was still trying to work out who was actually calling the shots. It didn't seem to be their chief.

"Yup," her colleague answered through a mouthful of croissant. "Even though Adrian said to deprioritise the case, I think it's worth a look. If she's there, we'll pick her up. If not, we put the case on the backburner."

"It's a shame the ISP was so slow in giving us the account for the IP used to post the video, then we wouldn't have to go behind the chief's back."

"He won't care if we bring her in." He took a slug of his coffee. He spat it out, spraying his shirt. "Fucking hot."

She watched as he dabbed the coffee with his tie. "When are we leaving?"

"That depends. Can you check the tides in Northumberland?"

"Tides? Are we going by boat?"

"Nope, car."


JESSICA HAD SLEPT so soundly that Anna had already left for work. She raised herself on one elbow. Her arms were covered with sticky notes; Anna must have used up a whole pad. Some were spread out over the duvet.

Looking in the dresser mirror, she noticed two stuck to her forehead. Removing and reading them one at a time, she discovered most had just a few words.

*You're amazing! Beautiful! Get up already! Property of A. Edison. I'll miss you today <3. Too sexy! Heroine of Holy Island* (underlined with squiggles). *Chill today!*

There were many more. Jessica smiled, covering her mouth with her hand. "She's nuts," she said, chuckling. A sticky note on the bedside lampshade made a request:

*stop by and see me @ 1:30, x.*

After doing the chores around the farm and work on repairing the last of the stables, Jessica showered and headed into town.

"Jessica!" someone called from behind.

She turned to see Beth, running towards her. Before she could protest, Beth wrapped her in a rib-cracking hug.

"How is your father?" Jessica asked, embarrassed by the greeting from someone she barely knew.

"He's a bit slow, and it will take a while for him to get back to normal. But he's alive." Beth gripped her arm. "Thank you."

An awkward few seconds ticked by as Jessica tried to work out what to say. "Beth, if you or David need help with anything—"

"That's kind of you... My brother, Daniel, is staying to help run the farm for the time being. But really, I owe you so much... If there's anything you need, or Abbie or Anna." Beth looked weary and tearful, despite her smile. The last few days had aged her thirty-something features.

She placed a hand on Beth's, where it still held her forearm. "Thanks for the offer."

Beth didn't seem to want to leave, and Jessica felt obligated to make conversation. "I was wondering is there somewhere I can take Anna for a meal that doesn't cost too much? It was her birthday yesterday."

"There's the Crown, but the food can be dire there. When did you want to go?"

"I was hoping Friday." Even though she felt better now she had a plan for dealing with the police, her head throbbed with the stress of knowing there was little time left. If she took John's advice, she should head back to London next week. At least she'd have the weekend with both Anna and Abbie.

Beth fumbled in her handbag for her phone. "I've an idea. Let me make some calls, and I'll text you. What's your number?"

"I don't have one."

"Okay," Beth said quickly. "Then I'll get David to drop by later and let you know. I'll try to sort out a place for you. Just the two of you?"

"Yes, and thanks so much."

Again, Jessica was crushed in a hug, "No, honey, thank you."

THE DOOR OF Priory's Cup opened, and Anna glanced over to see Jessica step inside. Her heart leapt, and the excitement lifted her out from the drudgery of her morning. Jessica looked so beautiful and mysterious. She stood out, being taller than most women, her edgy handsome features drawing attention. Anna thought back to when they had first met in the rain and wondered if it had been love at first sight.

Certainly, the connection had happened then; one that would never be broken. There would be more heartache to come, but at least she knew they were in it together. She ran over to her and wrapped her arms around Jessica.

"Ow! You're the second person who's tried to kill me with a hug in the last ten minutes."

"Are you telling me there's someone else?"

"What? No—"

"Does this other person know about your boyfriend?" Anna pointed out through the misty glass of the coffee shop.

"Boyfriend?" Jessica turned. Kermit was standing on the stone wall on the other side of the road. "At least he didn't try to suffocate me in my sleep with sticky notes."

"I thought, since not much sinks into your skull, they'd make it clear you're mine." Anna leaned into Jessica and kissed her. "There will be a test later. You better pass."

Jessica's cheeks turned red. The dozen customers in the café were all watching them. "Um, Anna, audience..."

Anna twirled away and grabbed her coat, before waving goodbye to the owner.

Outside, the sun was shining for a change, giving the air a taste of summer.

Anna tucked her arm into Jessica's. "I'm glad Linda let me work a short shift. My leg was starting to ache."

"We shouldn't go far if it's bothering you," Jessica said when they headed in the opposite direction to their home.

"I thought we could have a late lunch," Anna said. "My treat."

On the grass near the public car park was a converted, grey Citroen HY van. A list of pizzas was written on a chalkboard next to a hatch with a narrow, varnished pine counter. Cinders and smoke vented from a stainless-steel flue pipe protruding from the van's roof, while inside two women in black aprons cooked pizzas in a wood-burning oven.

"I didn't know this was here," Jessica said.

"They're here every year at this time for a couple of weeks, then they travel to different music festivals. The pizzas are fantastic. Pick which one you want."

Jessica scanned the menu. "A Margherita, please."

"What? No. Look, they have all kinds." Anna stabbed her finger at the board. "You can't have a Margherita just because it's the cheapest." She slipped an arm around Jessica's waist, nudging her closer to the menu. "How about this one?" She pointed. "Florentine, it has an egg."

"I like Margherita."

Anna kissed her cheek. "Okay, but—"

"Hi, how are you?" The older chef with short brown hair had turned to Anna after serving a customer.

"Hey. It's great to see you're back! I've been looking forward to this since last year." Anna leaned against the counter, accidentally nudging a pile of leaflets and causing a number to fall into the van.

The woman ducked down to collect them.

"God, I'm sorry," Anna said when the woman's head reappeared.

"It's not a problem. Here." She handed over one of the leaflets. "Perhaps you and your girlfriend might want to go. It's in July this year, and we'll be there."

Anna double-blinked, realising that someone other than herself had affirmed that Jessica was her girlfriend. A sense of warmth and belonging filled her. She then noticed the painted rainbow at the end of the van's name and, how since last year, it had changed to "MacNeil's." She scanned the leaflet—*L Fest, the UK's only lesbian festival, camping, families, music, poetry...*

"What would you like?"

Anna glanced up. "Um…" It took a moment for her to gather her train of thought. "Yes, a Margherita for my unadventurous girlfriend. And a Frenchfrio for me."

The woman released a hearty laugh, which echoed about the van's interior. "Both are good choices."

The younger cook scooted around to grab a plastic container of grated mozzarella, pausing for a moment when she was introduced. "I'm Wendy, and this is my wife, Nicole."

Anna held out her hand. "Anna and Jessica." Jessica came forward and shook their hands. "You changed the name on your van?"

"Yes." Wendy put an arm around Nicole. She wore a proud smile. "We got married in October last year, and Nicole decided to take my last name."

"Actually, it was because you couldn't spell mine," Nicole chimed in.

"Well, congratulations," Anna said quickly, unsure if the pair were about to get into an argument. "It must be idyllic travelling from place to place?"

"The life of a pizza gypsy. It has its ups and downs. But mostly, it's pretty fantastic. Of course, anything is with someone you love."

Nicole kissed Wendy's cheek with a big "mwah" sound and shuffled back to the oven.

"I better let you serve other people." Anna took a sideways step.

"Your pizzas will be ready in a few minutes," Wendy said before her attention moved to another customer.

Anna slipped her hand into Jessica's, and they went to sit on a bench under a beech tree a few yards away. "Maybe we could go?" She handed over the leaflet. "Abbie would love it. I have some camping gear somewhere in the barn."

Jessica studied the brochure for a long time.

"We'll assume we can go. All right?" Anna said, squeezing her arm tight around Jessica's waist.

"Sure."

"And I want you to play there. We can get that crappy band from the pub to play with you. What was their name? No Balls?"

One corner of Jessica's mouth was turned upwards. "We'll see."

"You know, I didn't realise they were a couple."

"Wendy and Nicole?"

"Yeah. Do many same-sex couples take their partner's last name when they get married?"

Jessica shrugged. "I don't know. I've not been married."

"*That* I can understand. No one's going to marry you if every time they get into your car, they get a wet ass."

"I'll get it fixed," Jessica said seriously.

In the corner of her eye, Anna noticed that Nicole was heading towards them, carrying two pizza boxes. Outside the van, it was easier to see that Nicole was at least ten years younger than Wendy. "You didn't have to bring them over. I would've collected them."

"It's cool." Nicole pushed her fingers through her auburn hair that had been cut in unequal tufts. A colourful tattoo poked out beyond the rolled-up cuff of her chef's shirt as she handed over the pizzas.

Anna pulled her purse out of her jacket pocket, but Nicole shook her head. "They're on us."

"I should pay."

Nicole wangled her finger. "Nope, you're a cute couple... Cuteness always gets free pizza. Just promise to see us at L Fest."

The unguarded friendliness of Nicole had taken her aback; she had found it so rare in the UK. Anna beamed. "Sure, we'll try."

"Good enough." Nicole returned the smile, spun around, and jogged back to the van.

Sitting down with both pizza boxes on top of her lap, Anna stared at Jessica.

"What?" Jessica asked, after enduring a few seconds of scrutiny.

"Why does stuff like this always happen when you're around?"

"What stuff?"

"Free pizza stuff." She leaned over and kissed Jessica's lips, while simultaneously passing her lunch.

"Hardly a game-changer."

"To me, it is," Anna whispered.

"What on earth is this?" Jessica had opened her box.

"Oh, that's mine. Pizza with French fries on top. A mortal sin, but I've not been cast into purgatory yet." Anna swapped their meals. "Here's yours, tomato roadkill."

"Just because you're feeling guilty about the calorie count, doesn't mean you should insult my pizza." Jessica reached over and grabbed a couple of Anna's fries, before popping them into her mouth.

"Hey! Eat your own toppings. Oh, but wait," Anna paused for dramatic effect. "You don't have any!"

"Seriously, you're still insulting my choice of—"

Anna stuffed a half a dozen fries into Jessica's mouth. "I'm taking you with me to chunky hips hell."


ON THE BANK of the Thames, The Prospect of Whitby, once known as the Devil's Tavern, was filling up with office workers.

Ira Kapoor leaned against the railing of the garden patio on the second floor, looking westward along the river as the sun disappeared behind a glass building. The London skyline had changed dramatically in the last few years. A mock gallows and noose restricted her view. It was part of the tavern's history, commemorating a seventeenth-century hanging judge who'd frequented the public house. This evening, Ira wished the gibbet worked. She would hang the bitch herself if the police didn't catch her first.

She'd thought the look on Jessica Cox's face when she was sacked would be enough, but the fact she hadn't been found or charged kept her seething with anger.

"There you are." Jason Carter, VP of Customer Support, had managed to find her, despite being completely incompetent. "We have a table downstairs."

She collected her glass of tonic water and followed him back inside.

There were two others at the table when she sat down with Brian. She flicked her long black hair over her shoulder, knowing the single motion would attract the attention of male onlookers. Females as well. She gagged at the last thought.

"So, any news?" she asked, loudly enough to overcome the din of the bar. "Come on, speak!" Ira pretended it was a joke but, really, she wanted to get out of the pub and away from the group as quickly as possible.

"No news, Ira," Brian, answered for the others.

"So we're stuck then. Still having to wait."

"It's for the best. But you're too impatient. We need at least a month after she's convicted before we should exercise our options," Jason said. "And even then, we've to stick to the schedule we agreed."

*Useless cowards.*

"Evening, gentlemen." A curvaceous redhead in a tight-fitting, blue business suit joined them at the table. Ira knew she was intentionally calling her a "gentleman" just to annoy her. Ira hated herself for being part of their scheme, but revenge and money would compensate for the indignity.

"Hi, Victoria," Brian said, before standing. "Let me get you a drink."

CHRIS HAD COME to The Prospect of Whitby to meet a friend who worked for Genism Systems. With Hokthorn going to hell in a handcart and especially now he reported directly to Brian Lopez, Jessica's old boss, he wanted to find out what it was like working for their competitor, and if there might be a job for him.

"Busy here," Chris said, sipping the foam off his pint before someone could knock it onto his shoes.

"Yup, it always is at this time," his friend said. "Most of Genism drinks here and most of them drink a lot. Did you get here all right?"

"Was a bit of a pain. Bomb scare on the DLR."

Chris's old friend from university shuffled closer. "Watch out, our CFO is behind you." He discreetly pointed to a woman with red hair at a table with three others.

Chris glanced behind him, and his jaw dropped. He recognised Ira Kapoor, the HR Director from his own firm, and Jason Chapman, Jessica's nemesis in all things QA-related. *They're all looking for new jobs? No...that can't be. They all hate each other.* "What the fudge?"

"What's up, Chris?"

"Hold my pint for a sec." Chris took out his phone and snapped a couple of pictures of the group. "You know I told you about my boss, Jessica, and her laptop."

"Yeah, sure."

"Those people with your CFO, they were all involved in sacking her. Except...wait...fuck." He rubbed the stubble on his three-day-old growth, before retrieving his drink and downing a third of it. "Jessica was acting nervous a few weeks back about a date with a redhead. You think your CFO was her?"

"I've no idea what you're on about."

"Take my pint again." He quickly passed it over, pulled out his phone, set it to record, and stuffed it in his back pocket so the camera lens pointed outward. He took his lager and backed slowly towards the table, waving his hand at his companion to follow him. Now only a foot away, the space they vacated instantly filled with new arrivals to the narrow lounge bar. Chris held up a single finger, a few inches away from his lips, telling his friend to be quiet as he tried to video the conversation.

He was at the bottom of his glass when a hand gripped his shoulder.

"Hi, Chris, I'm surprised to see you here." His new boss, Brian, stared back at him.

# Chapter Twenty-One

THE WOMAN AT the car hire company had offered him an upgrade, but he wanted the vehicle he'd spent hours researching online. Eventually, she came up with the goods, and he was able to leave Edinburgh airport. And, after a few near misses, he adjusted to driving on the left.

Once out of the city, the midday Friday traffic was heavy on the A1 as he headed southeast. She would pay for all she'd taken from him, all the time in prison and for making him stab Emma. After, he'd collect his daughter from her school. The few pictures he had of Abbie as a baby with Emma and a birth certificate should be enough to convince the girl she had to come with him. If it worked, they'd simply fly back to the States. *If it doesn't, well, she'll die with her aunt.*

WITH HER ARMS folded and resting on the bottom half of the endmost stable door, Anna watched as Jessica fixed the final plank that would make the interior safe for animals.

"When's Abbie coming home?" Jessica asked, picking up another screw.

"Not until tomorrow. The tides are a real pain right now."

"I was thinking," Jessica said. A yellow cordless drill hung in her right hand.

"You can think while working? Impressive."

Jessica pointed the drill at Anna and pulled the trigger. It whirled for a few seconds. "This has reverse. I can undo all the screws."

Anna formed a gun with her fingers. "Put down your weapon and step away." She opened the bottom half of the stable door and entered. Once Jessica had been disarmed, she drew her into an embrace. "So what were you thinking?"

"That you don't need to buy ponies."

"I should open a B & B instead, right? Four rooms, fresh bedding, and a complimentary salt lick."

"I'd stay."

"But you're a bit simple and easy to please."

"Do you want to hear my idea or not? Because I'm thinking I should save it for someone worthier."

"Pick me!" Anna hopped up and down next to her. "I want to hear."

"Okay, crazy girl. I thought you could open a livery."

"A livery?"

"You allow children to keep their ponies here for free, or nearly free, and then you can use them for your pony trekking. Everyone wins. And you don't need to care for them all the time. And you get ponies to use for your business. Your paddock is big enough."

With her lips parted, Anna gawked at her.

"It's just an idea." Jessica grinned.

"Well, it's a pretty good one." Anna moved closer. "I knew there was a reason why I loved you... But what was it again?" She tapped her knuckles on her forehead.

"Let me remind you..."

"Ahem." The sound caused Anna to break their kiss. David stood at the stable entrance with his face tinted red. "Sorry. Um, Daniel and I are moving the sheep across your lane." He swallowed. "And I remembered I was supposed to give you a message."

"Hi," Anna said, untangling herself from Jessica. "What message?"

"It's for Jess."

"I see." Anna gave Jessica a peck on the cheek. "I'll leave you to it." She headed across the farmyard, but when she saw a man who looked like a clone of Iain Foster in the neighbouring field, she changed direction. She wanted to find out how Iain was doing and guessed the man must be his older son, Daniel.

Fifty or so sheep were pressed close to a five-bar gate. Fairweather skirted around the herd, keeping them in place.

When Anna got closer, Daniel whistled then shouted, "Fairweather, hold." The dog obeyed and hunched down in the grass.

She watched as Daniel counted the plump woolly balls while they jostled for position. When he was done, she introduced herself. "Hi, I'm Anna. You must be Daniel."

"I am." He shook her hand with both of his. "We owe you and your partner a great deal. And not forgetting Abbie."

*Partner? Jessica? How does he know...? Oh, yeah, the gossips of Holy Island.*

She would have normally been angry about people knowing her personal affairs, but right now she felt proud and didn't mind who knew that Jessica was part of her life. She was about to ask how Iain was doing when a black BMW crossover pulled into the dirt lane where they stood.

"Police," Daniel said.

"What?" Anna squeaked. "How do you know?"

"Blue LED strips behind the grill and the small box on the dash."

"Jessica!" Anna said. She tried to move, but her brain froze her to the spot. She glanced at Daniel, knowing her eyes must be wild with fear.

"I see." He opened the gate to the field, allowing the sheep to spill into the lane. A few calls to Fairweather sent the rest of the herd towards the car. "Stay here."

A smartly dressed man tried to get out of the car but was forced back by the press of bleating animals.

Anna was being bumped left and right herself until the last of the ewes passed by. The fear of what was about to happen had kept her from reacting, and all she could do was stand still and listen. She glanced back to her farm, praying Jessica stayed in the stables.

Daniel made his way towards the car, effortlessly nudging sheep out of his way. Anna let out a gasp of surprise when she saw Kermit trailed in the gap behind him. As soon as Daniel got close, Kermit leapt onto the bonnet of the car and then onto the roof. He did a three-sixty, before settling down on his new vantage point.

"Clear them out of the way!" the driver yelled through the open window. "And get that goat off my roof!"

Daniel bent down to the officer. "You've taken a wrong turn. This is private land," He said calmly. "The causeway's to the right."

"Police business. Clear the fucking lane."

"My land, my sheep, my business."

The lane was Anna's, but she understood the message he gave.

The officer tried to open his door, but the ewes couldn't move, hemmed in by the stone walls on either side and Fairweather at the entrance.

"Hey. That's my livelihood you're ramming with your door. A reminder, I'm the person who puts milk in your coffee, bacon in your butty, and wool in your clothes." His tone was still calm but authoritative. "So, before you do any more damage to my animals and, unless you have some legal reason to be here, like a warrant, I'll help you back out."

"We don't need a warrant to enter land the public can access!" the officer snapped back.

Daniel frowned and pointed behind the BMW. "There's a gate. On the gate, it says 'Private.' It's open so I can move my sheep. No one has access along this lane."

Anna knew this wasn't true. She always kept the gate open and didn't mind at all when walkers used it as a shortcut to the sea.

"I don't know why you're here," Daniel continued. "But you might need to do some more paperwork."

The driver glanced to his po-faced female colleague in the passenger seat. "Fine," he muttered.

After clearing a space behind the vehicle, Daniel directed them back to the road.

Anna watched as the police car drove slowly towards the village with Kermit still on its roof.

With a few calls to Fairweather, Daniel sent the sheep in the opposite direction. He closed the gate at the entrance, before striding back to Anna. "One second," he said, pulling his phone from his pocket. "Hi, Simon, Daniel here. Can you do me a favour...? I need you to be fully booked for two unwanted visitors."

Anna listened, stupefied as Daniel described the two people in the car.

"Can you call the B & Bs as well? And the Crown? Thanks, mate." He ended the call and reached down to pet Fairweather between the ears. "At least you can have your dinner tonight."

"Dinner?" Her voice still trembled with the aftershock of what had transpired. She could have lost Jessica. Although Jessica planned to head to London after the weekend, the police just turning up like that to take her away felt so much worse.

"Ah, maybe that was a secret." He scratched the back of his neck.

Emotions swept through her, and she hugged Daniel without thinking. "Thank you." Embarrassed, she quickly released him.

"No problem. The island protects its angels."

THE ROAD WAS covered in water. At least three feet deep by his reckoning. His phone insisted he had to cross here to an island that looked nothing more than sand dunes and long grass.

Standing beside his rental, he took a long drag on his cigarette, wondering what the fuck to do. When a car arrived behind him and started a U-turn, he flagged it down.

"Hey, what's with the road?"

"It's the sea. Tide's coming in. Caught us out too. We'll have to get a hotel."

"When can I cross?"

The driver consulted his passenger before answering. "Around midnight, give or take a couple of hours."

Without saying thanks, he turned away. He flicked the butt of his cigarette onto the road and got back into his car.

His fist crashed against the steering wheel. "Fucking fuck!" He rammed the gearstick into first and slammed down the accelerator while having the steering on full lock. The car squealed in an arc, heading back the way he came.

At a budget hotel, he checked in. Pacing the dour, utilitarian bedroom, he tried to decide what to do about Abbie. It was two in the afternoon. If he was to collect Abbie now, with Anna still around, she could send one quick text and undo his plans. He had no choice, he'd have to risk it. *I'll take the kid with me. If she cottons on, then it's her own fault... Near the school, somewhere quiet. Then cross at midnight and wipe that fucking bitch off the planet.*

He stood up, grabbed his key card, left the hotel and got into his sedan. He'd find a hardware store or garage for a roll of duct tape, just in case his daughter didn't behave.

ANNA CHECKED THE time on Emma's watch. "Are you ready yet?" she called up the stairs.

Jessica had fitted the new strap she had given her as a present. And now it was firmly buckled to her wrist, alleviating the fear that she might lose it again and providing comfort that her sister was only a glance away. Inspecting herself in the hall mirror, she straightened the spaghetti straps of her burgundy dress.

When she saw movement behind her, she spun around. A vision of sheer elegance stood at the bottom of the stairs; a femme fatale ready to devour anything that approached her web.

"My God, you look stunning!" Anna stammered.

Jessica wore Anna's old Christobel Kent black cocktail dress. Form-fitting with lace sleeves, it showed off Jessica's toned physique perfectly. On Anna, it had been too tight around the hips and bust, and she'd only worn it once to a dinner party in Edinburgh.

"So do you." Jessica returned her smile and stepped down into the hall to place a hand on the curve of Anna's waist.

Anna smiled back as best she could. As much as she was looking forward to the dinner, it was tainted by the fact Jessica would be leaving soon after.

Anna was terrible at keeping secrets and had told her everything that had happened with the police.

"I think I should go tonight," Jessica had said. "The police might come back tomorrow or the next day. I don't want Abbie to see them taking me."

"Please! I want you to stay the weekend. You won't see Abbie. She isn't home until tomorrow. Beth is collecting her for me tomorrow at noon."

"I have to get this sorted on my own terms. I can't have the police dragging me away in front of the whole village."

In the end, Anna caved in. It would be their last meal together. Jessica would leave at midnight when the tide was out. She tried not to sigh and almost succeeded. "So, where are you taking me?" Anna passed Jessica her coat, before donning her own.

"You'll see."

In the moonlight, the ruins of the priory cast foreboding shadows. It was as if dead monks waited in the dark corners for a soul to come too close.

Jessica had halted. "This isn't the right way, is it?"

"Not unless the spirit of Saint Cuthbert is serving up a Sunday roast." Anna laughed.

"Shit."

"Where are we supposed to be going?"

"Well, the castle."

"This way, love." Anna spoke as if to a lost elderly relative.

After five minutes, Lindisfarne Castle rose before them on a pinnacle of rock. Light from the outside spotlights and windows illuminated and deepened its silhouette against the night sky. The air was still, and the sound of lunar-washed waves could be heard crashing along the shore.

"We're quite late," Jessica said. "I hope Beth isn't too upset."

"Beth?"

"She made the arrangements. She'll be cooking for us. Kind of a thank-you."

Anna checked her phone again. It was the third time in the last few minutes.

"Something wrong?" Jessica asked.

"Abbie's not texted me back."

"Give her a ring."

"It's okay. She does this a lot. Ignoring my texts is her way of rebelling. I'll give it a bit longer."

ABBIE BACKED AWAY from him, with tears streaming down her face. He'd told her on the phone he was her father. He'd sent her pictures of her real mother and her as a baby. She shouldn't have met him. Not here, not outside the school gates. She knew that now, but it was too late. Her hands trembled, and her whole body shook.

She ran, trying to dial a number as she darted along the empty country lane back towards the path leading to her school. The call didn't connect. She tripped as fear caused her legs to give way. He was right on top of her and snatched away her phone. He hurled it into the trees.

"No phones!" he snarled.

Abbie screamed for help as he slapped a hand over her mouth and carried her to the back of the car.

"Fucking behave!"

INSIDE THE CASTLE, the ten-foot-thick stone walls of the old fortress blocked out all radio waves, and Anna had no signal. She placed her phone face down on the table.

"This is awesome," Anna said, glancing around the ancient dining room. They sat at an oval oak table, lit by a chandelier hung from the centre of a low vaulted ceiling. At one end, split logs blazed in an open fire. She could easily imagine herself in the sixteenth century.

The meal went by quickly, and the food had been fantastic—leek and potato soup to start, followed by Angus beef, dauphinoise potatoes, vegetables, and a lemon tart for dessert. But Anna knew she'd not been good company. Her lover would be leaving in a few hours, and she would be alone again.

She took hold of Jessica's hand. "Thank you for this. Sorry, I'm not making this *lit*, as Sarah would say."

Jessica gave a half smile. "It won't be our last supper."

"I know." Anna wiped a tear away. "But it feels like it is."

"Let's thank Beth."

Trying to be as chirpy as possible, Anna said her thank yous and goodbyes to Beth, and they were soon walking hand in hand to the village. Moonlight provided ample illumination, ensuring they didn't venture off the path and into the sea.

Anna checked her phone.

"Is Abbie okay?" Jessica asked.

"I have a missed call from her." Anna tried to ring her, but there was no answer. "She must be asleep," she muttered to herself.

It was midnight by the time they got back, and very little had been said. Anna busied herself making coffee while Jessica got changed.

When she reappeared in the kitchen, Anna wrapped her in her arms. She kissed her tenderly while sliding her fingers into Jessica's hair.

"I love you. I'm going to miss you so much."

"I love you too. And I don't want to go... I'll ring you as soon as I'm in London."

"You need money?" Anna's sorrow touched every word.

"I still have eighty pounds. Enough for petrol."

Anna nodded. "All right." She tried to steel herself, even though every cell in her body told her this was wrong.

"I better go."

Anna released her and crossed her arms. "Call me every day?"

"Yes, my every day." The attempted joke fell flat for both of them, and an awkward minute passed.

Anna picked up a travel mug and handed it to Jessica.

Tears ran down Jessica's cheeks.

Anna brushed them away. "Drive carefully."

Jessica nodded, seemingly too emotional to speak.

Outside, Anna watched as the Saab drove off. She stayed there long after its taillights disappeared.

# Chapter Twenty-Two

STILL IN HER jacket and camisole slip dress from dinner, Anna wiped the already clean countertop for the third time. Then the tears came. She slid down the cabinets onto the floor. Bending her knees against her chest, she sobbed until her eyes stung and her lungs burned.

*Go to bed, this is doing no one any good.*

Dragging herself off the cold tiles, she snatched up the cordless handset and tried Sarah's number. Her friend would help her return to a modicum of normality. There was no answer, so she tried her mom.

"Hello." Her mom's voice enveloped her in a comforter of familiarity. Shutters of emotion supplanted any chance of coherence, and she was unable to speak. "Annamaria? What's wrong?"

Anna snuffled. It took a minute to find her voice. "What time is it there? It's not too late, is it?"

"Honey, it's just after seven. Why are you crying?"

Anna slowed her ragged breathing. "I have a lot to tell you," she blurted out with a sigh.

"I'm listening."

Between sobs, she started at the beginning, explaining how she'd met Jessica, how beautiful she was, before moving on to Abbie and the Fosters and how Jessica had fixed the stables, how Jessica was wanted by the police for something she didn't do and how she'd left for London, leaving her alone. Of course, she left out the kissing, the sex, and what Jessica really meant to her.

"I'm just upset, that's all." Anna wiped her nose with her palm. "I needed someone to talk to."

For a moment, there was no response

"Mom?" Anna asked, "Are you still there?"

"Yes, pumpkin." *Pumpkin?* Her mom hadn't called her that since she was ten. "So, you love this Jessica?"

It was Anna's turn to leave dead air on the line. She closed her open mouth and stammered, "I...well..." She paused, hugging herself with her free hand. "More than I can stand."

"She feels the same?"

Anna nodded to the receiver. Realising that wouldn't transmit, she added, "Yes."

"I see," her mom said in a measured tone. "Does Abbie know?"

"Yes, of course," Anna said harshly, now feeling defensive. She wanted her mother to understand they were a family. "We've not spoken about it directly. Abbie's just accepting, and she's better when Jessica is around. We don't fight... She's happy." The last words caused Anna to start sobbing again.

When Anna finally composed herself, her mom said, "You know, I suspected you might be."

"Be what?"

"Gay."

"Huh? Wait...you're saying, you knew? Since when?"

Anna's mom laughed. "Since you were fifteen or so, but I didn't know for sure. You never showed much interest in boys. If anything, it was the Dicksons' daughter that made you blush and go all doe-eyed. Do you remember her?"

Anna swallowed— she hadn't thought about Heather in fourteen years. Tall, smart, with chestnut hair, Heather had been a complete mystery to her. She remembered those awkward moments when Mom and Dad would have the Dicksons over to play bridge while she and Heather were left to watch TV. Even now, she cringed at how tongue-tied she'd been.

"But then Emma died," her mother continued. "And you lost your chance to work things out. When John came along, you saw a way to escape. Running was how you dealt with it."

"Jesus, Mom...why don't you lay it all on me now!"

"Look, a mother only wants her children to be happy. That's it. But I can't find yourself for you. You have to deal with things your own way."

Anna sighed. "Awesome. You could've said something, a hint perhaps?" she huffed down the phone.

"Annamaria, you must know from Abbie, you can't tell a girl from our family what to think or do. I couldn't get Emma to leave, that...that devil. You think I could've stopped you going to England just because I thought John wasn't right for you, or any man was?" Her mother's tone held no anger or accusation—if anything, sadness floated on her words.

Anna knew she shouldn't be blaming her mom for the crippling torture of Emma's loss, the fear of Abbie's father, and the choices she'd made that had moulded her life.

"Pumpkin, the past is gone. It shouldn't define your present. You've been unhappy for so long, and I prayed one day you would look in the right places. So, I suppose now you need to make sure you don't lose her."

Anna blew out the braid of hair she had in her mouth and wiped away the tears that still fell like a dripping tap. "Yeah. I need her to live."

"And how are you going to make sure you keep her?" Her mom's tone implied she was feeding a rhetorical question Anna should've asked herself.

She took a deep breath and explained what John had suggested and added Jessica would call her as soon as she could.

"You know, sweetheart, I don't trust him."

"Nor do I, but he's our best option."

"Just be careful... Oh, the time. I'm sorry, but I have to go. I have ballroom dancing in ten minutes."

"I didn't know you did that."

"It's Friday, I'm not staying in to watch reruns of *The Love Boat*. Phone me anytime. But not Friday evenings." Her mom chuckled down the phone. "Love you."

"Love you too." Anna hung up, feeling a lot better; things weren't as dark as they seemed. And although she hadn't planned it, she'd come out to her mom. "Who knew?" she muttered. "Mom did...and never said a thing!"

She put the handset back in the docking station and noticed the flashing message light. She pressed play, wondering if it was Abbie. A synthetic voice said, "Thursday 11:22 p.m.," before reading a series of letters: *H-T-T-P-S colon forward slash forward slash D-R-I-V-E...*"The letters continued, and Anna wrote them down. She knew it was a text message that had been sent to her landline by mistake. Her mom still did this when she got telephone numbers mixed up.

At her laptop, she typed the characters into her browser. The link was to a Google Drive, and it played a video of a group of people in a pub. She flicked a quick, *what-the-hell-is-this-about?* smile and was about to close her laptop when she heard Jessica's name. Stock options were then discussed, a question as to whether a laptop had been restored to normal, then, finally, a woman with long jet-black hair looked towards the camera and said, "Is that Jessica's minion?"

Anna wasn't sure what to make of it, so she watched it again, before emailing the link to John, with a message:

*This might be useful for Jessica's case. She's heading to London tonight. Please do what you can for her, thanks. Anna.*

THE COLD WATER woke Chris but, cruelly, only to tell him he was drowning. Sinking lower into the dark muddy void, with his air spent, he'd hoped he'd done enough. In the last, fatal few seconds, the events of the prior thousand rushed back.

Halfway to Shadwell Station, someone jumped him by a church.

He knew who it was. Brian had been buying him drinks all night and must have followed him when he left the pub. His boss had punched him hard in the neck and bundled him into the trees behind the church.

"I'm sorry, mate. But you shouldn't eavesdrop," Brian had told him while he'd lain winded on the ground. Pain from a tirade of kicks to his head caused Chris to lose consciousness.

He had woken behind the gravestones near the water of Shadwell Basin, too broken to move. He had managed to pull out his phone and dial 999, but his throat had been badly damaged, and he struggled to speak. When approaching footsteps echoed towards him, he'd desperately flicked to another app and selected "share." *Fuck you, Brian.* The video upload had completed, and he'd shared the link to the number Jessica had given him. *Fuck you to hell!*

THE CAUSEWAY WAS clear when Jessica crossed. And although the old Saab continued to tick over, she had shut down, locking out her emotions for Anna, Abbie, and the home she had just left. Kermit came to mind, more as a remembered smell than an image and she started to cry. Jabbing at the tears with her sleeves, she pulled into the first open petrol station.

A full tank would be enough to get her back to London. As the pump rattled off litres, she glanced around the forecourt. An unshaven, muscular man in a leather jacket and blue jeans, from the car opposite, had gone in to pay. She noticed the *Diesel* sticker on the petrol cap, which told her it was a hire car. As her pump spun past fifty, she watched as the rear of the man's car rocked of its own accord.

"Bizarre," she muttered and went in to pay.

The man was in front and spoke with an American accent as he ordered cigarettes.

"Is it now safe to cross to the island?" he asked.

"Yes, but you're cutting it a bit fine," the middle-aged woman behind the counter answered. "It's not unusual for tourists to misjudge the depth and have to be rescued. Last year, a couple died. The sea here is very cold."

"I'm not a tourist."

The attendant shrugged. "Visiting someone?"

"Mind your own business," he snapped.

The hairs on Jessica's neck stood on end. There was something very wrong with this guy.

She paid without waiting for change and tailed him out. By her Saab, she hesitated. The rear of his car bounced up and down again. "Sir," she yelled after him and raced over. She grabbed the frame of his door before he could yank it shut. "The attendant wants to talk to you. Says she got the tides wrong."

He rolled his eyes. "So can I cross or not?"

"I don't know. You need to talk to her."

"For fuck's sake," he cursed and stomped back to the kiosk.

As soon as he was inside, Jessica tried to open the boot, but it was locked. She tore to the driver side and searched for a boot release. The model had one, and she popped it.

"Hey, what the hell, lady!" the man's voice boomed from fifty feet away.

Jessica lifted the lid to see a mouth covered in grey tape and a pair of terrified blue eyes.

"Abbie!" Jessica's scream was cut short as a hand spun her around.

"What the fuck do you think you're doing!" He smashed the back of her head into the rim of the open boot.

Pain halted all her senses. Her vision split into colours of red, yellow, and blue just before she blacked out.


JOHN CLOSED THE book he was reading and picked up his phone. The hotel he'd been staying in for weeks now was taking on his odour; a sign he needed to get his act together and find a flat. *But why should I? If all goes well, I can get back together with Anna, and we can buy a place in London.* He remembered Abbie. *She can stay at the boarding school. It all works out.*

He absentmindedly flicked between apps before checking his emails, jerking to a sitting position when he saw a message from Anna.

After reading the email, he followed the link and watched the video with a raised eyebrow. "So, Jessica Cox is innocent." He frowned and tapped "*delete.*"

THE NOISE OF the BMW door slamming shut woke Nadia. The crick in her neck was getting worse. Why the hell they didn't just drive back to London, she couldn't fathom. After finding nowhere to stay, her boss had suggested they hang about and see if their visit would flush out Miss Cox. And so, next to a campervan in the main carpark, they'd been stationary for nine hours. The camper hid their vehicle from anyone leaving the island while offering a clear view of the causeway.

"I heard a car, was it Miss Cox's?" he asked as he made himself comfortable.

"Nope," she lied, having dozed off for the last ten minutes and not having a clue whose car it had been. "Where did you go?"

"To take a slash and see if I could find somewhere to get a coffee. But this place is fucked up. Nothing is open."

"I think we should go, or we'll be stuck here until tomorrow."

"And? Is that a problem?"

There wasn't any point in arguing, he'd just pull rank.

In the full moonlight, she could see him picking his nose. When he ate the fruits of his labour, it reminded her she hadn't had any dinner. The quixotic notion of working for the Serious Fraud Office had notched down yet another dozen points.

SOMETHING THE SIZE of a softball jabbed into Jessica's back. She opened her eyes with the throbbing pain from her head repeating, *I'm hurt, leave me alone.*

She could see nothing. When she tried to sit up, she bumped her ear against a hard surface. The jabbing behind her continued, then a larger thud against her shoulder blades. She tried to remember where she was and what had happened. In a flash of horror, it came to her. "Abbie!"

A muffled grunt replied.

"Abbie," Jessica whispered. "Is that you?"

A powerful blow from what she guessed was Abbie's knee knocked her an inch forward.

"Stay calm, stay calm." But she was near panic herself. They weren't moving, and Jessica could hear no other sounds except the occasional call of a bird and crashing waves somewhere in the distance. Those noises told her where she was, and her desperation grew higher. With no room to turn, she was only able to bend her elbow enough to feel around. *There must be a way to get out of here!* She searched for a latch: an emergency boot lever. Something glowed in the far top corner. She grabbed it only to discover the plastic handle was detached. If it had been the boot release, the bastard had snapped it off.

Abbie's screams, muffled behind tape, were getting worse.

"Abbie, darling, I know you're scared. We'll get out." Jessica's words trembled. She wanted to tell Abbie to take deep breaths but knew it would be impossible for her. "Slow your breathing. Think of something else, like riding, or when we sang together."

After a minute, Abbie went quiet. The interlude had given Jessica an agonising period to consider what that animal might be doing to Anna. The person Anna feared the most, the demon who had murdered her sister and left Anna for dead, Abbie's father, was out there. *Fuck! Fuck! I've got to get out of here!*

"Abbie! Try to shift back, as far as you can... I need to flip over!"

The space behind Jessica opened up, and she rolled over on to her back. She pressed her knees against the boot's lid, pushing has hard as she could. The metal creaked and buckled, but the lock wouldn't pop. "Shit," she whispered. Twisting to face the front of the car, she felt for Abbie's face and yanked off the tape covering her mouth. Abbie gasped in a deep swallow of air. Jessica quickly covered Abbie's mouth with her hand. "Quiet. Very quiet. All right?" She felt Abbie nod in agreement. "Are you hurt?"

"No, but I'm really scared," Abbie murmured with a sob.

"Shh, it'll be okay." Remembering she'd been able to release the boot from the driver's compartment, Jessica prayed the mechanism was not electronic. Flipping again, she pulled at the lining from the trunk's side until she was able to reach between the bodywork of the car. With her wrist pressed against a sharp edge of the steel frame, she fumbled further into the cavity. Grunting while ignoring the pain caused by the gashing of her skin, she hooked her fingertips around a cable. When she yanked down hard, the boot sprang open.

Tears of relief filled her eyes.

Their kidnapper had parked at the front of the house, rather than around the back in the farmyard. Jessica could see light in the bedroom window. A shadow that wasn't Anna's appeared. Her tears halted and her blood froze.

She half clambered and half fell out of the car. Her legs couldn't hold her weight, and she collapsed to her knees. Using the rear of the car, she dragged herself up and reached into the trunk to untie Abbie.

In her struggles, Abbie had bunched the tape that held her ankles and wrists into thick bands, making it impossible for Jessica to rip. Blood dripping over her fingers from the cut on her wrist had also made the tape slick.

"You can't do it," Abbie whimpered.

With dread driving her haste, she searched the boot, but there was nothing to break the bindings. She thought about running to the building where Anna kept her tools, but she couldn't risk the minutes it would take. *I've got to get Abbie out of here!* Attempting to clear her vision, she inadvertently spread blood across her eyes. *The car cut me!*

Frantically, she ripped off the rubber seal that ran along the edge of the boot, exposing a spot-welded lip of metal.

"Forward," Jessica demanded, dragging Abbie's wrists to the sharp rim. She rubbed the taut binding against it, and the tape was severed in a matter of seconds. Repeating the action with Abbie on her back and her knees bent, Jessica was able to free Abbie's ankles.

Abbie leapt out of the car and dove into her arms.

"Where's your phone?" Jessica whispered.

"He threw it away. He's going to hurt Mum! He's going to—" Abbie stammered, her whole body trembling.

"Listen! You need to go. Run to Katy's. Tell her mum what happened, but not to come here. Tell her to call the police."

"I, I can't... I'm too—"

"Be brave. You can do it. Go!" Jessica released her and pushed her away.

Abbie hesitated. "I love you," she said and tore off into the night.

# Chapter Twenty-Three

NADIA WAS PRETTY sure school finished earlier than after midnight on a Saturday. To her left, her boss snored with his head against the glass of the driver's door. The racket was only just preferable to his sexist anecdotes. She nudged him in the ribs.

He grunted, sat up, and wiped saliva from his chin. "What's up?"

Nadia pointed. "She's still in her school uniform. Where do you think she came from?"

"I told you this place is fucked up. Go find out."

She rolled her eyes and got out of the car. Jogging to intercept the girl, Nadia was forced to break into a sprint when she flew past. There was no way she was going to catch her. "Hey! I'm a police officer. Stop!"

The girl skidded to a standstill and spun around. "Help me!" she screamed.

THE WRENCHING FEAR for Anna's safety defeated its purpose. Jessica could barely function. She couldn't think or work out a plan. Instead, she bolted into the house. The cooker's hood light was on, dimly illuminating the floor, which was strewn with the contents of the kitchen cupboards and drawers. She froze when she heard a sound behind her and then grabbed for the nearest object—a

Tupperware cake box. Spinning around, she threw it in the direction of the noise.

It bounced off a goat's head.

"Kermit, get out of here!" she whispered through gritted teeth. Jessica heard a grunt from upstairs. She sprinted for the steps, knowing she was being reckless, but she couldn't, not for a second, allow Anna to be hurt.

As she shouldered into their bedroom door, her mind stuttered like a TV screen flickering to life.

"Jessica!" Anna yelled across the room. "Run!"

Anna was cornered next to the bed. Her eyes were filled with fear. Her pupils were impossibly large. A hammer shook where she held it in two hands.

Jessica scanned the room. He was there, pushing himself up off the floor, his hair matted with blood.

"You're going to fucking regret that," he swore at Anna as he got to his feet.

Jessica leapt in front of him and backed up in Anna's direction. "Look, just leave!" She pulled the hammer from Anna's quivering hands. "Or, God help me, I'll kill you."

"Fuck you." He took a step forward, as the crunch of tyres on gravel and blue lights pulsed through the window.

He glanced towards the window, then back at Jessica, his face twisted into a mask of rage. He charged, slamming Jessica into the wardrobe. Her hand went through the pine panel of its door, and the wardrobe toppled over. She tried to twist out of the way, but he shoved her underneath the heavy antique.

Unable to see, Jessica writhed in a frenzied effort to escape, but her left arm was twisted and pinned.

"You bastard, get out! The police are here!" Anna screamed.

"You're coming with me, bitch!"

From under the wardrobe, Jessica's hand reached the frame of the bed. Tugging, she managed to free her shoulders, but her arm remained trapped.

He came for her with the hammer.

"Stop it, I'll go with you! Leave her alone!" Anna yelled from somewhere behind him.

He was about to take a swing at Jessica when he was knocked on top of the wardrobe, dropping the hammer. Jessica's breath rushed out of her lungs as his extra weight pressed down on her. She sucked in air as he got to his feet again.

She could see four white furry legs beyond his. A stink of decaying plants confirmed Kermit was in the room.

"What the fuck!" he snorted. He took hold of Anna's wrist and hauled her into the hall.

Kermit stood a few inches away, his eyes unreadable. A strip of denim wobbled in his mouth as he chewed. Jessica lunged at Kermit and caught hold of his left horn. Startled, the goat shook his head and backed away from her.

With Anna's life depending on Jessica's grip, she ignored the intense pain, and the unnatural movement of her trapped arm as Kermit pulled her out. When, finally, her arm ripped free from the broken wood, she let go of the goat's horn and slid the rest of her body out from under the wardrobe.

She tumbled down the stairs and managed to get to the kitchen, only to see he'd taken Anna's car rather than go around the front to his, where the police had arrived. She watched him speed away with Anna slumped in the passenger seat.

Outside, Jessica rounded the corner of the farm. A black BMW was reversing. There was no time. Opening the rear door as it began to drive off, Jessica jumped in.

"He has her!" Her words were no more than strangled gasps.

"We saw," the woman in the front said, accelerating with blue lights flashing. "He won't get far. The tide's in."

ALTHOUGH THE PUNCHES had been painful, they weren't crippling. Anna pretended she was more seriously hurt. If he thought she was too weak to act, she might get a chance to escape. The seatbelt alarm beeped incessantly as they sped along the approach road to the causeway.

"Put on your belt, and it'll stop beeping!" she told him.

Mike cursed and plugged in his belt. Anna did the same but fixed it behind herself when his attention was on the road ahead.

After the long stretch through the sandbanks, they made a sharp left to face a great expanse of water. The small wave tops glistened under the moon as they moved swiftly north into the bay.

Police car lights flashed behind them. Now was her chance. She reached for the door latch.

"You're not going anywhere!" Mike elbowed her hard in the chest, forcing her back into the seat. And again, as he floored the small Ford Fiesta. Water sprayed up in great arcs on both sides of the car.

At this point, true panic set in. Anna's chest constricted, agonising her bruises, as fear took hold. Her breathing was now so shallow her head felt like it would implode. It was a fear greater than any she had ever felt. Mike had been a constant threat for most of her adult life. But in front of them was the merciless sea. For a split second, she was back on the dock at the cabin in Michigan. Her grandfather throwing her off to teach her how to swim. She had never learned. It would be her grandfather, as much as Mike, who sealed her end.

A wave rolled over the bonnet in a great bulge.

"Go back! It's too deep!" she screamed, reaching for the latch on the door again.

Then everything happened at once. The car shuddered to the right and, before he could correct it, they tipped into deeper waters. The engine stalled and the car pitched to the driver's side, floating for a moment in the waves.

The sea seeped in through the doors, the windows, and vents, filling the footwells.

Mike was struggling to unfasten his seatbelt. Its broken latch required a knack Anna prayed he'd fail to master. The car sank deeper, until only six inches on Anna's side were above the surface.

"Get me the fuck out of this!" Now up to his shoulders in the ice-cold sea, Mike yanked at the seatbelt, causing the inertia locks to further tighten the strap around him.

"Fuck you!" Anna said, unrolling the window, allowing a surge of water to fill the interior. Against the torrent, she heaved herself through the window into the frigid flow. The car moved beneath her as she tried to kick free, disappearing beneath the surface.

She felt his fingers take hold of her ankle. She was being pulled under. All her limbs desperately thrashed, but she couldn't escape. *This is it! I'm going to die!*

From above, a hand hooked under her armpit. She was being tugged in both directions before the grip on her ankle slipped away. Her head broke the surface of the water, and she gasped for air. Salt stung her eyes as she choked, coughing out a mouthful of brine.

"I've got you!" a shaky voice told her. She was hauled up onto the roof of her car, to stand next to Jessica. Waves from the sea rolled up to their knees. Jessica held her with an arm around her waist.

Anna clung on, her mind still many steps behind what was actually happening.

Twenty feet away, the undercover police car idled, with waves to the top of its wheel arches and its engine revving noisily.

A man swam towards them.

"Get a move on!" a woman shouted from the driver's seat.

"Mum! Mum!" Abbie called from the back of the vehicle.

"Abbie, stay in the car!" the female police officer yelled.

Underneath their feet, the Fiesta shifted. An air bubble popped around them as Anna's car disappeared beneath the water.

"I can't swim!" Anna screamed.

Jessica was struggling to keep both of them afloat when the male officer reached them. "Grab my neck!" he shouted.

"Jessica!"

"Go with him, Anna! I'm right behind you."

Anna felt herself being pulled through the water.

"Stand up!" The officer's voice rang loud in her ears. She straightened, finding firm tarmac beneath her feet. With the sea up to her thighs, she waded through the water to the police car, its blue light reflecting off the waves in dazzling pulses. Jessica was soon behind her and Anna leaned on her for support.

"Let's go!" the policewoman yelled against the roar of the engine.

Abbie flung the door open, and the male officer helped them both in, before skirting around the car. "Holy brass monkey balls, Nadia, that was cold," he said, jumping into the passenger's seat.

"What about the other person in the car?" Nadia asked, shifting into reverse.

"No hope in hell. He's fish food! I'll call it in. Now, get us out of here!"

"All right." She leaned to look through the rear of the car and backed up slowly in the direction of Holy Island.

"I know you can't see it. But, for God sake, don't go off the road," he said, cranking up the heat.

"No kidding," Nadia muttered.

Curled up against Jessica, with her arms around Abbie, Anna was grateful for the warmth of her body.

"I thought I'd lost you," Jessica whispered, her face tucked into Anna's neck.

Anna could feel the heat from Jessica's tears and reached up to caress her head. "You didn't, baby. You didn't."

In the sanctuary of Jessica's embrace, she half listened as the officers made phone calls, reporting the incident and requesting maritime support to recover the lost car. But beyond that, there'd been no mention of taking Jessica into custody.

As soon as they had pulled into Anna's drive, she directed them to park around the back.

"I'm going to call for an ambulance," Nadia said.

"No. We just need to get warm," Anna said feebly.

"It's my duty of care. I have to. But let's get you inside first."

In the kitchen, shivering in sodden pyjamas, Anna went to the thermostat and flicked it to maximum. The boiler fired to life. She was tired, bruised, freezing cold, and alive... Abbie was safe— *Why is Abbie here?*

Jessica had fetched a blanket from the lounge and placed it around Anna's shoulders.

An hour later, Anna sat on the sofa in the lounge. It was still dark outside, and Nadia had lit a fire. Her male counterpart sat opposite, close to the wood burner. He was wrapped in a duvet and wearing Anna's pink robe and matching slippers.

A paramedic from the air ambulance tended to her injuries while another spoke to Jessica. Two more police officers had arrived with the medics.

Anna gathered the full story of what had happened as statements were taken. Numb, she found it hard to process the details. The thought of Abbie trapped in the boot of a car—she couldn't bear to think about it. Jessica had saved her. She had saved them both. They were safe. That's what she had to keep in her mind. They were safe.

Next to her, Abbie slept with legs stretched out over Anna's lap and her head against Jessica's shoulder.

"I'd suggest a trip to the hospital," the medic said to Jessica. "But I can't see anything that needs immediate attention, beyond what I've already done. If you start to feel dizzy or nauseous, don't hesitate to call for an airlift."

Once the medics had left, Anna lifted Abbie's legs and went into the kitchen.

"I suppose you're going to arrest Jessica now?" she asked Nadia, who was adding sugar to a cup of tea.

Nadia returned a sympathetic smile and asked, "Do you want a cup?"

Anna lifted her laptop from the old farmhouse table and put it on the counter in front of Nadia. "I need to show you something."

Together, they watched the video that had been sent to Anna's phone.

"How did you get this?" Nadia asked.

"A message to my landline. I don't know who sent it. I'd hoped—" A tear fell, and she wiped it away.

Nadia pulled her phone out of her pocket. "I need to talk to my chief."


JESSICA WOKE AT ten and got dressed in the bathroom so she wouldn't wake Anna and Abbie. They'd shared the double bed after all three of them had managed to right the wardrobe. Pulling on one of Anna's old sweatshirts, she had to take care with her left arm, which was wrapped in a bandage. Her head still rang with a dull ache.

Downstairs, she found a pen and paper and started to write a note. Nadia came in from the lounge.

"I'm ready," Jessica said, scribbling furiously.

"For what?" Nadia asked.

Jessica's brow creased. "I thought you were going to arrest me."

"I have news for you." Nadia took a seat at the table. "It's best if you sit down."

The pensive look on Nadia's face told her whatever the officer had to say wasn't good.

"Early this morning, we took into custody Victoria Walsh, Brian Lopez, Jason Carter, and Ira Kapoor for manipulating the equity of Genism Systems and Hokthorn."

"What!" Jessica said, staring at her. "You're saying they...they—"

"They set you up. When Miss Walsh was brought in, she gave a full confession. It appears all of them were set to make a lot of money by raising the value of Genism Systems' shares. She also admitted to modifying your laptop before the incident."

"Victoria Walsh?"

"CFO of Genism Systems."

Jessica thought about the night they had spent together and how all she had wanted to do was send her home. She hadn't realised the woman was only there to frame her.

"I don't understand. Why did she do it? I mean, why me?"

"Apparently, your HR manager, Ira Kapoor, arranged it. She had a grudge against you."

"Ira? Why? I never wronged her. Or anyone."

"When Ira Kapoor was interviewed, she blamed you for an incident with her sister, Myra Bedi. And for bringing shame on her family. I was told her rantings were rather homophobic."

"Myra..." Jessica whispered. She remembered Myra saying her sister was hostile towards them, but she'd never realised the Ira from work was once Ira Bedi. "I, I didn't mean to hurt her—" Tears welled up in her eyes. The old guilt of Myra's injuries twisted her insides.

Nadia briefly touched Jessica's hand. "This means you're no longer a suspect. Anna showed me a video. It was enough to have the four brought in."

"Video?"

"It was sent to this number from a mobile phone owned by Chris Brayfield."

"Chris is a friend of mine," Jessica said, after a moment's hesitation.

Nadia's tired eyes had changed from chestnut to taupe, and she gave a barely perceivable nod. She went quiet for a few seconds, before sitting up straight. "I'm sorry to inform you, but at 7:42 this morning, his body was found in Shadwell Basin."

"My God..." The blood drained from Jessica's face. It was as if her chair was sinking into the muddy sea. The same sea she'd just spent fitful hours dreaming about.

"I'm sorry. Mr Lopez is being charged with the homicide and the others will be charged as accessories." Nadia turned to look over her shoulder.

Anna had walked into the kitchen. The previous night's ordeal had left her with a bruised cheekbone and a black eye. She came quickly around the table and put both arms around Jessica.

"Are you okay?" Anna asked. "What's going on? Why are you dressed?" Anna looked from her to Nadia. "I thought you said she wasn't a suspect anymore!"

"Anna, I'm not. I've had some bad news. Chris, my friend at work... The people who framed me killed him." Jessica started to cry.

"God, no. Oh, darling," Anna soothed.

She looked up at Anna and let out a sigh. "He was my only friend."

"Baby, you have me, Abbie, David, and Beth. This is your home. You never have to leave."

The idea took root. It hadn't instantly sprouted into an oak tree, but her gut uncoiled. The guillotine over her head was being dismantled, and she had Chris to thank for that.

"I want you to go back to bed. Please," Anna pleaded.

In truth, she didn't feel very well. The shock of hearing of Chris's death, finding out it was Myra's sister who'd framed her, and the throbbing between her temples had made her want to throw up.

Anna guided Jessica up, kissing her neck and cheek.

Upstairs, Jessica changed into a T-shirt and loose jogging bottoms and claimed the empty bed. Her body ached, and she allowed the fatigue to engulf her. Anna's words—*This is your home, you never have to leave*—stuck with her.

She was unable to doze. The events of the last twenty-four hours tore shadows through all her thoughts.

Abbie climbed in beside her and stacked a pile of pillows. Propping herself up, she balanced a laptop on her knees. A half-eaten pack of Mini Eggs was dumped onto the duvet.

"Jess, please watch this with me?" Abbie asked. A programme played on the screen.

Jessica buried her head in the pillow.

"You'll like it."

Jessica turned her head and opened an eye.

"Here." Abbie put one of the chocolates into Jessica's hand. "Watch it with me, it'll help you to forget things."

"Okay." Jessica stuffed another pillow behind her aching head. "What is it?"

"*Wynonna Earp*. It's about this cursed descendant of a gunfighter who kills zombies. Well, they're not really zombies but demons. The characters are pretty tough and smart, like you and Mum."

Jessica laughed. "Sounds bizarre."

"Just watch."

Anna entered and placed two aspirins and a glass of water on the bedside table.

"Can we have pancakes? It's Saturday," Abbie asked, popping another Mini Egg into her mouth.

"I have to go out for a few minutes. But definitely after that." Anna smiled, leaned over and kissed them both. She bent down to whisper in Jessica's ear. "I love you. I won't be long."

# Chapter Twenty-Four

ANNA'S YELLOW WELLINGTONS splashed through the sandy puddles on the edge of the tarmac. The sky was blue, and the sun warmed her skin as she approached a flatbed lorry with its hydraulic arm hanging above her Ford Fiesta. Two police cars and a grey van blocked both lanes of the causeway. Beyond, lines of cones marked its temporary closure.

Anna now understood why her car had sunk so deep. It had fallen into the channel cut by the South Low—a river from the mainland that emptied into the bay.

"You're sure you want to do this?" Nadia asked.

Anna nodded. "I need to be certain." She watched her car being lifted out of its depression with water streaming from its seams. After it was lowered onto the road, the door was opened by a policeman, and a body tipped out. Anna moved slowly forward with her arms folded.

A few feet away, she stopped and twisted a strand of her hair around her finger. It was him, and he was most certainly dead.

*It's over.*

She turned quickly and walked away. Her boots made a flopping noise with each step.

"Can you drop me home?" she asked Nadia.

"Yes, of course." Nadia matched her stride.

"Are you going back to London after this?"

Nadia was quiet for a moment and, as seemed to be her quirk, asked a different question, rather than answering. "It must be hard running a farm with only the two of you?"

"It's difficult." She sighed. "Especially when I also work during the day."

"You and Jessica should take some time off. You shouldn't make light of what you've both been through."

Anna nodded. However, in the back of her mind, she calculated how overdrawn she was. "Well, the animals don't feed themselves. I was hoping to get a volunteer to help on the farm. But now..."

"But what?" Nadia asked, opening the BMW's door.

"Well... With what has happened, I'm even more reluctant to let some stranger in the house."

"Understandable."

Inside the car, Nadia turned to her. "Miss Edison?"

"Please, call me Anna."

"I don't know much about farms, but I'm a quick learner, and I'm thinking I could help."

TWO WEEKS HAD passed since the tide had taken an evil from the land, and one of the first things Jessica did was to phone Anna's ex and tell him they wouldn't need his services anymore. John sounded dejected at first, before switching to speaking in a formal tone. She didn't explain what had happened. She was just thankful they no longer had to deal with him.

Anna had kept Abbie out of school for a week, and now the students had broken up for half term. Beth and Katy had visited most nights, bringing around meals after discovering what had happened. In fact, many of the villagers had popped over to check they were all right. The next week, it had quieted down; it seemed everyone knew they needed time to themselves. Except for David, who would knock every morning at ten, asking if there was something he could do for them. Jessica would pat him on the shoulder and send him on his way.

"You know that's going to make me need to pee," Jessica said, taking the travel cup from Anna. Jessica was steeling herself for a trip to London, where she would close out the chapter in her life that had brought her a career and money but nothing else.

"I'm hoping the caffeine will stop you from falling asleep at the wheel. So, you'll have to live with the side effects." Anna's blue irises had taken on a darker hue. "You'll drive carefully?"

"Of course."

"You'll call me every time you stop?"

Jessica waved her new mobile at Anna.

"And you'll be back next Saturday?"

Jessica laughed and hooked an arm around Anna's waist. "Yes." She slipped her fingers under the hem of Anna's top to touch bare skin.

"Okay, you can have a hall pass."

Jessica smiled. "You know I don't want to go, but I need to sort things out." With the case against her dropped, her bank account had been unfrozen, and she had been able to help Anna, despite her protests, by paying some of her outstanding bills.

"We're in this together, right?" Jessica had insisted.

"But I can't have you paying off my debts."

She'd cupped Anna's cheeks in her palms. "So, consider it an investment. An investment in us. All right?"

Anna hadn't responded, so Jessica had wobbled her head up and down, forcing a yes.

Together, they'd gone through Anna's business plan, her maxed out credit cards and what her outgoings were. Anna had covered all her money problems in a pall. It was a method of accounting that would've scared the Chancellor of the Exchequer. Jessica was determined to make sure their finances were viable so they could keep the farm and get Anna's pony trekking business off the ground. To do this, though, Jessica needed a trip to London to put her affairs in order. She had enough savings to buy the farm outright if she sold her sought-after London flat.

Anna's hands slipped up Jessica's back and, as they always did, sent shivers down her spine. "Try not to get kidnapped this time." Anna moved to press tightly against her, and they kissed.

"I could go a different week?"

Anna leaned back. "No. I don't want you worrying at the festival."

Jessica slowly slipped out of Anna's arms and picked up her keys. The old Saab had been returned after a few days, having been found at the petrol station on the mainland.

"Say hello to Sarah for me," Anna added.

"I will." They kissed again. Jessica got into the car and started the six-hour drive south.

EACH DAY IN London had been a challenge to get through and, when they ended, Jessica managed to close off her old life.

After being reinstated at Hokthorn, she resigned. At her flat, she packed her guitar and a few personal belongings, before calling a home clearance company to collect the rest, and then she put the property up for sale. At Somerset House, she met Sarah for a coffee and chat, before hooking up with a band from Brighton at a rehearsal studio off Denmark Street. Finally, on Friday, she collected her Saab from a garage in Brentwood where it had undergone extensive repairs.

It was around 9:30 p.m. by the time she arrived at her brother's house. *Well, it's still my house, but not for long. I should've done this ages ago.*

She waited for the sound of a passing train as it rattled over the level crossing to fade before she knocked on the door. Darren was his usual self, overweight, perpetually hungover, and cantankerous.

"So, you brought back my Saab," he said, looking through her.

"Hello, to you too. And, no, Darren, I'm keeping it."

"Like hell you are," he shot back.

"I'll do a deal."

He frowned. "What kind of deal?"

"The house for your car."

His eyes widened, and he started to rub the stubble on his cheek. "Really?"

"Let me in, so I can sign it over to you."

In the tiny lounge, she cleared a space on a dirty armchair by moving a tabloid paper and a few dubious magazines.

"Before I do this, I need to know about the guy who assaulted Myra."

"Fuck, that was years ago. But, okay, sure. No skin off my teeth." He offered her a can of lager.

"No, thanks." She paused and waited to get his attention as he opened his beer and took a slurp. "He still lives around here, right?"

"The old scrote moved to Potter's Bar, but he still uses the Black Horse as his local, if that's what you're asking."

"And he's there tonight?"

"He's there every night. He does a lot of duty-free business in the pub, so to speak."

A plump ginger cat waddled into the room and meowed loudly. Darren heaved himself off the sofa. "Let me feed Fatcat."

While he was in the kitchen, Jessica made a quick phone call.

He put a cup of tea in front of her and eased down on the sofa. "You know she still lives in the same house?"

"Who?" Jessica asked, picking up the tea.

"Myra."

Her hand started to tremble, and she put the tea down. "Myra still lives on Osborne?"

"That's what I said, wasn't it?"

They had managed a full hour in each other's company before Jessica stood. She stuffed the vehicle registration for the Saab into her pocket while leaving the signed deeds to the house on a stack of video games that littered his coffee table. "Well, see you."

He grunted and made no effort to rise. She made her way down the hall and outside.

It was dark, but she felt less spooked than a month ago, when she had been on the run from the police. She knew she need never return.

After ten minutes of walking, she arrived at a doorstep she hadn't frequented in more than a decade.

The house itself hadn't changed and looked the same as she remembered when she was sixteen.

She bit down on her courage, needing to know if Myra hated her after all the time that had passed. Not knowing had eaten away at her.

She rang the bell. After a few seconds, a light flickered on behind the frosted glass door. As the door edged open, Jessica considered bolting but, by the time she'd decided she would, Myra was standing in front of her, staring blankly. She hadn't changed, except perhaps her hair was longer and her eyes had lines at the corners where there had been none.

*She doesn't know me.* "I'm sorry. I shouldn't have—"

The space between Myra's eyebrows creased before a realisation spread across her delicate features. "Jessica."

"I'm sorry, it's late. I wanted to—" Jessica's head dropped, and she wrung her hands.

"It's been so many years! I'm so sorry about Ira. If I had known... Oh, I'm not being very polite. Please come in. I haven't seen you in so long." Myra leaned forward and kissed one cheek then the other. "Come in."

A boy, perhaps about ten, appeared at her side. Then a toddler climbed between Myra's legs, and she picked her up, balancing the child on her hips. "You two are supposed to be in bed." Big curious eyes stared at Jessica.

"It's late. I just needed to know everything was...okay with you."

"I should be asking you that after what my sister did—"

Jessica felt Myra's eyes burn into her soul. "I'm really sorry about what happened in the Chinese restaurant," Jessica blurted out. "I think about it a lot, and it was my fault." Her tone wavered.

Myra shook her head. "That was a long time ago. You need to forget about it. I have. But I don't see why you think it was your fault. There are bad people in this world. And, to my shame, my own sister is one of them. I'm very sorry for what Ira did to you."

An awkward few seconds passed. "Your children are beautiful..." She couldn't think of anything else to say. "I better go."

Myra reached out to Jessica's shoulder. "It wasn't your fault. Believe that."

Jessica nodded. Raising her chin, she focused on Myra's brown eyes for the first time. "All right. It was nice to see you again."

"You...too."

She heard the door click shut behind her as she headed back to where she'd left her car. A large BMW was parked a few spaces along. The passenger's window rolled down when Jessica approached it.

"Are you sure he's in there tonight?" Nadia asked.

"Yes. He's in the Black Horse every night until eleven and then drives home drunk."

"Okay. He has several prior drink-driving convictions so another will send him to prison for a while."

"Thanks for doing this for me, Nadia. I know it's not in your jurisdiction."

"It's no problem. One last arrest for me before I leave the force."

Jessica nodded.

"Best if you're not around when he comes out of the pub."

"Okay." Jessica headed back to her Saab and waited until he appeared and got into his car. As he pulled away from the kerb, the lights of Nadia's undercover police car flashed as it manoeuvred to block his vehicle.

Jessica got out to watch.

After breathalysing him, Nadia bundled him into the back of the police car. The moment before his head ducked in, he caught sight of her. Standing still, Jessica gave him a middle finger, then turned away.

IT WAS EARLY Saturday morning, and it had started to rain. Anna pulled up the hood of her bright yellow weatherproof. The chickens pecked furiously at the feed she'd dumped from a bucket on the grass near their roost.

The night before, Anna had spoken at length to Abbie about her mother and how she'd been adopted. Anna had expected Abbie to react with anger and storm off. But Abbie just blinked and said it didn't matter.

"I don't remember any of that. You're my mum." Abbie had then asked, "What's for dinner? I'm really hungry."

"Anything you like, my princess." Anna had hugged her for dear life and kissed her temple.

Thinking back, Anna couldn't help but be proud of her daughter. *Yes. My daughter.* She'd bounced back with only a few nightmares.

The sound of a car pulling up caused Anna to drop her bucket and run into the farmyard. An old Saab had come to a halt near the kitchen door.

As soon as Jessica stepped out, Anna ploughed into her, grinning from ear to ear.

"You're back!" Anna said, a little breathless.

"Yup." Jessica's fingers brushed Anna's cheek. Their lips tangled in a deep kiss. When they separated, both panting. Jessica said, "I need to show you something." She took Anna's hand and led her to the passenger door. "Please get in for a sec."

"All right, but why?"

"Please."

Inside the car, Anna waited for her. Once Jessica was in the driver's seat, Anna's curiosity got the better of her. "So? Where are we going?"

"Nowhere." A few seconds passed. Rain pattered on the canvas rooftop. "And everywhere, I hope," Jessica whispered. The car was already starting to fog up.

"You know, we have a perfectly good bed we can make out in if that was your plan."

Jessica took Anna's hand. It had a slight tremor as she turned Anna's palm upwards. "See?"

Anna knitted her brows together. "Not really."

"You told me once..." Jessica's fingers closed around Anna's. "That no one would marry me because they would get a wet bum whenever they travelled in my car. Well, it's raining and—"

"Oh, yes, you've fixed the leak." Anna focused on Jessica's different coloured eyes, which never ceased to captivate her. Jessica looked terribly nervous. Then Anna understood.

"Oh my God!" Anna cried as her heart leapt to one hundred miles an hour. "Jessica!" With her free hand over her mouth, she gasped when an antique diamond ring appeared between Jessica's thumb and forefinger.

"Anna," Jessica's words were shaky, but Anna didn't need to hear them perfectly, she already knew what her answer would be. She'd known after they first made love. "Will you marry me?"

Anna nodded slowly at first, tears streaming down her cheeks. "Yes, my angel. Yes!"

# Epilogue

CLOSING THE BOOT, Anna asked, "So, what have we forgotten?"

"It's impossible to remember what's been forgotten," Jessica said, leaning against the driver's door. The top was down, and Abbie sat in the back seat surrounded by camping gear.

"I'm sure you have everything you need." Nadia had wandered over, dressed in jeans and a navy T-shirt. "It looks like you're going on a safari."

It was a warm July morning without clouds and, to Anna, everything was right with the world. "You're sure you'll be okay running the treks while we're away?"

Nadia laughed. "I've been doing that for weeks now. It'll be fine. I've roped in David and Beth to help."

Anna had been surprised when Nadia volunteered to work for them at the farm. She'd said she needed a change and that the Serious Fraud Office wasn't quite ready for her. This Anna didn't understand, but she was grateful since without her help they wouldn't have been able to get her business off the ground. The other thing she didn't understand but also didn't care about, was John's reaction when she told him of her engagement to Jessica. He had gone silent on the phone, before hanging up on her.

Anna glanced around. The yard was busy; a gang of kids were mucking out their ponies while Beth was brushing down the latest addition to the stable, a black Dartmoor.

"We better get going," Jessica said, placing a hand on Anna's shoulder.

Anna nodded. "You have my number, right?"

"Yes, Miss-soon-to-be-Mrs Cox," Nadia said. She quirked a half smile.

"All right, see you in five days." She climbed into the passenger seat and looked back as they drove out of the yard.

"Everything will be fine," Jessica assured her.

After a four-hour drive, they arrived at L Fest and managed to cart all their gear to the camping area, without dying in the afternoon heat. Anna made a mental note. *Next time, less stuff!*

It didn't take long to erect their four-person tent, and they were soon heading towards the main stage.

The sun was still an hour away from dipping below the horizon as they sat on the grass listening to the first performances. Around them were other female couples, some with children. The festival was compact compared to others she'd been to, but this only made it friendlier and more intimate.

Sarah carefully lowered herself down on the ground. "You know they have hot tubs over there? I mean, hot tubs! Who has hot tubs at a festival?" She passed a beer to Anna and a Coke to Abbie, who put down her guitar for a moment to open the can and take a sip.

"I have my eye on the hammocks," Anna said.

Sarah turned to Abbie. "So, Jessica is teaching you the guitar?"

"Yeah, open chords for now. One sec." Abbie picked up her acoustic and strummed a simple chord sequence.

"That's lit!" Sarah clapped.

"Hey, Anna!" A voice called. Anna turned to see Nicole, who she'd met at the pizza van over a month ago. "You made it!"

Nicole hunched down on bended knees and tiptoes.

"Yes, just arrived."

After introductions, Nicole added, "Well, when you're up for something to eat and a chat, we're over there." She pointed to an area set out for food vendors. "I was hoping we could meet up after the dinner rush."

"Sure, that'd be great."

Nicole scanned the area. "So where is Jessica?"

Anna, impressed that Nicole had remembered their names, pointed to the stage. "She's getting ready to play." Anna smiled.

"Wow."

"She's very good," Sarah chimed in.

"Oh..." Nicole was looking at Anna's hand. "You're engaged now? I noticed your ring!"

"Yes." Anna beamed. "We've not set a date yet, but you're invited."

"That's great! Congratulations!"

A cheer spread through the crowd, drawing Anna's attention to the stage.

Jessica approached a microphone, shouldering a black electric guitar. "Hi. Before we start, I want to say thanks to Sarah and the organisers for allowing me up here. And lots of love to Anna and Abbie for making me whole again." Jessica turned to the drummer and nodded. The band began to play.

Anna wiped away a tear, but this time, unlike so many before, it was a tear of joy.

# About the Author

Alex is a novelist based in the UK. She grew up in Canada and completed a BSc degree, before moving back to work in central London. Alex has also lived in the United States. Since a young age, she has consumed a mixture of historical fiction, fantasy, and romance. Alex enjoys guitar, creating music, photography, and painting, but most of all, things she doesn't understand. For her, writing is a way to inspire virtues that should happen more often.

Twitter: @AlexSlorra

# Also Available from NineStar Press

# Connect with NineStar Press

Website: NineStarPress.com

Facebook: NineStarPress

Facebook Reader Group: NineStarNiche

Twitter: @ninestarpress

Tumblr: NineStarPress